In gratitude for the caricatures.

11/v/95

[signature]

THE 'MEES' OF TRE BOSCHI

A Story of the Abruzzi Region of Italy

R H 'GIMI' JORDAN

MINERVA PRESS
MONTREUX LONDON WASHINGTON

THE 'MEES' OF TRE BOSCHI
A Story of the Abruzzi Region of Italy

Copyright © R H 'Gimi' Jordan 1995

ISBN 1 85863 476 8

First Published 1995 by
MINERVA PRESS
10 Cromwell Place,
London SW7 2JN

Printed in Great Britain by
Antony Rowe Ltd., Chippenham, Wiltshire

THE 'MEES' OF TRE BOSCHI

A Story of the Abruzzi Region of Italy

ABOUT THE AUTHOR

After a lifetime spent in the service of the British Army both as a soldier and later as a Civil Servant, Gimi Jordan retired in 1973 and began to write in earnest. He had often written plays for the children at the various schools in which Jo, his wife, had been class mistress or, latterly, Head Teacher. Three volumes of verse owe their existence to him; all three sold fairly well, and so a long-suffering set of readers now have this latest book (his first full length story) inflicted on them. There have also been successful attempts at articles for various publications, most of them to do with the gentle art of motor caravanning.

Jo and Gimi now live quietly in Cromer, in Norfolk, but so far have managed to spend six or eight weeks every year in the Abruzzo, where they are elected members of five native families.

For the inquisitive, the name 'Gimi' is the Italian way of spelling 'Jimmy', there being no letters 'J' or 'Y' in their alphabet. And the 'Jimmy' derives from the fact that, in his Corps, all Jordans were awarded that name, which has stuck with him for well over sixty years!

More books are being considered, and if this present work sells well enough, will probably follow.

INTRODUCTION

This is a work of fiction. Although every place mentioned does in fact exist, (with the exceptions of Tre Boschi and La Poltrona), I have avoided giving specific descriptions of those places. I am certain that Fortalezza is not grand enough 'paese' to support a Carabinieri Barracks - if it does indeed have such an establishment, then I apologise without reserve to the troops there and to the Commandant himself!

No living person is represented. If anyone reading this discovers any resemblance to a person known to him or her, then that resemblance is purely coincidental and accidental. I cannot truthfully say that the characters are not based on people I have known or still know, but the originals are either British or Italian and the fictional characters an amalgam of both nationalities.

While Italy is a truly marvellous country, and the Abruzzi not the least beautiful of its many regions, there is, or was in the time that my tale is set, a maggot in the apple, a worm in the bud. Petty crime, and not-so-petty crime, seemed to be rife in the larger centres of the population; kidnapping for ransom, or to put pressure on influential persons, had, at the time my scene is set, developed into what amounted to a "fine art". Whether any band of villains would act as my little gang did is a point which verges on the moot, but my characters are fictional and cannot be relied to do things in the same way that more competent operators would go about them.

To the best of my knowledge and belief, there is no cave of the Black Madonnina up there below the sharp peak of the Corno Piccolo, but a glance at a relief map suggests that such a cavern could well exist, and on that premise I have based my tale.

I dedicate this book first to my wife Jo, without whose criticism I would have had to spend much less time at the typewriter, and secondly to all those folk of Italy and especially of the Abruzzi whom I know and love.

I am indebted to Andrew Church, the well-known North Norfolk artist and water colourist and others for the illustrations.

Pina

ONE

Sitting in a corner seat in a first-class compartment of the boat train in Victoria Station, Pina allowed her mind to range over the events of the past two weeks or so. Truly, she thought, Kevin had a lot to answer for! Had he not written that fateful note, she would not now be sitting here, quivering almost as much as the train panting to be off on its way to Dover. Fifteen short days had altered her life completely already, and she had only just started!

On reading that letter from Kevin, Pina's first reaction was to throw herself upon her bed and burst into tears. Her second impulse was to rush screaming around the room, breaking everything within sight and reach; her third was to read the note again, to assure herself that this was no nightmare; and her fourth, and most sensible impulse was to dash down to Cheyneys to discuss the matter with Mama.

Kevin had written, in that uneven and childish scrawl of his, "Dear Pina, I hope that you will not be hurt too much, but the truth is, I've found someone else. You don't know her. Thank you for the good times we have had together. I feel sure that you will soon get over me, and hopefully find somebody more suited to you than what I am really. Yours sincerely, Kevin." The "Yours sincerely" bit really hurt - he wasn't being sincere at all! Then, having obeyed her third reaction for the nth time, she followed the fourth impulse, and at the earliest opportunity that presented itself, took the train down to Cheyneys.

She found Mama, as usual, extended on the chaise longue in the lounge. In the few short months since Daddy had died so unexpectedly, Mama seemed to pass most of her days in that position. On a small table, near to hand, lay a half-empty box of those Italian candied fruits that she loved so much. Her nose was almost touching the pages of 'Donna' as she read. Mama stoutly maintained that there was nothing amiss with her eyes - she was much too young yet to require spectacles. Her trouble with reading was laid at the door of the printers - they *would* use such very tiny faint print! But this was a difficulty to be surmounted. How else could she remain in touch with the gossip and fashions of her native country, which she had left thirty years ago as a wartime bride?

As Pina entered the lounge, the copy of 'Donna' was flung away to join that of 'Oggi' where they lay together on the carpet. Mama's arms opened wide to enfold Pina in an embrace that expressed to the full her warm affectionate nature. Then, still without rising from her chaise longue, Mama held her daughter at arm's length and gazed intently on the woe-begone face.

"Ahime, tesoro mio, how good to see you again!" Once more Pina was pulled downward to be kissed. "But what has happened? You have been weeping! Is it on account of that great oaf, that zoticone, Kevin? Get shut of him, Pinina mia! You are far too good for such as that one!"

Pina burst into a flood of uncontrollable weeping as she buried her face in Mama's ample bosom, and sobbed out the news of Kevin's perfidy, and the contents of his letter.

"O Dio!" murmured Mama. "How ungallant that man is! But Pinina mia, look on the brighter side. And please do try to control yourself; my dress is quite wet all down the front! Remember what Daddy always used to say - there are far better fish in the woods than ever came out of them! I know you will find someone better than that Kevin!" The scorn Mama injected into the name was withering.

She had always considered Kevin to be a mindless lout, and made no secret of her opinion. Now with her daughter weeping so copiously on her shoulder, Mama comforted the girl in the only really effectual way, treating her as she would have treated a hurt child. The therapy was effective; soon Pina's weeping subsided into a few snuffles which she tried to wipe away with a limp rag that, minutes before, had been a lacy handkerchief. Pina sat on a small footstool, and rewarded Mama with a tremulous smile. The elder woman stretched out a podgy hand to ring a tinkly bell which stood on the table beside the chaise longue.

A small fair girl sidled into the room. She bobbed a curtsey to Mama and by some subtle chemistry managed to include Pina in her action. Mama ordered tea with much lemon. The maid bobbed once more and disappeared through the half-open door, to reappear very shortly carrying a tray on which were set a steaming pot and two dainty cups and saucers, together with a plate on which reposed slices of lemon. As the tray was deposited on a table which Pina had drawn near the couch, Mama murmured,

"Perhaps I didn't needing you some more today, Mary. Go home for early afternoon, eh?"

Thanking her, Mary left the lounge. Mama, with much groaning and puffing, gained a sitting position. She poured the weak tea and passed the lemon to Pina.

"Now," she said, "we can be human and forget that barbarous English tongue! Tell, Pina, do we get your brother Franco to thrash this briccone, this rascal?" She sipped her tea, and continued, "He deserves a leathering for this gross behaviour, and Franco would be happy to beat him a little, if not for you, then for me!"

Pina discovered that she could still smile. "Oh, no, Mama. These things are not considered as important as they were when you were a girl, and anyway, this *is* England, not Italy. I think I shall give up my post at the language school and try to find some position in Europe. It should be easy now that the Common Market is in full swing."

"Aha! I see you have given the matter some thought! But I still think Signor Kevin ought to have a sharp lesson. Please, Pina, let me set Franco on him, just to give him the teeniest little beating! No? Ah well, maybe you know best. Do you want me to write to any of my friends at home?" Mama always spoke of Italy as 'home' despite the years she had spent away from Naples. "To see if they can find you a post, you know."

"No, Mama," replied Pina firmly, shaking her head to emphasise her refusal. "You know how inquisitive your friends are, all of them. If you ask them to help me, you will have to explain why I want to change jobs. Your friends all have the same idea as you yourself, that it is a disgrace to be jilted by any man!"

"You have right, Pinina! If it got out that a man had so treated you, you might never meet another eligible man, especially in Italy. And you know how much I have always wanted you to marry a nice Italian boy, cara. These Inglesi you meet may be quite KO, as Daddy would say, but for you I would always choose an Italian!"

They chatted for another half hour or so before Pina rose to leave. In response to Mama's urgent pleading, she promised faithfully that any news she might have to tell would be transmitted urgently, and then, feeling a little more cheerful than she had been when she arrived, she set out to catch her train at the little halt half a mile from the house. As she strode down the drive, she turned to wave and was rewarded by a slight movement of the curtains at the window of Mama's lounge.

Arriving at the station, Pina found that she had a few minutes to spare before her train was due. The wind was chilly as it whistled along the open platform, and she sought sanctuary in a tiny waiting room. It was a mere cupboard of a place, with floorboards of rough wood, and some equally rough benches ranged against two of the walls. The grate held no welcoming fire. There was no other person in the room. A magazine lay on one of the benches, thrown there by some uninterested traveller, and for want of something better to do, Pina picked it up and idly leafed through the pages. It was a recent copy of one of those periodicals which are aimed chiefly at the younger woman. It was not, however, a comic such as many of its competitors seem so often to be. Pina was mildly interested to observe that towards the back of the journal, many small advertisements were displayed. Resisting the enormous temptation proffered by some person who was willing to teach her shorthand in three days, and spurning an offer, if she would but write for it, of a free gift of some unspecified nature that would astound all her friends as well as herself, she came by chance to a column devoted to 'Work offered and wanted'. One item caught her attention, and as the train drew fussily and self-importantly into the platform, she hastily tore out that page and thrust it into her handbag.

There were few passengers on the train, and in an empty compartment, seated by a grimy window, she studied the advertisement which had captured her attention. 'Wanted', she read, 'a governess/companion/tutor for a 12-year old girl. Applicants should have good English and a sound knowledge of Italian. The post is offered subject to the successful applicant being able to take up residence in Italy. Good salary offered. Apply to Box XYZ'.

She spent the whole of the hour's run back to town in composing a reply to the advertisement. As soon as she reached her flat, she typed out an application, and then, before she could change her mind, rushed out to post the letter. For the next three days, she went about her daily routine in a kind of trance. Omitting Kevin from all her plans had altered her way of life in a manner, and to an extent, she would not have thought possible. It astonished her to consider how his shadow had loomed over everything only a few days ago, when almost her every act was ruled by the consideration of what he would want to do, or where he would want to go. She was amazed at the air of freedom that had suddenly engulfed her, and that freedom assisted her to recover from her heartache much sooner than ever she would have thought possible.

On the fourth day after her application had been pushed into the pillarbox, a slim grey envelope was awaiting her in the porter's lodge of the block of flats. With trembling fingers, in the quiet of her room, she opened the envelope and withdrew a single sheet of matching paper. In a quaint and somewhat old-fashioned flowing Italian script, her correspondent had written, 'Gentilissima Signorina, Your application affords me much interest. I wish to receive, by return of post, testimonials and CV - I stress, by return of post, because my stay in England is drawing to a close. The post which I offer is near Teramo, where my residence is situated. Permit me to repeat that I require your reply urgently.'

Hastily she gathered together copies of references and CV. Fortunately, all were easily available, for her post at the language school was only a temporary one, and she could never tell when such things might be needed.

Quickly she parcelled the papers up, then dashed to the Post Office to ensure that they would be despatched at the earliest opportunity.

At the weekend, she went again to Cheyneys. Mama was in her usual posture, reclining on the chaise longue, with the inevitable box of candied fruit conveniently to hand, and the copies of Italian periodicals within reach. After the usual greetings, Pina showed her the letter that she had received, and described what she had done, Mama read the letter aloud, the Italian flowing fluidly off her tongue. At the end, she burst out with the only expletive she ever permitted herself, "Dio mio! But Teramo is in the Abruzzi! They are all peasants there, every last one of them! Why on earth did you not just ignore this letter?"

"Because, Mama mia, I'm very interested in the post. I simply must get away from town. I fear that at every street corner I may run into Kevin." Her eyes filled with the unbidden tears that *would* come without warning. "At least I should not run that risk in a place like Teramo. Naturally, I've looked up the town on the map. It's quite near the Adriatic coast, and there are masses of lidi all along the shore. If I had to, I could get back to England in well under twelve hours by taking a train to Roma and then flying on. If this man, Capriotti seems to be his name, offers me the post and the money is anywhere near right, I shall accept. Of course, it is by no means

14

certain that I shall be even short-listed - there must be dozens of girls who would jump at the chance of a post like this one. I'm probably just one among a whole crowd of applicants."

Mama shook a warning finger. "You can never be certain that you will not be offered the place. In fact, I am quite certain that you *will* get it, because every night I pray to Sant'Antonio to arrange for you a post in Italia! Now it is clear to me that he is working for us! Mind you, perhaps I did not pray quite hard enough. I didn't expect an offer from such a remote and backward region. However..." her voice trailed away.

Pina could not repress a smile. Mama had a deep and positively child-like faith in her patron saint, and over the years had plied him with all sorts of pleas, ranging from the trivial to matters of immense importance. In her heart, Pina almost believed in the miraculous powers attributed by Mama to Sant'Antonio, but only rarely could she bring herself to demand favours in the way that Mama did. But just this once, Pina allowed herself to breathe a tiny prayer. When she sat again in the train as it puffed its way out of the platform, she felt within herself a peace that she had not known for over a week - not since she had received that letter from the faithless Kevin.

She let herself into the hallway of the great block of flats, at the top of which she established herself in her tiny two-roomer. As she moved towards the lift, a man stepped from the darkness of the porter's office opposite the lift shaft.

"Mees Corrigan?" he asked, in heavily accented English. Pina, inspecting him, nodded briefly. He was tall, thin, and rather ordinary in appearance; he would pass in almost any crowd without being noticed. His speech, however, proclaimed to the world that here was a man who rarely visited England. His drab raincoat, unbuttoned in the warmth of the hall, was slightly open as he moved towards her, and Pina could see that beneath it, he wore some kind of grey half-livery which seemed to give the impression that he was some kind of superior serving man.

In rapid Italian, the man said, "I am majordomo to the Senatore Capriotti, with whom you have been in contact." Pina, having found her keys, dangled them from her hand as she nodded again. The unexpectedness of this encounter seemed to have robbed her of the power of speech. Looking over the man's shoulder as he spoke, she could see the burly form of Mr. Britten, the porter, who was watching

Luigi Passi - The Majordomo

this meeting over the top of his evening paper. Somehow she sensed that although the man's Italian was beyond criticism, it was not the speech he normally used; probably in ordinary conversation, he spoke some sort of regional dialect. He continued, "My lord is master of the estate of Tre Boschi, in the Abruzzi, near Teramo."

Again Pina nodded to signify that she understood.

"My lord, the Senatore, has sent me to inform you that he is pleased with your application for the post of companion to his daughter, and that he engages you immediately. The precise amount of your remuneration will be the subject of mutual agreement, but it will start forthwith; I am to add that it will be generous. I am also to pass over to you this package. In it you will find a first-class railway ticket from Victoria Station here in London to Giulianova Lido. The ticket is valid for any day within one hundred and sixty eight hours from tomorrow at six o'clock a.m.; your ferry ticket is also enclosed. The package contains a sufficient sum of money in French francs and Italian lire to enable you to travel in comfort. You will not need to stint yourself of anything you may require - my lord is a generous man to his employees. By your acceptance of this package, you signify your acceptance of the post he offers you, on the terms he offers. If you do not care for those terms, then you refuse the package and the matter of your employment will be annulled. Does the signorina agree?"

Had she been in her normal state of mind, Pina would have asked for more time to think things over. She would have said that she had much to do; that it would be impossible to move at such short notice; that she could not possibly be expected to close one chapter of her life so abruptly, and open another with so little time for preparation. Even so, there was a very slight trace of uncertainty in her voice as she asked, "Is your lord then an eccentric? He has not even seen me!"

"That is true, signorina. But my lord trusts my judgement, and I have seen you. Had I considered you even remotely unsuitable for this post, I would not have disclosed myself to you when you entered the palazzo where you live. I would have slipped away, and you would never have seen me! Please answer me, do you accept?"

"I am probably taking a very dangerous gamble, but yes, I accept. I shall be leaving London in six days' time. Shall I be met at - where is it? Giulianova?"

"Oh, sicuro, signorina. A car with driver will await your arrival."

"How do you know I am to be trusted? Can you be sure that I will not take the money and ticket, and go to Roma for a good holiday, returning home having never seen the skies over your region?"

"Signorina, as I have said, my lord trusts my judgement. I judge you to be an honest woman. But if I am mistaken, and you *do* harbour the thoughts you have suggested, you would do well to forget them quickly. The old ways still hold in the Abruzzo, and any treachery inevitably meets with its due reward... you understand me, I am sure." He gave her a little bow, thrust the package into her hand, replaced his hat, turned on his heel and left the hall, to be swallowed up in the traffic in the street.

Mr Britten lifted the flap which lay across the door of his cubby hole, and came across to Pina. "Was that geezer annoyin' yer, Miss Corrigan?"

"No. On the contrary." She flashed him a bright smile.

"'Cos if 'e was bein' a noosance, I'd a marked his book for 'im, see? I'd a knocked 'is block orf!" He gave her smile for smile. "Funny sorter geezer, w'an't 'e? Not English, if yer know what I mean. Eye-talian, I fought 'e was."

Pina, still smiling, thanked him for his solicitude. "Had he been waiting long for me, Mr Britten?"

"'Bout arf an hour, I should fink, miss. 'E di'nt speak much. Jist wanted me ter give him the orfice when you come in, like. Well, if that's orlright, then that's orlright, miss. I gives yer goodnight." He made a semi-military salute and returned to his sanctum. Pina pressed the button to call down the lift.

Once she had gained the comfort of her flat, she lowered herself into an armchair without even bothering to remove her coat. She gazed at the package which had been passed to her by the majordomo, and whispered to herself, "Corrigan, you're the biggest fool! You're a cretinous impetuous moronic idiotic foolish goose, and that's only some of the things you are! What on earth have you let yourself in for? Not," she hastened to reassure herself, "that threats will have the slightest effect upon my actions. Now," she admonished herself, "before you do another thing you great fathead, take off your coat, make a nice cup of tea, and then sit down to write to Mama to tell her all that has happened since you saw her a mere two hours ago!"

TWO

Mama's reply to Pina's letter had been uncharacteristically swift. 'Pinina mia, your letter tells me so much and so little! Such mysteries!! I shall pray every night for your safety all the time you are in the wilds of the Abruzzi!!!' Mama had always been lavish with her exclamation marks, and this time she had really gone to town. 'But you say that you have accepted these strange terms of your engagement, and you cannot in honour withdraw from that position! I have placed you even more under the protection of Sant'Antonio, and I shall pray for you every day, both night and morning, while you are in that uncivilised place!!! Take up your post, and if at any time you feel in need of help,' (and this part of her letter Mama had underlined no less than three times) 'ring your zio Giglio in Firenze, who will then rush to assist you.' Pina giggled to herself as she pictured Uncle Giglio in Florence rushing anywhere. He was almost eighty years old, and crippled with arthritis. She continued her reading of Mama's letter. 'I will write immediately to Giglio to inform him that you are on your way to a post in Teramo. As soon as you let me know your address, I will write to him again.' For another six or seven pages, Mama rambled on as only she could, and concluded, 'Now, remember to write to zio Giglio without delay. And also remember that I shall not rest happy until I know that you have arrived safe in Teramo.'

So here she was, installed in a corner seat on the boat train, which seemed to be shaking with impatience to be on its way. It was still early afternoon, but on such a dull wintry day, it could well have been midnight. Pina hoped that the weather in central Italy would be a little warmer than it was here in London, and that the daylight would be a little more powerful. Rain was streaming down the carriage window as she gazed at her own reflection in the glass. She saw a contorted image of a heart-shaped face twisted by the rain-streaked glass into a caricature of her true features. The face was framed by a halo of rich auburn hair, an inheritance from Daddy's Irish ancestors. Below arched eyebrows of a similar hue, her eyes held a colour that seemed to vary according to the light that struck them, now tawny, like the eyes of a tiger, now dark and brooding. Her nose was straight and aristocratically high-bridged, the replica of Mama's patrician organ, and her lips, again like Mama's, rather too full and sensuous for perfection. Her lower jaw was square and determined, the jaw of a fighter. Considering herself dispassionately, Pina thought that she was a typical product of a mixed marriage between a faintly Hibernian sire and a Latin mother. How lucky it was, she thought, that she had inherited the genes the right way round! She gave a wry smile as she thought of herself bearing Daddy's very roman nose with its mottling of small broken veins around the tip, combined with Mama's thick coarse jet-black hair and small black-irised eyes.

These thoughts were interrupted by the noise and bustle of the train pulling out of the station, and now that the die was cast, they flew immediately to speculation about what might await her in about thirty hours' time. Well, she would learn soon enough. In her mind there was no real fear of the future; there was just a lively curiosity, a curiosity intensified by the somewhat unorthodox means which had been employed to engage her. She soon gave up this line of thought, and settled to leaf through the magazine which she had bought at the station bookstall. There was little in it to excite her attention, though, and she soon allowed it to slip to her lap, and then to the seat beside her. It was impossible to see anything outside the window. Everything was totally blurred by a combination of rain, speed, and darkness. She abandoned herself to waking dreams of what her future might hold.

The ticket collector broke into her reverie. He looked closely at the slip of paper that she handed to him, then punched it expertly. "Cor!" he remarked as he passed her ticket back to her. "Rather you than me, miss! Wouldn't care to be crossing ternight! Blowin' arf a gale out there, it is, an' raining like the clappers! Reckon you'll be needing them seasick pills." He was chuckling at his own joke as he closed the door of the compartment, and made his way along the corridor.

When she alighted at Newhaven, Pina had to admit that the man had been right - it *was* going to be a rough crossing. The wind tore at her like a living thing intent on tearing from her body every stitch she was wearing. Staggering under the weight of her case, she made her way through passport inspection, where her document was given a very cursory glance from a languid young man whose mind seemed to be more concerned with the imminence of the end of his day's work than with his duty. She made her way to the ferry, stumbling up the gangplank, to report to the purser's office. A bored stewardess led her to the cabin which had been booked by her telephone call the previous day. Although the ship was still tied to the pier, she could feel it rocking as she threw her case upon the bunk. She removed her wet coat, ran a comb swiftly through her hair, then lay on the opposite bunk, secure in the knowledge that she would be undisturbed. Snug, warm, dry and not a little excited, she fell into a deep sleep. The sounds and notion of the ferry leaving harbour did not rouse her, and although she had fully intended to have dinner aboard, she did not recover consciousness until the stewardess rapped on the cabin door to tell her that it was almost four o'clock. She rose and made a rapid toilet, had a light breakfast in the almost deserted cafeteria, and went on deck to watch the process of docking.

The wind had dropped, and there was the promise of a fair day ahead. A disembodied voice over the tannoy ordered all passengers to prepare to disembark and before long, Pina found herself standing on the rough pavè of the dockside. With a bare handful of fellow passengers, she trudged through the customs shed and was quickly cleared to enter France. In passable French she asked for directions for the Paris train, and was rewarded with a jerk of a pointed beard along the dock. Taking the path thus indicated, she came to a panting locomotive to which were attached a dozen or so coaches. A conductor led her to her reserved seat, and she subsided on to the leatherette bench. So far, so good, she thought. She had crossed her personal Rubicon, and now her new life was starting in earnest. The locomotive emitted a hoarse snort, as if in distaste at the task that lay before it, and with much clanking and creaking lumbered into action. Slowly the dawn crept into the sky on her left; outside, things began to assume recognisable shapes. Pina dozed, waking briefly as noise levels altered when the train dashed through a small station, or banged its way over a level crossing while traffic on the road waited patiently to cross the line.

On arrival in Paris, her command of the language was adequate to find the Gare du Lyon. She had some hours to wait for the Simplon Express, and enjoyed a leisurely meal in a small bistro near the station. Finally, she returned to the platform and was conducted to her reserved seat by a smartly uniformed conductor, and swiftly set about making herself comfortable for the long journey before her, for this minute compartment was to be her home for several hours now. She would be travelling via Lausanne, Brig, and Domodossola to

Milan, and it could be fourteen or sixteen hours before she arrived at that final stop on this stage of the journey. It might prove difficult to occupy her time. She felt that she had had ample sleep now, and even the long-dragged out French railway meals could not possibly be stretched to fill all the hours of her journey. She decided to start a letter to Mama, detailing all that had happened so far, no matter how trivial. With her writing pad on her lap, she began work on a long screed. Her usually neat writing suffered badly from the frequent unexpected jolts given by the train from time to time.

Her literary effort was interrupted by the waiter calling the first dinner settings, and she was able to make that interlude last an hour and a half before she returned to resume her letter. Between this exercise, and frequent gazing out of the window, the time passed fairly quickly, and when the conductor came to make down her bed, she was quite ready to retire into it. She slept fitfully across Switzerland and part of Northern Italy before being roused by the conductor. A swift wash and brush up in the toilet room prepared her to face the day and her continental breakfast of roll and coffee.

As she made her swaying way back to her compartment, she thought she saw a tall brown clad man emerge from her door. On entering, she found that the bed had been made up by the conductor, and her case was resting on the seat. She concluded that he was the person she had noticed coming out. She sat by the window, watching the beautiful Italian countryside flying by. Brief tantalising glimpses of Lago Maggiore and the little towns scattered along its shores passed before her inspection and were gone, concealed by the swelling shoulders of the hills and mountains that tumbled down to the dappled blue water of the great lake.

In a hysterical shrieking of whistles mingled with the scream of tortured brakes, the train drew into Milano Centrale station. Case in hand, Pina alighted. As she started the walk along the full length of the train, her progress was arrested by a warning cry from a porter. "Signorina, your case! It is coming open! You are in danger of losing your property!"

Thanking the man, Pina stopped to replace a few scattered garments before shutting the case firmly. She noticed that on top of the contents lay an envelope that had certainly not been there the last time she had looked into the case. She removed the envelope and put it into her handbag, then stopped by a vacant bench to see what it was all about. The envelope contained a single sheet of coarse brown paper. In rough capitals scrawled on the paper was a message. 'You will be ill-advised to work for Capriotti. There could be danger for you. Return to your own land. Do not meddle in other people's affairs. This is the advice of a well-wisher.' There was no clue to the identity of the author.

Again she read the note. Then, putting the paper back into the envelope and the whole into her bag, she thought, "Pina, my lass, now what? Do you take Well-wisher's advice, or do you act like Daddy's girl and go through with your contract? Of course you will see it through! Any other course would be just plain cowardice!" Sticking out that firm little chin, she made her way to the small window marked 'Informazioni' and in a steady voice asked how she would best be able to get to Giulianova.

At such an early hour, with little to do, the young man behind the hatch was very happy to engage in conversation with a young woman, and to hold her attention for as long a time as he could. With the inexhaustible patience so often displayed by Italian males towards young women, and especially pretty ones, he outlined the options that lay before Pina.

"There are a number of trains which travel down the east coast by way of Bologna and Rimini. First there is the 'Rapido'. As the signorina is probably aware, this is the fast train, stopping only at main stations. It is of one single class, and all who travel by it must pay a supplement to the normal fare. One pays the conductor on the train, of course. Such a train will leave Milano in one hour, and will require four hours to arrive at Giulianova.

"Next comes the Espresso. This train carries both first and second class passengers. An espresso leaves here at nine hours. It will take a little longer for the journey, and you should arrive at Giulianova at fifteen hours.

"Then there is the Diretto. A two-class train, you will find it leaves Milano in half an hour. You would arrive at your destination at seventeen hours.

"Finally comes the Locale. That stops at every possible station, and some impossible ones and sometimes even where there is no station at all." He smiled with a flash of brilliant white teeth to show that he was making a joke. "The one leaving here will get you to Bologna, where you will need to take another to Ancona, and yet another there for Giulianova. A locale leaves here in ten minutes. Your journey by such means will occupy eight or even ten hours. If the signorina is holiday-making, she will not wish to waste so much of her precious vacation in such travel."

Pina agreed. She was torn between the espresso and all its advantages, and the diretto. She decided to use the diretto, because it left this station in only half an hour, and following the receipt of that note, she felt that she wanted to get away from Milano as soon as possible. The discovery of the note had unnerved her more than she was prepared to admit, and she felt that she might be safer in the train rather than in this noisy and as yet almost deserted station.

Thanking the young man, she took her leave of him, sternly resisting his languishing looks and smiles, and made her way along the low platform to where the diretto stood waiting to depart. She had to walk almost the whole length of the train before she could find a non-smoking coach. Such things are rare on Italian railways, since nearly every native from fourteen years old and upward is a confirmed smoker. In a place where smoking was forbidden, Pina felt that she might be secure from the attentions of would-be Romeos.

Sharp to time, the engine gave a peremptory toot of its whistle and began to muster up sufficient energy to leave Milan. The effort seemed to make it move in a series of jerks. Just as it gave one enormous convulsion, the door of the coach was flung open and a man fell headlong into it. He was carrying only a briefcase, and luckily sustained no injury. The train began to roll more smoothly, and the man picked himself up and dusted down his clothing. He came to the seat opposite Pina, and put his briefcase on the rack. Balanced lightly on his toes, he bowed slightly toward her. "I do apologise," he smiled.

Pina smiled. She had wished to be alone, but there was nothing she could do about this incursion - anyway, the man appeared to be quite a personable chap. Perhaps if she were to be coldly distant, he might move to another seat. "You were fortunate not to be hurt," she said, and turned to look out of the window at the passing suburbs of Milan.

He said, "You are not a native of these parts; your accent is not of Milan. Do I detect a certain - shall I say, foreignness in your speech?"

Carlo di Felippo

She turned to face him. "I am English," she confessed. "My mother, however, is Neapolitan." She looked more closely at this unwanted travelling companion. She judged him to be about thirty. That he was tall she had noticed, before he sat down, at least six feet, and he carried his head well set on broad muscular shoulders. His movements were quick and deft - had he not fallen when the train had jerked to precipitate him on the deck, she would have likened him to a cat, or, looking again at his physique, perhaps a tiger would be a more apposite description. He had removed his hat when he spoke to her, and she noted that his chestnut coloured hair was thick and wavy, expensively trimmed and shaped, and not greased into subservience as so many Italian haircuts were. He wore a short closely trimmed beard that lent a certain aura to his presence. His dark suit was unobtrusive, but quite obviously cut from expensive material. She thought he might be some kind of executive in a large international company. Many such companies had their Italian headquarters in Milan.

"English, eh?" he said, in that tongue. "Would you mind if I practised my English on you?"

"To judge from the few words I have heard, you need no practice. I would say that you would be understood anywhere in the world where English is spoken."

"Ah, maybe. But there are idioms which either I do not know, or which I use incorrectly. And my pronunciation is at fault often when I meet words which I know only from reading. You could be very helpful, if you would!" He gave her a piteous smile, acting like a small boy asking his mother for another sweet, and Pina was forced to smile in reply. Seeing her relent, he continued, "Shall we have a long time together? Do you travel far?"

"I am travelling to Giulianova."

"Ah! You are then a tourist, a maker of the holiday?" She shook her head. "Then perhaps you are courier for a holiday package, employed to see that clients enjoy themselves at all times, and if they do not, you press out all creases from their paths?" His interest was intense.

"No, nothing like that, thank God! I am going to take up a post as a governess in Teramo."

"Meraviglioso - marvellous! I, too, travel to Giulianova. I call myself Carlo di Felippo, and I am advocate."

The language tutor in her make-up took charge as Pina smiled at his enthusiasm. "We don't say, 'I am advocate'. We say 'I am *an* advocate'. And in any case, we rarely use the word 'advocate' in the sense that you use it. We prefer to use the term 'lawyer'," she corrected him. "My name is Pina Corrigan."

"Nice!" he beamed. "A pretty name for a pretty - no, for a very pretty, lady." He gazed at her boldly, as Italians will, and Pina flushed hotly. He continued, "And thank you for the correction. You see, already I profit by meeting you! And I like 'lawyer' - somehow it sounds more solid!" Again he gave her that beaming smile. "Tell me, you know the Abruzzi at all?"

Pina confessed her total and complete ignorance of the region, adding that few English people ever seemed to visit the area. In the hope of forestalling any lecture that di Felippo might feel disposed to deliver on the history and other aspects of the province, she added, "But I am sure it is a delightful part of this beautiful land, and I hope to make a thorough investigation of all its doubtless many and varied attractions in due course. Are you Abruzzese?"

"No, my family is of Cremona. You know Cremona? Bella bella citta! A most beautiful city. You must, you simply must, visit some time!"

The train was now running through the fertile valley of the Po and from the windows on each side, Pina could see prosperous farms, each surrounded by fields planted with various crops, for this is the great larder of Italy. In due season, the tomato plants would be heavy with fruit, each of which could weigh half a kilo or more, and corn would wave its silken tassels in the warm breezes that blew along the valley. Now, of course, the year was too young for such sights, but Pina had little difficulty in imagining what the countryside would look like later in the year.

"It is very beautiful, is it not?" said di Felippo, almost as though he could read her thoughts. "Always, when I have travelled, I am happy to return to the cultivated fields of the Po valley, in which Cremona is not the least important city. Ah, for me, there is no place like it!" He kissed his fingers and waved them at the passing scene in a gesture purely Italian, and Pina had to admire such fervour. "When you arrive in the Abruzzi, you will find it so different from here. First as we leave Rimini, there will be little hills, then they grow bigger, and finally, when you have crossed the Marche and are over the border into Abbruzzo, you will see the Gran' Sasso towering up into the sky; so tall that snow remains on the peaks nearly all summer! Below them the little fields are vertical rather than horizontal, and stony too, so that poor contadini have difficulty to wrest - is that the right word? Is it? Good - to wrest a living from the poor soil."

"I shall be interested to meet those people," said Pina. "You make them sound very interesting. Would you describe them as typically Italian?"

"What is typical Italian? Are the blonde people of the north typical? Or the brunette folk of Napoli? The Abruzzesi are as diverse as any other race. Their territory has been ruled in turn by Greeks, Normans, Sicilians, and even Albanians. Even today, in the deep South of the region, there are whole villages whose mother tongue has Albanian roots, and whose religion is Islam. Their chief heritage, the Abruzzesi's, I mean, as a whole, is mainly derived from the time when the province was part of the two kingdoms of Sicily, and the chief item in that heritage is a love of plotting and secret societies! They seem to be addicted to all sorts of signs and passwords; they love to plot and scheme. I have always thought that the leading members of the Brigate Rosse, you know, the Red Brigades, must be Abruzzesi! It would be completely in character. But the smaller bandits do not have the training that the Brigate members undergo, and thus they indulge in more petty crime, and then, having made some foolish mistake, which leads the lawmen to them inevitably, they wonder why such calamity afflicts them!" He smiled deprecatingly. "But I am delivering a lecture! Let us be kind and say that they are really amateurs, or perhaps even children!"

The train rattled over the great steel bridge that spans the Po, and then drew up in Piacenza. With a murmured "Permesso? May I?" di Felippo threw his briefcase on to the seat, and laid Pina's coat beside her on the opposite bench. He then stood sentry at the ends of the seats. "This will, I hope, preserve our privacy," he said. "So I will be able to practise my English on you without interruption from other people, and anyway to speak a foreign tongue in a crowded carriage is not easy, nor would it even be polite."

The ploy was successful - nobody attempted to occupy the seats thus engaged. After a short halt, the train proceeded. He replaced the briefcase and coat to their appropriate positions on the racks, then resumed his seat opposite Pina.

She said, "You speak of the Abruzzo sometimes in the singular, and at other times of the Abruzzi in the plural. Why is this?"

"Oh, it is terribly complicated! The whole province is rightly known as Abruzzo and Molise, but that is in the South; I mean, Molise is in the South, and when that is included, you use the plural. When you speak only of the North, the singular takes over, but the stranger never really learns properly..."

She fell silent, and resumed her gazing out of the window, while he, aware of her abstraction, studied her profile. To Pina, the countryside seemed to be unchanging. On either hand, the fields stretched away to the horizon, with only a few poplars or aspens to break the monotony of the landscape. Some fields near the railway were being worked by small bands of toilers, and from time to time the great motorway approached to allow her to see the heavy traffic that ran ceaselessly in either direction. At times a village flashed by, marked by a tall church tower piercing a sky empty of any cloud. The villages seemed to huddle round the church like chicks crowded round a mother hen as she protected them from dangers real or imagined. One such village possessed a tower surmounted by a gilded ball on which perched an angel of the same metal. Both angel and ball gleaned brightly in the sunlight.

"Of course, this is all pure Guareschi, isn't it?" he said, breaking in on her reverie. She turned to look at him, and seeing the unspoken question in her gaze, he went on, "You must have read 'The Little World of Don Camillo'?"

"I'm sorry. I was lost in thought, and had for the moment forgotten that Guareschi was the author of 'Don Camillo'. Yes, I have read him, both in the original and in translation. I thought that the translation lost a little something of what he was trying to say." As he nodded, she continued, "I must confess that it had not occurred to me that the tales were set hereabouts."

"Hereabouts," he repeated, savouring the word on his tongue. "That is a new word to me, but it translates easily enough. Yes, Guareschi wrote heresabout - I mean, hereabouts. Not about any particular village, you understand, but any or every one of them could be Don Camillo's 'Piccolo Mondo'."

The train approached Bologna. As it did so, di Felippo strewed the packages on the seats as he had done at Piacenza. He then told Pina, "The train stays here for ten minutes. Will I get for you a cup of coffee or maybe a gelato, an ice cream?"

"I'd love a cup of coffee, please!"

He rose and left the coach, and soon Pina could see his tall figure battling through the crowds that thronged the platform to where a small trolley, operated by a woman who sported a magnificent cavalry moustache, was dispensing refreshments to the passengers who milled about her. She saw him force his way to the front of the crush - the Italians, she thought, never queue in orderly fashion - and then, as he began to return, bearing two paper cups from which rose plumes of steam, he was lost to her view as the crowd swallowed him up. At that precise moment, a short portly man, clad in a grey mackintosh, entered the coach and approached Pina.

"Signore, I have to inform you that these seats are occupied," she told him.

The Man in the Train

THREE

The man ignored her protest. Roughly gripping Pina's shoulder, he turned his face towards hers and approached it within inches. His breath was a foul compound of cigarette smoke, garlic and cheap liquor as he muttered hoarsely, "Why don't you take heed of the warning you have been given, you little fool? Listen to me. Get off this train. Cross the line and take the next Rapido back to wherever you have come from. This is the last friendly warning you will get. And stopping your young man friend meddling would be a service to him, for you will both live to regret it if you continue on your present course!"

He was interrupted by the appearance of di Felippo. Carefully depositing the two cups of coffee on the floor of the corridor, he seized Pina's assailant with a strong brown hand. With an oath, the man drew from the pocket of his raincoat a vicious-looking knife. He cried out in pain as di Felippo gave a twist to his wrist, and the knife clattered to the floor.

"Pick it up, Pina," ordered di Felippo. "We must not let little boys play with such dangerous toys, must we?" He gave the man's wrist another bone-jarring jerk, and a yelp of pain came from the man's throat. "Now, who are you, and more importantly, why are you assaulting this English signorina? Is this a sample of our celebrated Italian hospitality to our foreign guests? I'm ashamed for you!" He turned the man round as the train gave an asthmatic hoot and lurched into motion.

The sudden jerk made both men stumble. The portly man gave a twist of his body, and leaving his raincoat in di Felippo's hands, dashed to the door of the coach to leap out as the train picked up speed. Too late di Felippo sprang after him - the man had disappeared among the throng.

Di Felippo returned to where Pina sat, and found her inspecting the knife which he had ordered her to pick up during the scuffle. He took it from her unresisting fingers and turned it over once or twice, looking closely at both blade and hilt. "H'm, we shall not learn a lot from this! You may buy one like it in any store for five thousand lire or so. Here, you keep it for a memento!" He passed the wicked-looking stiletto over to her. "I'll buy you a sheath for it later on.

Then you'll have a fair paperknife to remind you of this most peculiar
incident! Be careful with it - it is very sharp, but it is of too poor
quality to keep an edge for long. Wrap it up in the meantime, for
safety's sake."

Pina did as she was bidden, and dropped the tissue-wrapped knife
into her handbag. Her nerves were now beginning to appreciate what
had happened, and she felt sick in her stomach and almost ready to
cry with delayed fear. Meantime, di Felippo was examining the
raincoat. Turning it this way and that, he said, "I apologise for using
your given name, Miss Corrigan. It just slipped out in the heat of the
moment. But may we not get on to first name terms? I should very
much like to hear you call me Carlo, or, even better, Charles!"

"I think I would like that, Carlo." She ignored his request for his
name to be anglicised. "And thank you for arriving in the nick of
time. I was terrified of that horrid man!"

"I thought you were very brave, Pina. It was certainly an
unpleasant experience for you."

"You dealt with him very effectively, Carlo. Do you deduce
anything from that coat?"

"Very little. It's just a raincoat of very cheap price, bought from
Standa, the multiple store, well worn and dirty about the collar and
cuffs. Nothing in the outside pockets. Aha, just a moment, there is
something in this inside pocket. Aha, this is the sheath for that knife.
There, now you have the complete thing! Faugh! the coat stinks of
stale smoke and other filth. I shall throw it out of window!"

"Wouldn't it be better to keep it and report everything to the
police? The coat might give them some clue to its ownership."

"It might be unwise to consult the police. They will consume a lot
of your time and all to no purpose. This is not England and the Yard
of Scotland, you understand and life here is not an Agatha Christie
novella. No, I do assure that it is better to remain silent, and to try to
forget the whole incident."

Well," she said, doubtfully, "You are a lawyer, and know what
you are talking about, but I don't really like to leave things in the air
like this. I can't understand why I should be the object of such an
attack, though."

"Believe me, I am not going to let the matter rest, Pina. I have
connections, and will get to the bottom of all this hassle within a few
days. Meanwhile, this coat goes out of window." He rose and went

to the door, and flung the coat out into the air. A gang of workmen engaged on line repair, stood aside to allow the train to pass, and as di Felippo returned to Pina, he said, "Some poor labourer has gained a new coat! Not often are wearable articles of clothing flung from trains!" He gave her a smile with those wonderfully white teeth. He picked up the cups of coffee which Pina had retrieved from the floor and placed on the little table under the window. "I feared that we might have knocked them over during the argument," he said. "But they are still drinkable, though not whistling hot - is that right? Oh, piping, is it? I understand, piping hot. Well, the coffee is not piping hot, but it is still potable - I mean drinkable." He passed one of the cups to Pina, and each took a contemplative sip. The liquid was only tepid, as he had said, but they drained their cups with relish.

The journey continued across the flat plain until they reached Rimini. Here the line turned southwards, wending its way through the many seaside resorts so well known to British holidaymakers. Riccione, Cattolica, Pesaro, Fano, all came and went in their turn. Then as Carlo had predicted, the countryside began to swell into little hills, which grew bigger and higher as the southward run continued. Through Ancona they ran, then skirted the mountain that rose above the city. To their left, the blue sea laughed and sparkled in the bright sunshine. The coastal road that ran between the sea and the railway was busy with traffic of all kinds. The couple in the coach were both silent now, she absorbed completely with all that came into view, while he was intent on the play of expressions that flitted over her mobile features.

After a very brief stop at San Benedetto, the journey was resumed, and Carlo began to stir. "Nearly there," he told her. "Less than a half hour will see us at Giulianova." He stood and lifted down her case from the rack where it had travelled from Milan. The train rumbled through a few small stations, disdaining to halt at any of them but greeting each with a hoarse blast of the whistle. Then, gently slowing, it rolled over a level crossing where many people on foot and in cars were waiting its passing with more or less patience, and with a final squeal of brakes halted in a long station, equipped with about eight long low platforms. Di Felippo carried Pina's luggage to the door of the coach, and then leaping lightly to the platform, handed her down. Once safely on earth, she held out her hand.

Sandro

"Goodbye, Carlo. I have enjoyed travelling with you. And don't worry about your command of English - it is excellent. Once again, many many thanks for rescuing me from that awful man." She gave a mock shudder to underline her gratitude.

He took her soft little hand in his own brown strong one and let it lay there as he replied, "No, Pina. This is not goodbye. We shall meet again, because I intend it to be so. I have the matter of the assault to clear up, among other things. Listen! I shall be staying hereaboust - I mean, hereabouts - for some time. You may contact me at any time at the Albergo Regina Victoria, As soon as you are settled in your new home, please telephone me and let me know the name and number of your new address. Then perhaps on your free days I may be permitted to take you out and show you something of the countryside. I suppose in its quaint mountainy way it could be quite interesting to you."

Gently she freed her hand from his grasp. "Very well, Carlo. I will let you know where I am. But please do not get any funny ideas of romance. Friends, yes. But nothing more."

With a broad smile, he drew his finger across his throat. "I promise only not to try to rush you. Until you say otherwards, friends only shall it be. My chief worry is that you may be in some kind of danger; why else should you have been attacked on the train? I believe that you may yet be glad to have as many allies as possible - as many as you can find. So for now, think only of me as an ally, and for the present, I will be content. Now, may I get you a taxi?"

"Somebody should be here to meet me. I'll make enquiries at the station entrance. Meanwhile, arrivederci, Carlo. I promise to keep in touch." She made to pick up her suitcase, but he forestalled her, and together they walked across the line as their train pulled away, bound for Pescara and other exotic places. In the entrance hall, a young man dressed in denims stood smoking a black cheroot. As the pair approached, he threw away the butt and sauntered over to meet them.

"Signorina Corrigan-a?"

"Yes, I am she." Pina once more shook hands with Carlo as the young man relieved him of her case and moved out of the station, with Pina and Carlo in tow, as it were. He led them to a big Fiat, the door of which he opened with a flourish after he had deposited her luggage in the boot. After ensuring that Pina was comfortable, he strolled to the front of the car and took his place at the wheel. Pina wound down the window to give a last wave to Carlo as the motor started, and the vehicle drew away from the entrance portico.

The driver said, "Don Stefano Capriotti sends his greetings to the signorina and welcomes you to Giulianova. My name is Alessandro; people all call me Sandro. I am employed as a sort of general help about the house and estate of Tre Boschi. I also drive a car when necessary." He steered the car the wrong way round the central island on the station approach, coming to a halt at the traffic lights.

"When I ferry someone somewhere, I am called the autista, the driver. Luigi Passi, the majordomo, says I talk too much, but there is always something to be said, and never enough time to say everything! You speak good Italian, signorina. I wish I could talk in another tongue. I *do* have a little German, which I use in the summer when the Germans and the Austrians crowd our coast, and we boys want to speak to the girls. But mostly they laugh at the way I say their words, so there is little communication." In the mirror, he leered at her suggestively. "But it is normally enough! The girls like handsome young Italiani!"

He continued, "This car is a Fiat 2000. It is our middle car. Don Stefano has a Rolls Royce, which I am not often permitted to drive. There is also a Mickey Mouse of a car, a Fiat seicento. That vehicle I do not like too much. Like every seicento, it is too cramped and too slow." He banged a clenched fist on the rim of the steering wheel, "Come *on*! Change! These lights are always against me! If I come down the hill from Giulianova Alta, they stop me when I want to get to the station. They are red when I want to turn right as I come from Ancona, and red again when I come from Pescara. Now they are stopping me from crossing the main road. Do you have traffic lights in England? It must be very dangerous to drive there - I mean, people tell me that they drive on the left! I should be terrified to see all that traffic coming towards me on the wrong side of the road! Ah, we go at last! The lights change! Andiamo!" The big car leapt forward like a frightened deer, and they were mounting a steep hill before any other drivers realised that the lights were about to change.

"Now we go up the hill to Giulianova Alta. This town is Giulianova Lido, you know. The upper town is very nice, but rather small. I prefer bigger towns like Teramo, or Ascoli Piceno, or even L'Aquila. Get out of my way, you fool! Do you want all the highway?" This in parenthesis to an old man trying to cross the street. He shook his fist at an unfortunate driver who had momentarily put a wheel over the central line on a hairpin bend. "Some people scare me when they drive. But I am a very good driver, and I know how to deal with those who take up more than their share of the road! I am the best driver in the whole district of Campli! Are there fast drivers in England? Do you know Stirling-a Moos? I am told that English drivers are well-disciplined, quite as much as the Germans, per esempio. Is that true, do you think? But we Italians are the sort that need no law. We drive as though the car were an extension of our bodies. I tell my mates that there are only two states a car can be in when I am in command. One state is going as fast as it will, and the other is parked! Now we are coming to a fine panorama over the harbour. Look to your left, signorina, and you will see."

Sandro slowed his headlong dash slightly. Pina was able to see, far below, the tiny houses of Giulianova Lido and beyond them, the blue Adriatic Sea. Toy cars moved along the streets, and a toy train stood in a model station. Far away on the horizon, a few miniature ships moved slowly over the flat calm sea. The apparatus which projected from their bows showed them to be fishing vessels, and she resolved, as soon as she was settled in her post, to try to visit the harbour and see it and the ships at close quarters. As she looked down at it now, the harbour seemed to be crowded with white ships and boats, moored to the quays three or four deep.

Soon they were proceeding through the upper town. Sandro turned into a long piazza with a central island on which grew glossy palm trees surrounding a tall bronze statue. Round the bases of the trees, and the plinth of the statue, seats were strategically placed to afford as much shade as possible. Here some older people were sitting, chatting and enjoying the cooler air of the early evening. Cars lined the sides of the carriageway, seemingly abandoned rather than parked, and effectively reducing the usable width of the roadway to about half that which the town planners originally intended. Sandro threaded his way through with a careless ease. Glancing to her right, Pina saw a large domed building which was obviously the cathedral. Sandro turned right at the top end of the piazza, violently wrenching the steering wheel and causing the tyres to emit a squeal of protest as they scrabbled at the warm asphalt of the road surface.

"This is the road to Campli," he told Pina. "Soon we shall pass over the autostrada. Are there autostrade in England? I like very much to drive on them, but Don Stefano says I go too fast. Also it is expensive to pay the tolls. Do you also have tolls in England? I cannot understand my master's attitude, for he must be quite the richest man in this province, well able to afford a few autostrada tolls! But there it is. I suppose that those who are not careful do not long keep their wealth. As for me, I have to obey orders. On my salary I could never afford to pay tolls for a big car!

"Now we come to the top of a ridge along which the road runs. Do you see the little town perched on the hill top there on the right? That is called Colonella - the other little town to its left is Controguerra, an odd name for a town, I always think. If you split the name into 'Contro' and 'Guerra', you get the term 'Against War'. Imagine living in a place with a name like that!

"Now the road becomes a little uninteresting for a while, but soon we shall begin the climb up to Tre Boschi. I believe Tre Boschi is truly the biggest estate in the whole of southern Italy! Don Stefano has many hectares of vines, and even more of maize. In the wet bottoms, he also grows much fennel. Oh, he is enormously rich!" He paused for a while in silent admiration of his master's immense wealth, and the glory reflected on all who worked for him, not least of whom was Sandro! During his moment of worship, Pina was able to devote her full attention to the passing scene.

They were now well into the rural area behind Giulianova. Occasionally Pina would see an old woman striding along the roadside with a basket perched on her head while her bare feet raised little clouds of dust from the dry verges. In some fields, despite the late hour, tractors were still working; in others oxen pulled carts or ploughs, their heads nodding in time to the slow pace of their march. She was fascinated by the scenes around her, by the kaleidoscope of the long narrow fields coloured by the different crops sown in them. She was falling in love with the small towns hanging by their eyelashes to the steep hills. She knew that they were so placed for defensive reasons for this region was a fruitful source of riches, as well as for female slaves, for the raiding corsairs of history. So steep were the hills on which the towns stood that roads could not be built directly up to them, but had to be formed of a series of loops and bends which lay coiled like snakes about the slopes.

Fronti

Before them as Sandro drove her towards her new home, the sun was setting behind the high hills to the west, and in the valleys the shadows were lengthening rapidly; there is not much twilight in these southern latitudes. Pina glanced behind the car, but it was raising too much dust from the unmetalled road for her to distinguish anything. Sandro had not abated his speed. Bends in the road were greeted by a blast from the Fiat's triple horns. If no similar warning was received in answer, he took the bend on the left with the same aplomb as he drove on the correct side when a reaction to his warning was received. But even then, he seemed to drive always as close as possible to the centre of the road.

The route began to climb yet more steeply. Sandro drove under an archway and wended a rapid course through a series of narrow streets. "This is Bellante," he told Pina. "It is a very ancient town, with a wonderful belvedere from which you may overlook the whole valley to the North. I have two old aunts who live here. They own a little shop where they sell things like tablecloths and napkins and other materials for the household. When they die, I shall have the shop, because I am their only close relative, as far as they and I know. I would quite like to be a shopkeeper and sit at the door to welcome customers. I could become rich quite quickly. Look, the shop is just down that street there, halfway down the slope. It is sad that I cannot take this car down there, but it is too wide for the street. Now, the seicento would go there with ease. Look, signorina, if ever you need sheets or table linen or curtaining, tell me, and I will see that you get a good discount from those old biddies, my aunts!"

They emerged from the cool darkness of the streets onto the main road again. Sandro glanced at the dashboard clock and exclaimed, "Oh, it is still quite early. Will the signorina do me the honour of stepping out of the car to look over the belvedere? The light at this time of day is just right, and you would find the effort well worth while."

In spite of her travel fatigue, Pina assented, as he seemed so keen to show her the wonderful view, and he drew to a halt at the kerb. He rushed round to open the door for her and when she had alighted, conducted her up some steps to a long wide paved surface. A red-painted scrolled iron railing protected the daring from falling from the belvedere. Sandro put his hand under Pina's elbow and steered her to the railing.

"See," he cried, with infectious enthusiasm, "is not that a bella vista - a beautiful view? Look, straight across the valley there you see the lights of Sant' Omero coming on. To the right you can see Corropoli and Nereto, and yet further to the right is Tortoreto Alto. If you dare to lean ever so slightly outwards, you can even see the Adriatic! Then to the left are the mountains behind which lies Civitella del Tronto. Ah, when the old aunts die, and I am a rich man, I shall spend many hours up here, for I love it so much!" He kissed his fingers and waved them towards the view.

Pina could not disagree that the view was stupendous. Though the light was fading so rapidly, she could plainly see how magnificent was the country that lay before her. While she stood in silence, a man approached. An elderly man, as Pina considered him to be from her vantage point of twenty something years, he spoke to Sandro.

"Buona Sera, Sandro! A grand evening, nevvero? And is this the English miss of whom you have told us so much? How do you do, signorina? It is a great pleasure to meet you, after all that has been told about you!" He held out his hand and Pina shook it automatically. "Ah, signorina, you have a very soft hand! Softer far than I should have expected when I think upon the duties for which Sandro tells me you have been engaged!"

Pina looked at him in enquiry. "Ah, you are surprised! But we all know about your duties; Sandro is a very talkative young man, as you may already have noticed! But even so, he has failed to introduce us! I am Matteo Fronti, a sort of distant cousin of our young hero here. Not that that means a lot, for we are all cousins in these parts, you know. Even the mighty Don Stefano is related in some degree to about ninety per cent of the population. In the past, we were a very close community, and none of us travelled far from our native heath. Now, of course, things are different. The young people go to Teramo and Ascoli Piceno on their mopeds; some even go as far as Ancona or Pescara to bring new blood into the community with their spouses from afar. But there I go, chattering away like the cattle-dealer that I am. Come, let me escort you to your chariot of fire, the ever-faithful Fiat maintained and driven by Sandro!"

He gripped her firmly by the bicep and began to lead her to the car, Sandro following a few paces behind them.

"My dear young lady!" cried Fronti. "But you have no muscles at all! In no way do you resemble the Amazon that Sandro has led us to expect! You obviously have some secret, such as karate, or kung-fu or another martial art of which we have no knowledge! Of course, we have heard of such things - the cinema, is ubiquitous you know!"

By this time, they had arrived at the car. Fronti opened the front door for Pina and ensured that she was comfortably installed. He lifted his hat as Sandro started the engine and roared away with his customary violence. Pina glanced at the young profile to her left. "What on earth was he talking about? What sort of stories have you been telling him, Sandro? Allow me to inform you that an English governess does not require physical force to keep her charges under control!"

Sandro shrugged. "They have so little to talk about. Nothing ever happens up here, and their lives are empty of incident. All the evenings they sit out in their chairs before their doors, and they talk. And with every recital, things grow bigger. Fronti is a fool!" He pushed down harder on the pedal, and the big Fiat fairly leapt forward.

Much later when Pina had gained some knowledge of the country and its geography, she wondered why Sandro had taken such a circuitous route from the station to Tre Boschi. She wondered, too, if it was purely coincidence that Fronti had appeared on the belvedere while Sandro was showing her the views.

FOUR

Night had fallen as Sandro turned off the road on to a narrow lane, winding and completely unpaved, which led up a steep slope to the right. After a hundred metres or so, the lane straightened out. Pina gasped with sheer delight at the scene revealed to her by the light of the moon. The house of Don Stefano was long and low with whitewashed walls and black woodwork. It stood at the end of the drive, which expanded to make parking and turning places for vehicles. A few dim lamps illuminated the front of the house, and two wing walls on either side of it. One of these walls was pierced by what she thought to be a pair of heavy doors - later inspection revealed that the 'doors' were in fact two large wall ovens, intended to be heated by huge logs thrust into them and withdrawn when the heat of the oven was adjudged to be sufficiently high for cooking to commence. Much later Pina discovered that the ovens were used only when there were guests in the house, much as a barbecue would be used in England, to give the guests an experience out of the ordinary, or when the whole workforce of the estate were given their annual treat by their employer.

Sandro drove round the open space to the front door of the house, where he halted the car with a heart-stopping jerk. Bellowing "Elsa!" he dashed round the car in order to assist Pina to alight. As he conducted her to the door, a small bustling woman, who appeared to be some five years older than Pina, emerged from a door. This person, who was clad in the fine grey gabardine which seemed to be the uniform of the household staff, hurried to meet the new arrival.

"Welcome to Tre Boschi!" she cried, holding out both hands in greeting. "We have been looking for you for such a long time! Are you very weary? I know that you have had a long journey."

Pina took the woman's extended hands and pressed them warmly. "I am going to like this girl!" she thought. Aloud she said that she was only a little tired, but that she would certainly be glad of an opportunity to wash and to change her travel-stained clothing.

In response to Elsa's invitation, she followed her along the hall, and after ducking through a low door set in an arch, the pair mounted a steep and winding, though mercifully short, staircase which led to a little room. A divan bed, which looked as though it might be very comfortable, stood against the wall opposite the door. In one corner stood a dressing table with a triple mirror, flanked by a wardrobe built into an alcove. In another corner, most welcome sight, was a hand basin with towels hanging from a side rail. Rugs were strewn at random over the gleaming dark wooden floor, and curtains which matched the bedcover were still undrawn over the window which pierced the fourth wall of the room. The walls were colour-washed in deep cream distemper which had been applied directly to the rough plasterwork. The general appearance of the place was a symphony in blue and cream, set off by the black woodwork.

Pina clapped her hands together in admiration. "Oh, it's so beautiful, so elegant!" she breathed. "I do not know what I expected to find, but it was nothing like this!"

Elsa smiled her pleasure at Pina's enthusiasm. "It's quite nice," she agreed. "It is sad that there is no attached bathroom, but a few steps along the passage will bring you to the guests' bathroom, which you will have to use. These older houses do not readily lend themselves to allowing a bathroom to every bedroom. Now, in my brother's house in Teramo, there is a bathroom on every floor, five bathrooms in all! But that is a very new house."

Pina smiled. "This will be wonderful," she said. "I am quite sure that it will not hurt me to walk a couple of metres to a bathroom." A thought struck her. "Do you often have house guests?"

"Very seldom, now, signorina. Since Donna Maria died, this has been a cold house, warmed only by the presence of Stella who has been looking forward with much excitement to meeting you. She is a darling child, and all the servants love her as much as we feel she loves us. As you probably know, she is Don Stefano's only child, and none of us think there will be another; we are all quite certain that her father will never marry again.

"But you must be aching for your toilet! I will leave you to clean up, and then, when you are ready, please ring the bell by the bedhead, and I will come and conduct you to Luigi Passi, the majordomo, whom you have already met." With merest hint of a curtsey, she withdrew.

Pina set about tidying herself after her long hours of travel. Regaining her bedroom, she was running a comb through her hair when there was a knock at the door. No one came in when she called the person to enter. Opening the door, she found her luggage standing at the top of the staircase. She pulled the case into her room, but did not bother to unpack it. Seated on the bed, her mind was a wild turmoil of thoughts. How strange it was that her new charge had not been at the door to meet her! Surely most children would be more than curious about anyone who had been engaged to be companion and tutor to them, but it seemed that Stella had no such curiosity. It could be that she was timid about meeting a stranger, and a foreigner to boot. Perhaps she had been given orders to allow a weary traveller time to find her bearings before rushing to meet the newcomer.

But whatever the cause, Pina felt that the child's behaviour was a little odd. Maybe it was the way of the Abruzzesi. Fronti had said, on the belvedere, that the locals were different from the usual run of Italians - more inbred, was the term he had used, and it might be that their manners and customs were old-fashioned. She would uncover the answer to that riddle in due course, Pina told herself. In the meanwhile, she was delighted with the quarters allotted to her, and she felt that she could quite love Elsa, who, besides giving an impression of cheerful efficiency, appeared to be a warm and affectionate character.

For ten minutes or so, she unpacked and safely and tidily bestowed all her few possessions in their appointed places. Giving a final glance round the room, she tugged the bell pull as Elsa had requested her. Very shortly the housekeeper was there, and Pina was being conducted down the stairs and along the corridor. Elsa stopped at a door and rapped sharply with her pudgy little fist. A voice bade them "Enter!" and Pina was ushered into a room which appeared to be part office and part sleeping apartment, sparsely furnished and severely decorated in plain buff with the apparently usual black-stained floor and other woodwork. The principal article of furniture was a large desk which stood precisely in the centre of the room. Behind the desk was seated the man whom she had last seen in the hall of the flats - the man who had engaged her for the post she was now taking up.

As the two women entered, Passi rose, and extended his hand to Pina. She was surprised at the lack of warmth apparent in his handshake, but then, from the first she had thought him to be a cold fish. He gave her a thin-lipped cold smile and said, "Welcome to Tre Boschi, Miss Corrigan. I knew that I had judged you correctly, and that we should meet again here. I hope that the room Elsa has prepared for you is to your taste."

"Oh, yes, it is utterly delightful... er... er signore."

Again he favoured her with that thin smile. "Please do as all the rest of the household do, and call me Luigi, Miss Corrigan."

She thanked him and continued, "Yes, my room is, as I say, quite charming. I am very happy to be here, and am most anxious to meet the signorina Stella as soon as possible."

"You shall meet her tomorrow, Miss Corrigan. Meanwhile, if there is anything you need, please ask Elsa for it, and I am sure that she will do all in her power to ensure that your wishes are met. You must understand that you are the first Englishwoman to stay at Tre Boschi, and we are not absolutely sure of what your needs may be, although we have endeavoured to anticipate them."

"You have certainly succeeded, signore... er... Luigi," she assured him. He replied with an almost imperceptible bow, responding to her bright smile of thanks with a bleak stretching of his lips. With an air of dismissal, he began to shuffle the papers laying on his desk. Both women took the hint and withdrew. Outside in the corridor, Elsa said, "If the signorina will come this way, I will show you the dining room, and then give you something to eat. I am sorry that this evening you must eat alone. Stella eats in her room, and we servants in the basement. Luigi has every meal in his office. So," she continued, "as Don Stefano is not at home, tonight you must eat solo. I hope you like pasta. I have made for you some typical Abruzzese spaghetti alla chitarra, using the machine we call the guitar, so that in effect you will have square spaghetti. There is a meat sauce to garnish the pasta, a bottle of wine made on the estate and for dessert, fruit such as apples, grapes, and figs. We are very ignorant about how the English people eat, you know. Perhaps when you have been here a little while, I shall be able to present English dishes for you. I have already bought a recipe book!" She smiled an apology.

"Please do not let that worry you, Elsa. We eat much the same as you do, and anyway, I am half Italian, you know! My mama is a Napolitana."

Elsa heaved a visible sigh of relief. "I have been so worried," she confessed. "You cannot know how happy I am that you will eat my food!"

She led Pina to a medium-sized dining room. The heavy dark furniture made the room appear gloomy, but much of the gloom was dispelled by the light of the fire that burned in the large grate, the logs crackling merrily. The whole table top was covered by a sheet of plate glass that fitted perfectly to protect the highly polished surface so that neither cloth nor place mats were necessary. The chairs about the table were old-fashioned and high-backed; all were fitted with decoratively embroidered cushion covers. The table was set ready for one, and Elsa drew up a carver hair, saying, "Please be seated, signorina. You shall eat in five minutes. While you wait, please try an aperitivo. It is very good!" The door closed softly as she slipped away, leaving Pina to her thoughts.

She poured a glass of the wine from an antique decanter of exquisite cut and design. Rolling the drink round her palate, as Daddy had taught her, she was agreeably surprised at its quality, and quickly drained the glass to pour another and fuller supply. She was grateful that Daddy had taught her to appreciate wine. Mama's method was to slosh it out and gulp it down without really tasting it. To Daddy, wine was almost a religion, and the drinking of it assumed something of the importance and solemnity of a rite.

Before she had emptied the second glass, Elsa arrived bearing a dish of steaming pasta. She set the dish before Pina, and with a murmured "Buon' appetito", left again as quickly as she had entered. Pina helped herself to a plateful of the spaghetti. Suddenly, she found that she was hungry, and in a very short time had demolished two plates of the light yellowish pasta with its rich sauce garnish. Then she sat for a while, glass in hand, twirling it by the stem to catch the light of the dancing flames as she mulled over the events of the past two days of travel from rainy cold old London to this tranquil and beautiful house in the Abruzzo. Could there, she asked herself, be a greater contrast? In the middle of her reverie, Elsa again entered the room.

"Oh, signorina!" she scolded. "You have not eaten half enough! Did you not like the pasta?"

"It was truly delicious, Elsa. Perhaps I should have told you that I am a small eater - I have to watch my figure, you know! But the spaghetti were superb, and the sauce exactly right to accompany them. One day soon, I shall ask you for the recipe for both!"

As she cleared away the debris, Elsa blushed hotly. "I would be very happy to teach the signorina, but I fear that she mocks me. It was rough country fare, and not truly fit for an Englishwoman! But here is some fruit to complete your supper. There is also cheese.

Both fruit and cheese come from the estate. We are justly famed for both products." Pina nibbled at a piece of the strong cheese and then selected an apple while Elsa completed the task of clearing the table. "Does the signorina require anything else?" she asked, adding that she now had to prepare the supper for the staff.

"Nothing more, Elsa, thank you. Oh yes, there is one thing. Is there a telephone I might use?"

"There are two, signorina. One is in Luigi's office, and another in the corridor near the stairs to your room. There is a third, a public callbox, on the main road, just up the hill a little way, but for that you will need gettone, the tokens, you know."

"Thank you, Elsa. It was an excellent meal, exactly right after a long journey. I shall just finish this apple, and then shall retire."

"As the signorina desires. You must be very weary after travelling all the way from Londra. I quite expect that you had to change trains somewhere. I get worried when Don Stefano calls for me to go to the house in Roma. I should think Londra must be even further than that! But I do not care for trains and travelling. I am a peasant, and happier far when I am in the country! I wish the signorina a good night, and a good rest. We shall meet, again at breakfast, which for the staff is at six thirty. You will obviously wish to eat later than that!"

Pina agreed. "I think about eight would be better for me, if possible." Elsa nodded. "Good night, then, Elsa, and a thousand thanks for your kindness."

Elsa disappeared with the remains of the supper on a tray. Pina toyed for a moment with her fruit, then rose from the table and went to her room. It was such a cosy little room! Someone had lighted a fire in the hearth. The logs glowed redly, and Pina thought how considerate was that person to have lighted the fire; it grew cold at this altitude so early in the season. A sweet smell of burning applewood hung in the air. Little sparks detached themselves from the logs from time to time, and flew up the chimney. Pina recalled how Daddy used to tell her brother and herself that these sparks were really messages to the fairies, who, if the person seeing them had been well-behaved, would convey a message to anyone anywhere in the world. Sleepily, Pina wished a message to Mama, to tell her that all was well here at Tre Boschi, and another to Carlo di Felippo in his hotel down there on the coast. Really, she ought to have kept her promise and telephoned, but somehow she had grown suddenly very weary. Half asleep, she undressed and crept into bed. Then she knew no more.

FIVE

Faintly, from a distance, a bell tolled slowly, insistently, sensed rather than heard through sleep-filled ears. Sheep bleated in their pens. The treble voices of lambs replied to their dams' baritone notes. Cattle lowed to welcome the burgeoning day. Nearer to hand, in the courtyard below Pina's room, a cockerel crowed, throwing out a challenge to the whole poultry world. Pina awoke slowly to these rural sounds, opening her eyes and wondering, for a moment, precisely where she was, and what she was doing in this strange bed. Then with full wakefulness came recollection and she sat up, running her fingers through her tousled hair. A wide uncovered yawn revealed a set of perfect teeth. A small clock on the dressing table showed that it was just after seven. Now fully awake, she rose from the bed and crossed to the window. She drew back the curtains and flung open the casement.

The view made her gasp with delight. Immediately below her window lay a courtyard. Unlike the front court, this yard had no oven doors. Instead, each of the three walls that Pina could see was pierced by doorways that gave entrance to storehouses. The doorways had no doors, and from her vantage point of height, Pina could look right into the interiors of the stores. Two were stables, she saw, and it was from these that the animal sounds were emanating. The third was stacked from floor to ceiling with neatly cut logs. Between the two animal shelters, a great gate afforded access to the outside world. And what a world that open gate revealed! She could see nearer things through the gate, but above the wall farther vistas showed in the soft morning light. Dimly in the far distance the peaks of mountains, their tops covered in snow, reached upwards through the morning mist. The peaks seemed almost to pierce the bright blue sky. Even as she looked, the mists rose higher, and within moments the mountains were lost to view.

Closer to hand, low rolling hills approached the mountains. On the tops of these hills, in sharp relief, stood toy-like farmhouses, surrounded by fields which ran vertically up and down the hills, a patchwork quilt of long strips of material rather than the more usual squares which she knew in England. In the fields, the grey-green of olive trees marched cheek by jowl with the bright green of young corn

- maize, Pina thought it might be. Hedges made of bright green vines separated the fields. Far away, a tractor crawled slowly up the field it was ploughing, giving to the patchwork a tone of reddish brown newly turned earth. Far to her left, Pina could catch a tantalising glimpse of the sea. The terrain between Tre Boschi and the coast was hilly, but here and there deep valleys ran towards the coast, drawing the eye inevitably towards the deep blue of the Adriatic. Many of the higher hills were crowned with small settlements, as she remembered from the drive of last evening. Each village had its tall church tower or spire, matching an equally tall water tower, and each town seemed to be approached by a white road that had to coil round the hill to gain altitude. Behind the blackness of the three woods that gave the estate its name, the top of a church tower stood proud; it was from here that the bell she could hear was tolling.

She turned her gaze to the right. There was a repeat of the view which she had just been admiring, except that the mountains were not so tall, nor were they garnished with snow. In the morning sun, they appeared to be a purple-grey in colour, with huge masses of rock which could have been granite, she thought. She wondered how often such great masses rolled down the steep hillsides, and what damage they could cause if ever they lost their anchorages.

A movement in the courtyard below brought her attention to nearer things. An old man, erect and tall, entered the log storehouse and emerged bearing a wicker basket full of fuel like that which had warmed her last night. The man's hat was perched precariously on the back of his head, and he moved with the sprightly dancing step of the cavalryman, a gait much like that of Daddy, Pina thought. He was dressed in the almost universal blue denim trousers and blouse of the peasant, and his bare feet were thrust into wooden-soled sandals with only a thin strap across his toes. Pina thought he was the odd-job man of the staff. As he strode across the yard below her, she was unable to see his face, but instinctively she knew that his face was like that of other Italian peasants she had seen - nut-brown, wrinkled like a walnut, and blessed with sharp dark brown or black eyes. Probably, she thought idly, his teeth were badly nicotine-stained and he suffered from halitosis. She continued to watch until the man disappeared from her line of sight, then withdrew her head and began to prepare for the coming day.

She found the bathroom to be well furnished with fine soft towels and was agreeably surprised to discover that scalding water gushed from the hot taps. In her experience the marking of a tap 'caldo' was more normally a pious hope than a certainty. Another pleasant surprise was that the shower actually worked, and it was a much refreshed Pina who returned to her room some twenty minutes later. It was nearing eight o'clock, and her stomach was beginning to remind her that a healthy young woman required sustenance from time to time. She descended the stairs bent on search for Elsa and breakfast.

The noise of pots being banged about guided her steps to a small scullery where she found a young girl cleaning the huge pan in which last night's pasta had been cooked. The evidence was plain, for pieces of sticky pasta were clinging firmly to the sides of the pan, giving the girl some trouble to remove them. She was so engrossed in her task that she failed to hear Pina's approach, and had to be tapped on the shoulder before she ceased working, and with a gasp, turned to face the Englishwoman.

"Oh, scusi, signorina! I did not hear you come in. How can I help?"

"Good morning. I am looking for the kitchen and Elsa."

"Ah, yes, the kitchen. But surely the signorina would prefer to go to the dining room and ring for service?"

"On the contrary. I would much rather greet Elsa in her kitchen! By the way, what is your name?"

The girl bobbed. "I am Rosa, signorina. The kitchen is through that door." She indicated a door with a nod of her head.

Thanking the girl, Pina left her to her duties and entered the kitchen. She found herself in a large square room with a cement floor. Against one wall stood a gas cooker flanked by its fuel supply, two great cylinders of bottled gas. In another wall, a wood-burning stove of unimaginable age stood, emitting a welcoming and cheerful warmth. Elsa was busy with a small saucepan which seethed on the gas cooker, and she turned to greet Pina as she entered.

"Buon'giorno, signorina! I trust you slept well?" She pointed to the wood-burner. "There is coffee in the mocha machine there, if the signorina does not mind helping herself. I am sorry that at this moment, I cannot serve you, but I am preparing Stella's eggs, and they must be just right to tempt her appetite, so I dare not leave them. There are cups and sugar on the tray on the table."

Pina poured out a cup of the thick black coffee, sugared it well, and took an appreciative sip of the scalding liquid. "Thank you Elsa. I slept wonderfully well! I've just passed a pleasant ten minutes gazing out of my bedroom window. What glorious scenery there is up here!"

Elsa sniffed. "We don't think much about scenery here. After all, what is it but land? Sometimes it is flat and easy to work, sometimes it is rugged and steep and can only be cultivated with great trouble. But certainly we don't think about it being pretty. Except perhaps Sandro looks at it with different eyes than ours. Of course, I remember when Donna Maria was alive, and we had many guests from the city, they used to rapturise about the scenery, so I suppose you have to be educated to appreciate it! For myself, I would rather see a good meal well cooked and properly served, to be eaten by people who are hungry and appreciate my work! But I fear that sounds ungracious. And speaking of hunger, what would the signorina like for her breakfast?"

Pina, well aware that in the main, Italians do not eat large breakfasts, replied; "I would be quite happy with a roll, with a little oil and salt, and some more of this delicious coffee."

Elsa dropped her ladle and clapped her hands in glee. "Ah, but the signorina is almost pure Italian! Bread, oil, a little salt and some two or three cups of good coffee will carry anyone safely through the morning! If the signorina will not mind waiting, I will just run up with Stella's breakfast, and then I will prepare the dining room."

"Please do not go to that trouble on my sole account. I will happily eat in the kitchen. I love kitchens and always think of them as being the heart of a house. And yours is a splendid example."

Elsa beamed. "I *am* proud of what you are pleased to call my kitchen, although it is really Don Stefano's. You will be very welcome to eat here. I'll just take up Stella's tray, and then I shall have some moments free."

Deftly she turned the eggs that she had been cooking on to a plate. Quickly, with an economy of movement that denoted long practice, she loaded a tray with the equipment needed for one person's breakfast and as she swept from the kitchen bearing the tray, she swept up a small coffee pot that stood on the stove. Pina began to prepare her own breakfast and by the time Elsa had returned, had managed to find all that she needed and was seated at the table ready to eat. It was quite ten minutes before the housekeeper returned. She poured out a cup of coffee for herself and then sat opposite Pina at the table, resting her elbows on the scrubbed white wood.

"Stella is not so well today," she told Pina. "Of course, you understand that she always has pain, more or less, and today is one of the days when she has more. But she endures it well; she is a very brave girl. You have been told about her, naturally."

"I know nothing at all about her, but I am anxious to learn."

"Well, she is a cripple now. Two years ago she was thrown by her pony in the valley below the hill we call La Poltrona, because it looks like an arm-chair. Sadly the pony fell too, and rolled on her. She lay for two, three, maybe four hours before she was found. Of course, we quickly called in the local doctor, but he was powerless to help, and I should think Don Stefano consulted every surgeon in Italy about her, but it was all fruitless - every one of them said she was incurable. As I said, she bears up very well, but it is hard on a child, once so active, to be confined all her days to a wheelchair or hobbling about on crutches. It was Annibale, the odd-job man, who found her, and now she thinks the world of him. He is an ex-cavalryman, very wise in the way of horses, and he always seemed to know what any horse will do in any circumstances. You will not yet have met Annibale, of course."

"I think possibly I saw him from my bedroom window, carrying a basket of logs."

"That's right, that would be Annibale. Well, that is the sad history of Stella Capriotti. Twelve years old, and condemned to a lifetime of crutches and wheelchairs. And she is so cheerful and undemanding." Elsa's arms were upraised in admiration. "To see her, you'd think she was twice her age, so wise she is! It was her accident that really killed her mother, too, because she was so upset about the accident to her only child, and she unable to bear a son for Don Stefano. She took to her bed and sort of pined away until one day I took her breakfast up to her, and she was dead in bed. Poor Don Stefano has had a hard two years, believe me!" She sighed. "I have to tell you that Luigi says if you will go to his office at about half past nine, he will introduce you to Stella and then you might discuss your duties with both of them."

"Thank you, Elsa. You have prepared me well. I might easily have registered shock on seeing an invalid when I expected to see a whole young lady. I will be in Luigi's office sharp to time. Now, as I have half an hour or so to waste, are there any places in the grounds where I may not go? I should like to see it in daylight after seeing it so briefly in semi-darkness last night."

"Faccia pure, signorina - do as you please. Will you take more coffee before you leave?"

Declining the offer, Pina left the kitchen and found her way to the door that led on to the rear yard. The heavy black door was ornamented with iron nail heads, just like a church door at home, she thought. She entered the yard and found herself, as she had expected in the courtyard below her bedroom window. Crossing the yard, she tried to push open the now closed great gate, but it resisted all her efforts and she quickly gave up the unequal struggle. She then peered into the open stables. In one of them, a pair of oxen were suckling a calf apiece. They regarded the intruder with questioning brown eyes and a tossing of their heads, from which sprang huge wide and fearsome horns. Quickly retreating, Pina entered the other stable, and there found six sheep behind hurdles. The sheep had lambs resting beside them on the rushes which protected them from the cold stones that formed the floor of their pen. Each lamb had been fitted with what appeared to be an old sock tied round its muzzle. Plainly this was a device to prevent the lamb from suckling, but Pina could not see the reason for this deprivation, and resolved to make enquiries as soon as she met someone who could enlighten her.

The woodstore was occupied by logs stacked around the walls, some of them being two metres in length, plainly awaiting the attentions of the big circular saw that stood in the centre of the floor. Logs already cut to size were standing ready for transportation into the house. At some time during its existence, the logstore had been a stable, for it was fitted with a hayrack and old pieces of tack; the leather, turning green through lack of use, still hung from hooks set into the walls. She turned and looked back at the house. Immediately below her bedroom, there was another of the stores, but unlike the rest, this one had a rough door set into the frame. She walked over and pushed at the door. It yielded to the lightest pressure of her hand, and swung open to reveal a cell-like room. Opposite the door, set against the wall, a truckle bed stood, the bedclothes neatly folded on it. A shelf above the bed held a number of books. On her right, the whole wall space was covered by large pictures, each secured to the

Annibale

rough wall with sticky tape. Above a portrait of Stalin another portrait, this one of Mao Tse-tung, which stared out across the cell at a small slow combustion stove.

The sight of the portraits brought her up 'all standing', as Daddy would have said, for a moment, and she stood gazing at them, hand to mouth. Never would she have expected to see such pictures at Tre Boschi. A light step behind her made her turn and she found herself confronted by Annibale.

"Buon'giorno, signorina. Can I be of assistance?"

"Oh, I do so beg your pardon," she gasped. "I did not mean to intrude upon your private accommodation!" She went on, "Elsa told me that I could go anywhere in the yard. She did not tell me that you lived here."

Bright blue eyes twinkled as he smiled at her. His teeth, she noticed were white and well brushed, and his general aspect far removed from her estimate of him as she looked from the bedroom window. "Elsa was correct, signorina. There is nothing private here. You, of course, will be the new governess? I thought so. Well, be careful and ride her easy, signorina. She is a young and spirited filly and has a soft mouth. Ride her on a slackish rein and all will go well. Try to bully her, and she will unseat you. All of us here at Tre Boschi love her very much, and I, Annibale, love her more than most. It was I who found her after her fall, and it is to me that she runs whenever she is in trouble. I do not mean literally that she runs to me, although I wish to God that she was able to do just that. Now I suppose she will transfer her affections to you, and will forget old Annibale!"

The old soldier looked so woe-begone that Pina's soft heart was touched. Impulsively she reached out and took the man's hand. I am certain that she will never forget you, Signor Annibale. Elsa has told me of the great debt she owes you for finding her when others could not. Rest assured that I will never do anything to wean Stella's affections away from you!"

He bowed and removed his hat. His hair, she noted, was not at all grizzled, but snowy white. "I am pleased to have your reassurance, signorina. Would you care to enter my quarters?" He motioned her to enter, and she, fearful of giving offence, stepped over the threshold. "Here, you see, I keep my few household goods, my lares and penates, as you might say. First my books - oh yes, even a tough

Elsa

old horse-walloper may read and enjoy great writing. I have some of your English authors - in translation, of course; that is understood. See, there is Dickens, Hardy, Shaw, and the marvellous Shakespeare. I have Italian writers, too. People like Dante, Leopardi, and in my own untutored opinion, lesser lights like Soldati, Moravia, Gadda, and Pratolini. I saw you inspecting my art gallery. Those pictures are there solely to annoy Passi, the majordomo, who stands as far to the right in politics as he thinks I stand to the left! It is an old man's little bit of fun, you understand."

Pina smiled as she replied, "Thank you for letting me see your house, signore. Now I must go to see that same Passi, who is to introduce me to my charge and to instruct me in my duties."

"Ah, the much-loved Stellina!" He kissed his fingers and waved them in the air. "There are few here at Tre Boschi who would not lay down their lives for that young lady! She is as kind and thoughtful as she is beautiful! I do assure you, signorina!"

Thanking him yet again, Pina made her way back into the house and to Passi's office. Bidden to enter when she knocked, she did so, and found him seated behind his desk. Beside him, in a wheelchair, sat a young girl. She had a heart-shaped face; her complexion was a creamy coffee colour, while her hair and delicately arched eyebrows were of an intense raven black, almost a dark blue where the light shone directly on them. She wore her hair long enough to fall in rich profusion about her slim shoulders. A faint smile, half fearful, half bold, played about her well-shaped mouth as she propelled the wheelchair forward to meet Pina, crying at the same time, "Welcome to Tre Boschi, mees! May I call you 'Mees', or would you prefer some other form of address?"

Extending her hand, which was grasped and shaken enthusiastically by the girl, Pina answered, "All my friends call me Pina. And since I am certain that we are going to be great friends, why not call me by that name? In return, perhaps you will allow me to call you Stella."

"Oh, but I should be very happy to have it so! I have wanted so long to have a friend! Elsa and Rosa are very kind, but they cannot talk about things that really matter, such as fashions and art and music. Elsa never has time to stand and gossip, and as for Rosa - well, she has no conversation at all beyond the cinema in Teramo, and dancing, and the annual festa in her village. It will be wonderful to hold intelligent conversations again!" She clapped her little hands as Passi looked indulgently on this first encounter between tutor and pupil.

"If I might interrupt the signorina, I would like to tell Miss Corrigan what Don Stefano expects of her - and of you, too, Stella! Miss Corrigan will act as companion to you at all times when she is in the house. She will be free during your daily rest times, of course. Stella has to rest every day for at least two hours," he explained to Pina. "There will be not less than one hour of formal tuition in English daily, save for Sunday. Miss Corrigan will also be free on that day every second week, and is to have a half day free weekly, on a day to be decided between you mutually. Now, Stella, to further your acquaintance with Miss Corrigan, perhaps you will show her round the place - the house and grounds."

Stella nodded. "A good idea, Luigi. Before we leave you to your work, may I ask you to make it known to all the staff that they will address Pina as 'Mees'. That will help her to remember England, you know."

"All the servants will be so informed, Stella."

"Now," cried the girl, "that's all fixed, then! Remember that you also are to call Pina 'Mees', Luigi! Come, Pina, let us away! But you may have to help me over the bumpy bits!" She gripped the wheels of her chair and steered a course for the door. Pina followed more sedately, thanking Passi as she left the office.

Stella was adept at managing her chair. She mounted the low step in the hall with practised ease, but was balked by the high step that led to the front courtyard. Here, safely arrived with Pina's aid, on the drive, they made for the outer gate and the world outside. After they had gone twenty yards or so, Pina turned to gaze at the house. "It is very beautiful," she said.

"Yes, it is. Once it was a convent. That's why there are those great ovens in the wall, and the little cells like the one that Annibale lives in, and the store sheds. Have you met Annibale yet? I owe my life to him, because he was the one who knew where to look for me when Lampo threw me. Wasn't that a good name for a pony, Pina? What do you say in English for 'lampo'?"

"It means 'lightning'. Was your pony so very fast?"

"Oh, yes, indeed he was! He would go like the wind! That is how I came to fall off, you know. We were going very fast and he tried to jump over the shadow of a tree or something, and we both fell. But it wasn't his fault!" Pina was touched by her swift defence of the pony. "Annibale says it could happen to the best of mounts."

"Do you still have Lampo?"

"Sadly, no, because Papa said when I was hurt, he would not have the pony near the house any more. I did not know that at the time because I was too ill to be told. If I had known, I would have been very cross, because I loved Lampo so much. But Papa ruled that he was to be sold. I don't know who bought him. Papa has no time to ride, of course, and since I cannot ride any more, I quite see that it would have been dreadfully wasteful had *we* kept my pony. Horses have to eat you know, even if they might never again be ridden." She said this with a knowing adult air that Pina found attractive.

"Yes, I can see that, Stella." Pina gave the chair a little push and they started to move along the drive that led to the main road. The trees that grew on either side gave a pleasantly dappled effect in the strong sunlight, and in the growing heat of the day, the shade was welcome. After they had gone some fifty metres or so, Stella put the brake on her chair.

"Here, just inside the bushes, there is a little fountain - a spring gushing from the rocks. It is the house's own source of mineral water. Papa says that when the nuns had the convent here, they used to sell the water to cure all kinds of illnesses. Now we sometimes have the water on the table at mealtimes. It has a not unpleasant taste, but it does not mix well with wine. When he first bought the house, Papa had the water analysed. The chemist said it would be indicated in cases of gout, stomach disorders, and fevers; sadly it will not cure a crushed pelvis or broken and twisted legs!" She gave herself a little shake. "But I am not to pity myself. There are many worse than I. Some poor bambini have to spend their whole lives in hospital beds. At least I am able to be here at home, with Luigi and Elsa and Annibale, and now you. I believe that we are going to be very happy together, Peppina! You won't mind me calling you Peppina sometimes, will you? Already I feel that I have known you for ages, and it is so lovely to have a real friend at last!"

Pina smiled down at the small frail form in the chair. "I should like to think that you liked me sufficiently to call me by a diminutive, Stella. I like you, too, and feel that I am anything but a paid companion! I am so very glad that I saw your Papa's advertisement in the paper, and answered it!"

"I believe that these things are meant to be," rejoined Stella, with a gravity that sat oddly on her youthful appearance. "Had I not fallen from Lampo, there would never have been a vacancy at Tre Boschi for a companion and tutor. I should have been packed off to some school in Switzerland by now, and I know that I would have been very unhappy in such a place! I could not bear to be long away from my home in Tre Boschi! How do you say 'Tre Boschi' in English, Mees?" She smiled mischievously up at Pina.

"We would say, 'Three Woods'."

"T'ree Woods-a." Stella savoured the taste of the words on her tongue. "No, I prefer Tre Boschi. You can see the woods if we go round the next bend in the drive. Then we must return to the house for my morning milk. Elsa will scold both of us if I am late for it. Will you join me in a glass of milk, Pina?"

"I shall be delighted to do so, Stella." She found this girl oddly attractive. At times quite adolescent in her manner, at other times she assumed a wisdom and behaviour far beyond her years. Clearly she was of an affectionate nature, with a great love not only for her sire, but also for all those with whom she came into daily contact. It seemed strange that, so far, she had not mentioned Sandro, who must, at some time or other, have taken her out in one of the cars.

After they had attained the bend in the drive, and Pina had dutifully admired the three woods (although at home they would only have ranked for the title of 'copses', being so small), they retraced their steps to the house. An agitated Elsa was waiting at the front door. "You are a quarter of an hour late," she scolded. "Your milk is served in the dining room, Stella, and I have also put coffee in there for the signorina."

The girl thanked her politely, and apologised for their tardiness, pleading that Pina was really enthralled by the sights she had been shown. "Has Luigi told you that Mees Corrigan-a is to be addressed as 'Mees'?"

Elsa agreed that she had indeed received that instruction. "And," she added, "I have told Rosa the same. Will that be all right, signorina?"

Stella reached out with one of the light metal crutches that were carried in brackets attached to the wheelchair. She gave Elsa a light tap on the arm with it. "If you keep forgetting to say 'Mees', you will receive another thrashing like this, Elsa!" she threatened severely.

Elsa giggled. "I'm sorry. I'll try hard to remember. Please don't be too hard on a poor ignorant peasant girl, signorina Stella!" She ran laughing into the kitchen.

"I love Elsa a lot," observed Stella. "She is always ready to joke and pretend that I am a grand lady whose every whim must be obeyed."

"She is a good person indeed. Now, into the dining room with you, drink up your milk, and let us get to work. I have to earn my salary, you know!"

Stella looked downcast at the prospect of work. "I must not be pressed too hard, you know! Every afternoon, I have to rest. My back is all strapped up, and Rosa comes to unharness me and help me to get comfortable. Rosa is a good girl, but a little flighty. That's what Papa calls her. I don't know what 'flighty' means, but it cannot be good, or Papa would like it! Shall we make the dining room our classroom? It would be more comfortable than any other room in the house. But on nice days, we could go outside to work."

SIX

Pina soon discovered that Stella was a bright pupil, but erratic and very tiring to teach. Her impish sense of the comic was forever bubbling to the surface; this prevented Pina from obtaining the discipline so necessary for effective tuition. But on the whole, she was content enough. Such tuition as had been absorbed by Stella had sunk well into her mind, and Pina felt sure that when Don Stefano came to test his daughter's progress, he would be if not exactly astounded, at least satisfied.

On that first day, both tutor and pupil were relieved when Elsa entered the dining room and suggested that she would like to set the table for lunch. However, Stella refused to eat there, saying that she was weary and in pain from her harness. She would rather eat in her room after Rosa had helped her to get into bed, and therefore, as soon as Elsa had made the necessary arrangements, Stella propelled herself out of the dining room.

Once more Pina ate in solitude, and when her simple but satisfying meal was over, went to her room. She lugged a chair up to the window, and sat hungrily devouring the superb view. It was, she told herself, a truly glorious part of Italy, and many people would have paid a high price for the privilege of sitting to gaze at such scenery. The builders of the convent surely had an eye for beauty when they sited the building in that particular spot.

Her train of thought was broken by Elsa, who came to inform her that she was wanted on the telephone. For a moment, Pina wondered who could possibly know that she was living at Tre Boschi. She hastened to the corridor and lifted the instrument. The thin disembodied voice of di Felippo greeted her ear.

In English he said, "You owe me an apology! You promised to phone me!"

"But I didn't say *when* I would call! Honestly, I've been so busy that the time has simply flown! In any case, now that I think about it, I don't recall that I ever did promise to call you!"

"Oh yes you did! But I forgive you. Listen, may I come to see you this afternoon? There are certain things I would like to discuss with you, if you will agree to meet me. I've hired a car, and I could run you round to visit some of the hill towns if you would like that. I am sure you would be amused!" His tone was pleading and persuasive.

She thought quickly. Teaching was over for Stella for the day, and for the rest of the afternoon, her time was her own. It would be very pleasant to have a conducted tour of the district. "Very well, Carlo," she said. "I will meet you at the end of the drive to the house in an hour. But please, Carlo, don't get any romantic ideas. I just do not want any emotional entanglements at this time."

"I promise to be good. It would surprise you to see how good I can be when I have promised!" The line went dead with a click.

She returned to her room in a pensive mood. Carlo was clearly keen to continue their acquaintance. Of that, she was glad, for he was quite the nicest man she had met for a long time. But all men were untrustworthy. The wounds inflicted by Kevin were still sore, and she was determined that she would not expose herself to a similar experience for a long time. She decided that she would let Carlo see that she was happy to meet him again, but she would not make her pleasure too obvious. Mama said a girl should always keep a man guessing, and Pina resolved that she would follow that advice to the letter.

She laid out her few clothes on the bed, the better to decide what to wear. She selected a red sleeveless dress with a flared skirt. Having changed into the dress, she sat before the mirror and put her make-up into a state of repair. As always the amount of powder and lipstick she applied were minimal. Satisfied that she was looking as well as Carlo could expect, she descended to the kitchen and informed Elsa that she was going out for an hour or so, but would be back in time for dinner.

Carlo had not arrived when she reached the main road. A large stone, half-buried in the grassy bank beside the shallow dry ditch made a convenient seat. She was at first struck by the absence of bird life, of which there ought to have been a lot so near the woods, but then she recalled that Italians usually shot everything that flies; even the tiny tuneful thrush found its way into an Italian stomach quite often. The peace of the afternoon was broken only by the shrilling of cicadas. Distantly, she hear a tractor hard at work, even though this was the hour of siesta, when all right-thinking Italians ought to be resting, if not actually asleep.

Round the bend lower down the slope, a white Fiat came rushing towards her, pursued by a cloud of dust. The car drew up with a flourish, and Carlo leapt out as Pina rose from her seat. He neared her, then taking both of her hands in his, planted a kiss on each of her cheeks. She flushed a bright scarlet.

"Oh, I am sorry!" he cried in Italian. "I quite forgot myself! You know we Italians always greet our friends, men or women with at couple of kisses. But then, you are half English and half Italian. Perhaps I should have greeted you with one kiss only!" He grinned widely.

"You took me by surprise! After all, we have only known each other a bare six or seven hours when we were fellow-travellers." She scrubbed at her cheeks with the back of a hand. "I am not accustomed to such fast work!"

"I will try to remember. But you look so beautiful that I was quite carried away. Please forgive me - it was only a venial sin, I hope?" His eyes crinkled at the corners as he looked down at her.

"I forgive you this time," she murmured. "But please do not let it happen again." Then seeing his smile broaden, she smiled back at him. "Do you always work as fast as that?"

"No. I am normally a very slow and placid animal, somewhat like our native oxen." He guided her to the car and saw her comfortably installed. Then he tucked his long legs into the driver's position. "It's rather a cramped little car, but it's cheap and cheerful. I would much have preferred to have here my own Alfa Romeo. Had I known that we were to meet, I certainly would have brought it. But there again, had I done so, we would never have met on the train, eh?" He turned the car round in the drive. Nodding towards the house, he asked, "Shall you be happy there?"

"Yes, very happy, I think. My charge is a twelve-year old who was crippled when her pony fell on her two years ago. In spite of her injuries, she is a bright little button who seems fairly keen to learn - more to please her father than to please me, I think! But it seems that we are going to be good friends."

"Who could fail to friends with you? Now, I do not intend to talk a lot more. I will drive slowly so that you will be able to look about you and observe the scenery; it is very beautiful, though I, being Cremonese, prefer my scenery horizontal rather than vertical."

"But I have skied up there in the Gran'Sasso, where in winter there is plenty of suitable snow. My firm has a branch at Teramo as well as at Giulianova, so I am not utterly a stranger to this area."

He drove well, and Pina was grateful that he drove, on this occasion, so much more slowly than did Sandro. She was able to look about her in comfort, and to all her questions, Carlo was able to give well-informed replies. They ran down the hills to the coast road, where Carlo turned north. After a few kilometres, he turned inland again along a tree-lined road that took them once again into the hills.

In the square at Colonnella, he parked the car. Taking Pina by the hand, he led her up a stepped street to a belvedere above the town. Marble seats were scattered here and there about the belvedere, some of them quite close to the railings that protected the unwary, or perhaps the suicidal, from a hundred feet drop on to the roofs below. With his handkerchief, Carlo dusted one of the seats before he left her, to return in a few moments, with two large ice-cream tubs.

They sat in the sunshine, spooning out the coolness of the rich confection. He said, "Now I will tell you a little of what I have discovered so far since we parted on the station.

"I have been going round the bars in Giulianova - not in the flashy tourist bars, which anyway are not opened yet, because the tourist season is yet to start, but in the flea-pit bars that the locals use. I think, or rather, I hope, that what I have heard is lies or exaggeration - most probably the latter. Somebody has been spreading stories that you have been engaged as a bodyguard for the young Capriotti. You will no doubt be astonished to learn that you are a black belt in karate, and a proper little Annie Oakley with either pistol or rifle! Having met you, I don't believe a syllable of it, but the locals who have not seen you, accept the tales as fact.

"Before you appeared, the young woman, like all children of wealthy and important men, stood in some danger of being kidnapped. Her father is a powerful figure in the Government. Kidnapping his only child would give a great lever to such a body as the Red Brigades to get certain laws altered or abrogated, or even to get a few terrorists released from prison. But your arrival, far from affording protection for the kid, has placed her in even greater danger. If Senatore Capriotti considers it necessary to hire a bodyguard for his daughter - well, do I have to spell it out for you? The gang, or gangs, are not yet quite sure of themselves, nor are they absolutely certain about where exactly you come into the picture. That's why you have been subject to those mysterious goings-on, like being accosted by the knifeman in the train. They were trying to scare you off, just in case. And your determination to get to Tre Boschi has not made things easier for you. They are still uncertain.

"These are murky waters in which we fish. The thing is, I'm worried about you, and I wonder to what extent you realise the danger you have put yourself in by coming here at all."

She stared at him, open-mouthed. "Carlo, I do assure you that I am nothing more than a companion and tutor to Stella. I don't know the first thing about combat, armed or unarmed, and I am frightened of firearms - always have been. Whoever has put these rumours about is an unmitigated liar!"

"Yes, I assessed you as being exactly what you say you are. But the fact that these stories have no foundation will not save you from being involved in whatever game is being played by Don Stefano's enemies. Have you any means of protecting yourself? A gun? Anything?"

"Certainly not! I wouldn't know how to hold a gun, let alone how to shoot it off! Surely if these gangsters thought things out, they would be able to see that I am not in any way fitted to protect Stella from violence and danger; that the best people to act as bodyguards are those who work on the estate and are known to the girl. Surely the servants would be far quicker to spot danger then ever I could be!"

Carlo crumpled up the ice-cream tubs and tossed them accurately into a nearby litter bin. "That's exactly the reasoning I used myself! I know that you have been in the house only a matter of hours, but would you say that there is any person who could act as a regular bodyguard for you and the child?"

Biting her lower lip to aid her thought processes, Pina said, "There is Sandro."

He interrupted her quickly, "No, not him! I have already discovered that that young man is too free with his tongue. What we need is a somewhat more solid citizen."

"I know," she cried. "Annibale!"

"Annibale? Who's he?"

"He's the odd-job man about the estate. He is oldish - over sixty, I would think, and when I was looking in his room, I saw a shotgun hanging on the wall - one like my father used to use in the season. And I know Annibale thinks the world of Stella. Yes, I am sure that he would be far and away the best person to be a bodyguard to

Stella." She rested her elbow on the stone-topped table in front of their seat and lowered her chin into the palm of her hand. "But this is silly chatter! We are living to the twentieth century! This is not the Middle Ages!"

"That's exactly the point, cara. We *are* living in the twentieth century, and living with us are the Mafia, the Red Brigade, and countless other lawless types, none of whom would have the slightest compunction in putting pressure on Senatore Capriotti or anyone else, by any lever they could get their hands on, if by that means they could achieve their particular object, whether the object was a political one or they were motivated by just plain old-fashioned greed!"

"It's absurd!" she protested.

"No, it's deadly serious. Life today is what it is, and not what we would wish it to be." He thought for few moments, then, "Does anyone know that you are out with me this afternoon?"

"No. I doubt if I was seen walking down the drive. I simply told Elsa that I would be out of the house for an hour or so. That was all."

"I see. Do you think, when I take you back to Tre Boschi, I might walk a little way with you along the drive? I would like to see this Annibale without anyone else being aware of our meeting. Could you arrange that?"

"It might be possible. There is a little fountain hidden in the shrubbery at the side of the drive. I could ask Annibale to meet you there, but I could not guarantee that he would be willing. Can't I tell him why you want to see him?"

"No. I want to judge him for myself before enlisting him. For all we know, he might be one of the gang!"

"Impossible!" She was shocked at the suggestion.

"Don't be too sure, cara. This fountain - is it in use?"

"Yes. The family draw from it for table water. Rosa fills the carafes every morning."

"Ah. Well, when you get back to the house, see Annibale and ask him to get you a fresh bottle of water. I guess he will think it an odd request, but if pressed hard enough, he will probably do it. I firmly believe that any old soldier will do almost anything to get a smile from a pretty girl!"

Pina blushed as they rose from the table and made their way down the steep steps to the car. Di Felippo drove much faster than he had on the outward journey to Colonella. Pina, absorbed in thoughts, was surprised when she suddenly and unexpectedly found that they were at the entrance to the drive so soon. After she had dismounted, she waited while Carlo drove the car round a bend a little further along the road, and then rejoined her. Together they walked to where the fountain lay. She pointed out to him the almost completely concealed path that led to it.

All around them the woods were silent save for the shrill rasping of the cicadas. As she made to leave him, he caught her by the shoulders and drew her close. "Be very watchful, cara. There might be much risk here, and the most precious thing is yourself. You are becoming dear to me!"

She wrenched herself free. "Now, Carlo! You promised!"

He released her instantly. "I shall wait here half an hour, no longer. If by that time Annibale has not come, I will leave. I will ring you again tomorrow, and if necessary, we will rethink our tactics. Meanwhile, go cautiously, cara."

Glancing at her watch, Pina was astonished to see that she had been absent from the house less than an hour and a half. It was still early afternoon, and people were only just beginning to stir from their siesta. In fact, Elsa had not yet descended to the kitchen, for which she was thankful. She rapidly crossed to the courtyard door, and went towards the cell where Annibale lived. Tapping on the door, she wondered if she was not making a great fool of herself agreeing to participate in Carlo's melodramatic plan, but as she had left him at the fountain, and since she could hear Annibale stirring in response to her knock, she felt that she was now too deeply committed to withdraw.

Annibale came to the door. He was rubbing the sleep from his eyes. Pina thought that he looked far too old to act as a bodyguard, even if he accepted the role. "Mees?" he asked.

"Er, I... er... I wondered if you would be good enough to get me some water from the fountain?" she stammered.

He gazed at her in astonishment. "But there is plenty of water in the house, isn't there?"

"I looked, but Rosa has filled all the carafes for dinner, and I couldn't find another container."

"But this is unprecedented! Wood for the fires, yes; gas cylinders for the cooker, also yes; but water from the fountain I do NOT fetch! That is for Rosa to do!" He made to slam the door in her face.

She summoned up all her histrionic powers. A limpid tear rolled down her cheek; her shoulders slumped in despair. Annibale found it impossible to resist, as Carlo had forecast. Gruffly, he said, "Oh, very well. But please regard this as very unusual indeed! I refuse to carry water up to your room, lest I run into Elsa or Rosa on the way, so when I return I will whistle from the yard here, and you will have to descend to get your so-urgently needed water! Really, I have never heard of such a request!" He was still grumbling as she left him and fled to her room.

Once she had reached her sanctuary, she kicked off her shoes, opened the window so that she could hear his signal, and then fell into a chair. She thought again about what Carlo had told her. Clearly he was worried about Stella's safety. But that was not the whole story. He was more concerned for her, Pina's safety, and only incidentally about Stella. Pina doubted strongly if his fears had any firm base. He could so easily be inventing all this in order to get a closer relationship with her. But against that, although their acquaintance had been so short, she had a feeling that he was to be trusted. She had no idea about who or what might be the source of the rumours about her, but she recalled the remarks made by Fronti only last evening as he had assisted her into the car at Bellante. It could be that Carlo had some slight grounds for his fantasies.

But young Englishwomen, whatever their situation in life, did not have such things happen to them in Italy, or anywhere else, for that matter. They might perhaps have small unimportant adventures, but rarely anything so vile as kidnapping and violence. Was Carlo making all this up, so that he could start a passionate affair with her that would fizzle out as soon as his business in the region was finished? All this talk could so easily be infantile raving; was Carlo in fact the type of man Mama has so often warned her about? But he could not possibly be like that! He was too nice a man to indulge in such callow tricks. Perhaps he *was* sincere! Oh what a mess everything was becoming, when she was hoping to begin really to enjoy life! Her musings were interrupted by Annibale calling from below. "Ahi, Mees, please come down. I have your cool water here!"

She moved quickly to the window. "Una momentina, Annibale - just a moment." She hastened down to the yard. He was standing in the doorway of his cell and invited her to enter. He motioned her to be seated while he straddled the stool that stood near his table. Unwinking, he stared at her for what seemed like an eternity.

"Well," he said at last. "here's a pretty coil! I met your friend. A typical northerner, isn't he? All push and go, and never a minute for rest and reflection! Whether there is any basis or fact for the rigmarole he told me, I don't know, but he seems to be quite convinced that Stella has to be guarded, and he has appointed me, Annibale Coccia, late corporal of cavalry, and later partisan fighter, to be her bodyguard. Therefore you are now to inform me whenever you and the signorina Stella leave the house and grounds. You are to tell me exactly where you intend to go, and if I think it necessary, I am to accompany you - armed!"

"I am never to be more than fifty metres from you, and I am always to carry the little barker that you see hanging on the wall there. And should you go in a car, much as I hate the things that go round frightening horses, then I am to sit in the back seat. So there it is, mees. Your northern friend has enlisted me to watch not only over Stella, but also over you! Thank the buon' Dio I am a light sleeper, and that your room is directly above mine! I will rig up a bellpull so that if you need me at night, you will only have to heave on a rope to rouse me. That I will do this afternoon, if you will allow me to enter your room for ten minutes."

Pina agreed that it would be possible for him to enter her sanctum, and he continued, "I am positive that those who live on this estate are to be trusted. Elsa has always been employed here; Rosa has worked in the scullery since she left third grade at school; Passi has been in the service of Don Stefano since a few years after Noah's flood; Sandro has also been here all his life, as a son of one of the farm workers. All of the farm workers and their history is an open book to me. No, there will be no traitor on this estate. Should I ever find one, I Annibale Coccia, will tear his liver out and make him eat it fried for breakfast!" He looked so fierce that Pina could hardly suppress a smile. He caught the smile and looked a trifle sheepish. Handing her a flask of water, he added, "Now we go about our daily tasks as though everything is normal, as I firmly believe it to be, for your northern numbskull has got all things muddled up. Those people up there seem to think that we southerners are all either crack-brained or mafiosi, or perhaps both! But remember that my orders are that you are to keep me informed of all your movements whenever you leave the house, be it with Stella or alone. Yes, even if you are only going about with your boyfriend!"

Pina thanked him and returned to the house carrying the flask of water. In the kitchen, she ran into Elsa, who told her that there was not the slightest need for her to fetch water from the fountain - that was Rosa's duty, and the girl would be offended if Pina went for water herself. Leaving the flask in her room, she went in search of Stella. She would tell her nothing of what had occurred this afternoon. Lessons would continue as the girl would expect them to do. There could be some difficulty in accounting for Annibale's presence whenever they left the house, but Pina hoped that she would be able to cross that bridge when she came to it. She had been at Tre Boschi less than twenty-four hours! If so much could happen in so short a time, what on earth could three or four months produce?

SEVEN

Life began to flow very smoothly. As the bright warm days passed, the thought of crime receded into the back of Pina's mind, and existence became pleasant to a degree that Pina would never have thought possible. Stella was making progress with her English as well as with all her other subjects. Pina, with frequent conversations with Rosa, and occasionally with Elsa - though the latter seldom had time for idle chatter, it seemed - was acquiring the basics of the local Abruzzese dialect.

Annibale looked on Pina's dialect studies with scorn. "This barbarous speech will wither and die now that everybody has wireless and television. Then, when we have one single language throughout the whole country, the dream of Garibaldi will be realised, and Italy will be truly one nation. Oh, yes, I concede that Abruzzese was the only tongue of my forefathers, but it is doomed, doomed! And therefore all your effort is wasted. In a few short years the only people using dialect - any dialect, will be hermits, who are without the means of mass communication, or dry and dusty scholars locked in unfrequented libraries!"

In addition to learning the talk of the peasants, Pina was able to absorb other matters that engaged her attention from time to time. She caught Elsa in a rare moment of stillness, and asked why the baby lambs were muzzled with what appeared to be old socks. The housekeeper gazed at her astonished at her ignorance.

"But, Mees, it must be obvious! The muzzles, which are indeed old socks or stockings, prevent the lambs from guzzling continually from the ewes. They are so greedy, those lambs, that we can only permit them to suckle two or three times a day. How else could we get the ewes' milk to make our famous cheese, pecorino?"

Pina had also found that the little Fiat seicento was very simple to drive. She soon arranged to take the national driver's test, passed with consummate ease, and was now the proud holder of a patente which permitted her to drive on public roads. She was thus enabled to take Stella out for short trips, with Annibale, ever-watchful, sitting stern and erect in the cramped back seat, nursing his 'barker' between his knees. Stella had accepted without question Pina's reason for the man's presence, that she had to have help to unload the wheelchair because it was too heavy for her to lift single-handed, and also because he could help to push the chair along the steep rough tracks where grew the wild flowers that the girl loved to collect.

Besides visiting the remote fields on these trips, the trio had gone to Teramo, where Stella was ecstatic to be able to remake acquaintance with the silver-fronted altar in the cathedral, and Pina had been enchanted with the Roman remains that were scattered about the older parts of the city. They had been to Giulianova to watch the fishing fleet put out to sea which they did every evening at six o'clock, because the Adriatic is almost tideless. They had bought from the women with the barrows at the port gates, fish so fresh that they still wriggled as the women tipped them into the scales. Elsa had been glad to receive this addition to her menus, because usually she had to rely for fish supplies on the man who travelled round the villages in a lorry, playing loud music from a tape recorder to advertise his arrival. The three of them had picnicked in the hills above Campli, staying long enough to watch the purple shadows race down the hillsides as the sun went down behind the twin hills that stood to the west of the town. They visited the lidi that lay all along the coast from Alba Adriatica to Monte Silvano, and had watched how, on all the beaches, the foreign tourists and holidaymakers allowed themselves to be sunburnt to a searing painful redness, painful even to the beholder. As her skill and confidence in driving improved with practice, Pina had even ventured into the port area of Pescara, where she and Stella had watched the ferries unloading cars and lorries and passengers from exotic parts like Yugoslavia and Greece, and even more fabulous places, places which Stella diligently sought out in the atlas when they returned to Tre Boschi.

The memory of Kevin faded as Carlo began to loom ever larger in Pina's thoughts. He telephoned her at least twice a week, and when they were able to meet, he invariably took her to dine in some little hotel or ristorante up in the hills where the food was prepared and cooked in true local style, and ladled out in true peasant quantity. He scorned the 'eateries' along the coastal strip, saying that they were geared only to the needs of visitors who more often than not were unwilling, if not actually afraid, to sample any dish that they did not know. He described their style of cooking as truly international - a hotchpotch of tastes German, Austrian, Dutch and Italian, and true to the traditions of none of them; a nauseating medley of all four styles fit only for the palates of those who knew no better.

His manner towards her was always deferential, warm and kind. He had not repeated his earlier mistake of attempting to kiss her. Instead, when they met, or when the time had come for them to part, he would take her hand and make a little bow over it, the inclination of his head concealing the hunger in his eyes. At times as they strolled through the crowded streets of some small town, he would take her by the hand on the pretext that he wanted to prevent them from getting parted by the throng. On her part, she respected his restraint, and liked him the more for it. In some queer way, she would have liked him to kiss her again, to kiss her properly, as she described it to herself, but the cautious English side of her character overcame the impulsive Italian streak, so that mostly she retained her cool yet friendly attitude when they were together. She reflected that Mama would have laughed at her, telling her that she was being altogether too British, too cold by far.

In the weeks that she had been at Tre Boschi, Pina had not met her employer, Don Stefano. Apparently he was a very busy man, much involved in politics. From time to time, Stella would receive cards he had sent from some of the Italian cities he had visited, and once there was even a letter from far-off America. At times, Stella would be called into Passi's office to take a telephone call from Papa. Pina had never spoken to him, nor even heard his voice. Her salary, a generous one, she thought, was paid into an account which Passi had opened for her with the Banca Provinciale di Teramo. Her needs were few, and her opportunities of spending limited, so her bank account was developing into at sizeable nest-egg. She hoped that she was considered to be earning her salary, and contented herself with the thought that if Don Stefano was dissatisfied with her work, he would not have qualms about informing Passi of his doubts and the message would be rapidly passed to her. On the credit side, Pina could see the way in which Stella would prattle away in rapid, if rather novel, English, while Elsa, although not understanding a single word of what was being said, would hold up her hands in adoring admiration.

September crept upon them almost unobserved. Now the vines hung heavy with ripening grapes. Apples and other fruit fell from trees to be left ungarnered for cattle and sheep to devour. Grain grew golden in the fields - maize, wheat and oats. Tomatoes, some weighing half a kilogram, hung heavy on the plants. All nature was ripe for harvesting, and the farm workers were toiling from dawn to dusk and beyond to get the crops into storage against the winter.

Days grew sultry. Sometimes great black clouds would roll up from the sea and pass overhead, without depositing any of their load of rain. When they ran up against the mountains, they would rear up in threatening attitudes, but would be beaten back towards the sea which gave them birth. Then the skies would be rent apart by savage flashes of lightning accompanied by great rolls of thunder which seemed always to be right above the roof of the house. Huge drops of rain would fall, singly at first, then increasing to a deluge which would bounce on the floor of the courtyards as high as a man's knee. The sheep and cattle would fall silent; cockerels would cease to challenge all the birds in neighbouring farmyards; even the garrulous ducks would stop their clamour until the storm had passed, as it would in an hour or so. Then the ducks and hens would become active again, calling excitedly as they turned up some dainty morsel that they had found in the muddy puddles. As the clouds retreated further, the sun would break through, watery at first, but gaining strength with every passing minute.

It was odd, thought Pina, how the storms always seemed to arrive in the afternoons. She and Stella would work hard all morning, and as a reward, Pina would promise that they would go out after Stella had had her siesta. But so often their plans would be negated by the rains. Stella would become peevish. "It's not fair," she would grumble. "Before Lampo fell on me, I loved to ride in the rain! Now I have to await the convenience of others! All because I cannot go out alone."

Immediately she would grasp Pina's hand in contrition. "Now I am being truly ungrateful! Before you came, I rarely went out at all except when Sandro took me in the big Fiat. And then he drove so fast that I could see nothing I wanted to look at! I know that there are many girls who would like to have all the advantages I possess. I am naughty to complain so. Let's go to the dining room and play two-handed briscola! I like to play cards with you; you are such a poor player, and I always win! You may be clever enough to teach me school lessons, but at cards you are hopeless! Well, here in the Abruzzi we have a saying, 'Lucky at cards, unlucky in love'. Perhaps the saying goes by opposites. You might find a nice Italian man, marry him, and settle down near here where I shall be able to visit you and all your children, and we shall all be happy ever afterwards!" Pina would feel the hot blood rushing to her cheeks when Stella spoke like that, and she would hope that her colour did not betray her inner most secret thoughts. If it did, Stella made no remark on her blushing.

In early October, Luigi put Elsa into a state of near panic, relaying a message from Don Stefano that he intended to visit Tre Boschi for three days, and to bring with him a gentleman guest. From the moment of receipt of the message, poor Rosa was given little peace. Everything in the house had to be polished, and repolished and polished again. Bedding had to be laid out in the inner courtyard to air, sheltered from any possible rain by the eaves of the storesheds. Menus had to be planned and discussed with Luigi. Wood had to be carted in from the estate for Annibale to cut into the right sized logs for burning on the fires. The air was rent by the screaming of the circular saw as he worked in the woodstore. Sandro had to go to the blacksmith to order a supply of gas cylinders, lest one gave out at a critical moment and perhaps ruin a soufflé. Then Elsa made him return to the forge to make sure that the order had been fully understood. Every man, woman, and child on the estate was kept on the go from dawn to dark. Stella could not restrain her happiness at the imminence of a visit from her Papa. She went about the house like some pale little mechanised wraith, singing in a thin piping voice and getting in everyone's way.

At last everything was declared by Elsa to be in satisfactory order, after she and Luigi had stalked through the house and its immediate environs seeking non-existent traces of dust or pockets of grime hitherto unseen. Elsa's work force was stood down from their exertions, and Luigi was able to announce a return to normality until the hour that Don Stefano was due to appear.

It was during this period of comparative quietness that Sandro asked Pina if she would care to accompany him on a visit to Bellante and the aged aunts of whom he had spoken on the day of her arrival at Tre Boschi. Excitement had given Stella a headache, and she had been put to bed by Elsa and given a tisane to cure her trouble. Pina was consequently free of further duty that day. Since Carlo was not coming to see her, she accepted Sandro's offer; she was interested in what she had heard of the old ladies. After lunch, she and Sandro set out in the seicento, Sandro driving with his accustomed verve along the narrow dusty roads.

He was his usual talkative self. "How are you settling in, Mees? Luigi told us all that we are always to say 'Mees' when we address you, or even when we speak about you to each other. Luigi is a very clever man. He looks after the estate most carefully. Don Stefano is lucky to have such a majordomo! My father, who drives the great crawler tractor, could do the work quite as well as Luigi, as far as field work is concerned, but he knows little about keeping books. My father says Luigi knows as much about farming as any man in the region, or even the province. Maybe if my father could read and write, he would be able to do Luigi's job. But years ago, when papa was a child, Mussolini was not interested in educating the children he wanted the women to produce; all he wanted was soldiers for his army and more children from the girls of the families. I have been told this by my papa, who is a very wise man. And what did Benito's schemes come to in the end? Just a hanging by the heels alongside the Petacci! Much good his eight million bayonets did him!" He spat out of the open window of the speeding little car, "And now Italy is in the same position as when it all began! Too many parties bicker about power when they should be getting on with government. All the banditry, all the crime we read about in the papers is the natural result of a weak government. I am not a communist like Annibale says he is, but sometimes I think that a few years of rule by Stalino might set the country on its feet again. The trouble is that when you elect a dictator into power, you cannot unelect him out of it, my father says, and he knows. So your dictator just sits there and perpetuates and compounds all his errors, as we learned to our cost in the thirties. Of course, I was not born then, but I listen to the older men talking, especially my father.

Annibale is not really a true communist, but he says he is, just to annoy Luigi, who is very strongly of the Right. Once those two talked politics a lot, but now they never do. When they did, I would try to listen and learn from them. Annibale is very well-read, you know, but he used to hit a cynical note too often for Luigi's liking. Once I heard him say to Luigi that politics, besides being the art of the possible, is also the ability to prove beyond all doubt that the inevitable is the result of human ingenuity. I don't rightly know what that means, and when I asked my papa, he didn't know either. But it sounds very clever and cynical. Ehi, it's a strange world we live in today!"

As he uttered this profound and original thought, Sandro was driving the car through the narrow main street of Campli. He had not reduced his speed by one iota. They cruised rapidly down the centre of the carriageway with the driver's thumb pressed firmly and continually on the horn button. Pedestrians were compelled to leap out of his path. Many of them shook a fist at him, but he merely laughed, negligently steering the car with one hand while making a gesture with his left arm. As soon as they were safely through the town, he said, "Please forgive me! I should not have made that sign, especially with you beside me in the car."

"It's not a gesture I understand."

"It was very wrong of me. It is an obscene signal, but I did not think what I was doing. I was so amused to see those people all jumping about because of me!"

"You must admit, Sandro, that you were going very fast in such narrow streets. You might have killed someone!"

"Never, Mees! They all know this seicento and also they know who is driving it. They know my style. No, there would be no serious hurt to anyone save in their self-pride because I caused them to move faster than they wished. I am truly a good driver. Why, once I went from Rimini to Milano in under three hours! True, at that time I was driving the big Fiat on the autostrada. But then, nobody ever passes me on the autostrade - I would not permit it! Eccoci Bellante - here we are at Bellante!"

The little car was arrested by a brutal application of the brakes as they entered the little town. Pina saw the belvedere where she met Fronti, and she begged Sandro to allow her to look over the railings once more. Quite politely he stopped and getting out of the car, led her by the arm to the edge of the belvedere. Once again the view took away her breath. It was just as magical as it had been that last time - no, it was more beautiful, for now she knew the lay of the land better, and besides, it was broad daylight, whereas then, dusk was falling. Today fleecy white clouds drifted slowly and majestically across the bright blue sky, throwing shadows which raced across the earth at a speed which seemed to be infinitely faster than the dignified march of their cause. The little hilltop towns gleamed white in the sunlight. This was an area that she had now come to know more intimately, for

Carlo had taken her to many of the places that were now set out before her. She could easily make out the belvedere at Colonella, where they had eaten ice-cream, and he had told her of his fears only a few weeks ago. She stood almost breathless at the railing, photographing the scene on her memory, until a light touch on her arm brought her back to the present.

"Come, Mees. We will go to meet the aunts." He guided her across the main road into the maze of narrow steep little streets that made up the greater part of the town. This was an area that Pina did not know at all. Whenever she and Stella had gone through the town on their way to the coast, they had kept strictly to the main road, which, at least, was sufficiently wide to allow of easy passage. She did not believe that Sandro was taking her by the most direct route to his aunts' shop, but was showing her as much of the town as he possibly could. They descended streets far too narrow to accept anything bigger than an ass equipped with panniers. A person leaning from one of the top storey windows in any of the houses could easily touch another person opposite, she thought; there seemed to be hardly sufficient width to allow daylight to enter. Tiny windows at street level revealed, upon inspection, that they were really shop windows in which were tossed haphazardly the type of goods sold by those shops. Here was a tangled mass of leather goods, there a heap of intimate clothing, elsewhere a pile of cartons in which food was once packed for sale. Pina thought that the goods thus displayed could not really be intended to attract custom; they were more likely to be heirlooms exhibited as an indication of what the shops once sold, years ago!

On the whole, she thought, Bellante was a most interesting place and worthy of further exploration. She would bring Stella one day soon, and they could inspect the town thoroughly and at leisure. There were tiny courts that seemed to exist solely for the purpose of holding the houses together. Annibale would be useful here, for he could help them to manoeuvre the wheelchair up and down the slopes.

Having whetted her appetite for his town, Sandro stopped outside one of the tiny shops. He pushed aside the chenille curtain that hung in the doorway and shouted, "Ehi, 'allo! It is I, Sandro, with the mees!" He ushered Pina into a small space made even smaller by a counter that ran from the entrance to the opposite wall. The counter was strewn with bolts of all kinds of material, but the shop was so dim that Pina, having been in the bright sunlight outside, could not distinguish colours or types of material. Other bolts of cloth were pushed into a sort of pigeon holes in the wall behind the counter; the aunts certainly carried an enormous stock of materials. As she began to recover her power of sight, a door opened at the far end of the shop, and framed in the backlighting, an old woman leaning heavily on a walking stick entered.

"What a noise you do make, to be sure, Sandrino!" she complained. She inspected Pina. "Welcome to our small establishment, signorina," she said. "Please enter the kitchen. Will you take a cup of coffee, or a glass of wine?" She extended a bony claw which Pina took in her own hand and shook warmly.

"A cup of coffee, please. What a fascinating shop you have, signora... er... er..."

"I am Signorina Capriotti Romina - unmarried, you see. Sandrino tells me that you are now almost one of the family, up there at Tre Boschi, so you had better call me 'Mina' as all the rest of the family do. Please come and meet my sister Maria. I expect that Sandrino has already told you that my sister and I live and work together in this shop. I do the selling, but Maria, although she has had a stroke, does all the buying. She is a shrewd buyer, and before she grew so old and frail used to have a stall in the market down there in Giulianova Lido."

Mina stood to one side to allow Pina to enter a large rectangular room, much larger than one would have thought possible after the tiny frontage. The walls were white-washed, and in the centre stood an immaculately white wooden table. Four chairs stood precisely opposite each other, two each side of the table. In one of the chairs sat zia Maria. She appeared to be an exact replica of her sister. As Pina entered, Maria made small deprecating motions of her head, indicating that she could not rise to greet their guest. Zia Mina said, "This is the English signorina of whom Sandrino has so often spoken."

Pina held out her hand, but Maria made no move to take it. She peered up at the younger woman with rheumy eyes, nodding all the while like one of those Chinese dolls that Pina used to play with in her childhood.

Zia Mina said, "As I told you, she has had a stroke and her talk is difficult for strangers to understand. I have to translate everything for her, even when she is buying for the shop. She can understand you

Mina

when you speak, but only Sandrino and I can catch her speech, and he does so only with great difficulty. Sister Maria is very intelligent, you know. In her younger days, she could speak both German and French, and even a little Albanian. She will be interested in anything you say, not only because you are the first English ever to enter our shop, but also because Sandrino has told us so much about you. She will shake her head, or nod to signify that she has understood you. Talk to her while I put on the mocha machine."

Pina now entered on a bizarre one-sided conversation while Mina put the coffee maker on the gas cooker that stood against one of the walls. She turned up the gas to its highest, and flames rose all round the pot. Sandro exclaimed impatiently, "You never listen, do you, you old... zia Mina! When the flame rises all round the pot like that, you are wasting gas! You do not have so much money that you can afford to throw it away!" He went to the cooker and lowered the flaring yellow flame to a more respectable blue hue. "This one is always the same," he told Pina. "She wastes gas as though the cylinders grew on trees in the backyard! And then she complains about the cost of refills!" There was little kindness in his tone, and Pina smiled nervously while Maria shook her head violently. Sandro had revealed that he was not the tender loving nephew he pretended to be. Pina felt sorry for the old women. Their lives, she thought, must be very drab. Perhaps Sandro's visits were the only bright spots in their lives. If that were true, she hoped he was not always so rough-spoken as he had been over the small matter of gas wastage.

Conversation with Maria was well-nigh impossible. The watery eyes fixed so intently on her face seemed to dry up all Pina's flow of small talk. Whenever she asked a question, Sandro leapt in with a reply before his aunt could offer any kind of response. The arrival of coffee was a welcome relief. Mina handed round three small cups of scalding black liquid, bitter as gall, together with the little sweet biscuits that in every Italian household accompany the drink. Sandro stood leaning against a wall, despite the pressing pleas of his aunt Mina to take a seat. He refused all offers of coffee, but went to a wall-cupboard and took out a bottle of whisky from which he poured almost a tumblerful of neat spirit, tossing it down his throat without blinking. The first dose was followed by an equally generous second helping, which he held in his hand, twirling the glass so that he could see the light glowing through the amber spirit.

"We do not care to see Sandro drink so much and so heartily," said Mina. "But there it is - he is a man, and a man will not be denied, or so we have been told by those who should know. Always we tell him that he would be better to drink coffee."

Sandro shrugged, and took another sip at his whisky, "How can a couple of old hens know what a cockerel needs? Had either of you married, I might listen to your advice!"

Maria nodded away, smiling vacantly. Mina fluttered round the table, offering Pina another biscuit, just one more; another cup of coffee. Uncomfortably, she sat at the table, wondering how she might terminate this visit, which appeared not to be running to plan. It was extremely difficult to achieve any form of communication with Maria, and Sandro, to say the least, was not being helpful. Some moments of deep silence broken only by the ticking of the wall clock ensued, then Sandro drained his glass at a gulp, and left the room without a word. "Men!" said Mina, and there was a world of scorn in her tone.

In minutes Sandro returned, accompanied by the man Pina had met on the belvedere, Matteo Fronti. He went straight to Pina, seized her hand, and raised it to his lips. "Ah, the beautiful young mees!" he murmured. He retained her hand for just a second too long before relinquishing it, and then turned to the old women. "Ciao!" he greeted them. Mina pushed a cup of coffee towards him. Without acknowledgement, he picked it up and drained it noisily. "I suppose Sandro here has been showing you our countryside?" he asked.

Sandro interrupted Pina's reply. "No, the mees has been out in the seicento with the Signorina Stella. The mees has acquired a patente, you know, which I think is a very smart thing for a foreigner to do! She has not been out with me as guide since her arrival here - not before today, that is." He brooded on this injustice for a time, then added, in dialect, "Sometimes she goes out with a fellow from the town."

Fronti nodded. He replied, also in dialect, "I know. She has been seen. Do you know what he is, or what his business?"

"No, but I should think you have the sources to find that out."

Fronti shrugged. To Pina he said, in Italian, "Oh, do please excuse us signorina! We lapsed automatically into Abruzzese; not to affront you, but because your Italian is so good that we forgot that you are not a native! I asked Sandro if he had yet taken you to Ascoli Piceno, which is a city well worthy of a visit." He smiled ingratiatingly. For some reason, Pina found herself shuddering. She decided that she did not like Signor Fronti.

Sandro poured himself a third whisky and drained it at a gulp. Then he stood away from the wall where he had taken up his position after his re-entry with Fronti. He stretched himself luxuriously and said, "We had better be getting back, mees."

Pina rose and gave Maria a last smile. The old woman nodded and appeared to make some effort to speak but no sound came out of her twisted lips. Zia Mina held out her claw, and Pina repressed another shudder as she tried to shake hands in friendly fashion. "Thank you for the coffee," she said. "It has been very pleasant!" To herself she added, "Cross my fingers for telling a lie!"

Fronti again held her hand for a moment too long before allowing her to follow Sandro into the street. He took her to the car by a much shorter route than they had used before and he slipped into his seat without bothering even to open the door for Pina. All the way back to the house, she was thinking how glad she was that she had not told him that she was learning the dialect; there apparently something was going on which put Carlo's fears in a different light, so that she resolved to tell him about what she had heard at the shop. As for Sandro, he did not utter a word throughout the journey, but sang to himself a bawdy song in dialect, of which fortunately Pina understood rather less than half.

EIGHT

Back at the shop, Fronti helped himself to another cup of coffee. Seated at the table, with his elbows resting on the scrubbed surface and his chin cupped in his hands, he lapsed into deep thought. During this time, the sisters dared hardly breathe for fear of breaking his concentration. After ten minutes of deliberation, he rose and shook himself as a dog might after a dip in the sea. Zia Maria had miraculously thrown off the effects of her stroke, and now stood beside the cooker.

"Well," said he, addressing himself mainly to Maria, "I am fairly convinced that the Englishwoman is not a bodyguard for the young Capriotti, but is what she says she is, a tutor, even though at times Sandro has been convinced and informed us all otherwise. That young man ought to visit the cinema a little less frequently. Nearly everything he says is coloured by his cinematic experiences. His idiotic prattling has cost us dear; we have spent money needlessly in probing the woman's motives and reasons for being here at all. I am thinking of the pair that we put on the train to attempt to scare the woman off. Useless expense, but perhaps it *could* have been for good reason. Sandro will be taught a sharp lesson, but that is by the way. We can afford to let him wait while we deal with bigger game!"

"I am concerned about the fellow who threw Patrizio off the train and is now escorting the Englishwoman all over the region." Maria went on without a trace of speech loss, "He seems to be rather more practised in street fighting than any advocate I ever heard of. My advice is that you investigate him thoroughly and as soon as possible. As for Patrizio, we must wash our hands of him - he has turned out to be the worst type of bungler, and is to be rewarded as bunglers usually are. There are plenty of ditches around Piacenza which could hide a body long enough for our needs. See to it, Matteo!" She seemed to attach as little importance to Patrizio's expectation of life as she would to that of a fly beneath the swatter.

Fronti nodded. He took out a small notebook and made a brief note. "Ever the meticulous Matteo!" sneered Maria, "I hope you never lose that book! You've got enough there to put us all away for the rest of our lives!"

"I take too much care of my book for anyone ever to see it, but even if I did slip up, erevything is written in code, and only I can read it. Now, about this di Felippo. I've had a tail on him for a month now. He stays at the Albergo Regina Victoria in Giulianova Lido, and frequently visits the offices of advocates and notaries in Teramo, in Pescara, and in Ancona. He is smitten with the Englishwoman, and visits her as often as twice a week, but there is no regularity in the visits; they are completely at random times. I feel that we could forget him. As for his treatment of Patrizio, I think that was the normal reaction of a young red-blooded male when a girl is accosted somewhat roughly in a train."

"I just hope that you are right, Matteo!" Maria eyed him shrewdly. "I have to allow that so far all has gone as you predicted, but this is the biggest thing we have attempted so far. But you are in charge of the outside jobs, and in this one, you are the capo!"

"Another shipment has been arranged for Thursday night," said Fronti, ignoring the barb in Maria's remark. "Salvatore will go out with only one member of crew. He will return at four in the morning with the goods.

"The question is, where do we store the load? If it is to come here - no problem. I can pick it up with the light van before daylight. Put you are getting a bit overstocked here, and if I have to take it up north, I must make more detailed arrangements."

"Mina, get the ledger!" commanded Maria.

Mina scuttled into the shop remarkably quickly for an old person who was almost crippled when Pina was present. She returned with a thick book which she laid on the table. Fronti opened it and ran his finger down a list of items. "Milano is pretty full up. There have been difficulties at Bologna, and things will be worse in Piacenza when Patrizio has to retire from active life. There's not a lot coming in, really, only about half a tonne. Can't you take it in?"

"Just make sure that it is broken down into handleable packages," said Maria, "and we will manage. And this time make certain the packages are the right shape. We can't hide the square packs at all, and as you know, Mina and I were up half the night repacking the whole of the last lot you brought in. We were shaking in our shoes all the time we were working in case anyone should see the light on and come knocking to see if we were all right!"

Fronti made another note in his book, and Maria repeated her warning about taking care of it. "I want to live to see Mina and me

Don Stefano

safely installed in that little house we intend to build below the belvedere. As soon as this consignment is accepted, and the big job safely done, we shall have enough cash to buy the ground and get things started. Then Sandro gets this business, and what you do with the organisation will be up to you - your ideas are getting to be too grand for us! It's a lot of trouble to me, keeping up this paralysis thing, and Mina is not the actress she needs to be really!"

He grinned. "But what a superb job you make of it, dear Maria! The world of stage and screen lost a great actress when you decided to go into this line of business! The whole town will rejoice with the pair of you when you have visited Loreto and made your complete and miraculous recoveries!"

Maria smiled at the thought. "I have determined that the Church shall benefit greatly on that happy day! Certainly to the tune of a quarter of a million!"

"A sensible figure, Maria! More would cause people to think about where the cash came from; less would be low ingratitude to the Saints!"

"Get these two jobs successfully completed, and I shall do it! Meantime, the old wooden coffer under my bed is stuffed with bank notes. They make the softest mattress my old bones could want!"

The shop bell tinkled. Immediately Maria relapsed into the invalid that Pina had seen such at little time earlier. Fronti winked at the shapeless mass that had collapsed into her chair. "Farewell, my dear cousin. I shall visit you again ere long." He brushed past a customer as Mina hobbled out to serve in the shop.

NINE

Don Stefano came home to Tre Boschi on one of those warm sunny autumn days that seem to be left over from summer. The huge Rolls Royce purred up the drive, occupying the whole width of the carriage way, and drew up in silent majesty before the front door of the house Stella had been assisted down the steps by Pina, and with a squeal of delight, the girl launched her chair across to the car, almost crashing into her father. He stepped aside adroitly as she braked and then bent over her to kiss her long and tenderly, putting his arms round the thin body and pressing himself close to her tiny form. While he was enjoying the welcome given by his daughter, Pina was able to inspect her employer for the first time.

She saw a slight figure dressed immaculately in well-pressed white sports trousers and a white silk shirt open at the neck. Inside the collar of the shirt, a scarf of crimson foulard was carefully arranged to look as though it had just been thrown into place. His hair was iron-grey, brushed straight back from a high forehead. His nose was aristocratically roman, high-bridged, and when at last Stella allowed him to stand up straight again, Pina saw that his eyes were bright and brown, and very shrewd. He stood erect, to counteract his lack of height,

"I presume that you are Miss Corrigan," he said, in excellent English. Pina admitted that she was indeed the bearer of that name and title. For no good reason, she blushed furiously as she did so.

"Oh, what a poor hostess I am!" cried Stella. "Papa, may I present Miss Corrigan? Not only is she my tutor, but she is also my best friend, as I have often told you on the telephone. Don't you think she has taught me well?" She spoke in English.

"I am happy to meet you, Miss Corrigan. I perceive from her accent that you are making an excellent English speaker from this little wretch!" He gave Stella another squeeze.

Still blushing, Pina said, "Oh, but she is a very quick and apt pupil, signore!"

Stella giggled, "You mustn't say 'signore'! Have you forgotten that Papa is a senator? If you have to be all polite and formal, you have to say 'Senatore', but since you are my friend, you shall be allowed to call him 'Don Stefano.'" This time, she spoke in Italian.

She had been assiduous in learning her first little speech in English, but thereafter her excitement at her father's home-coming proved too much for her to recall much else that she had learned.

Don Stefano waved a slim brown hand towards a young man who had dismounted from the car during the family reunion. This man was now approaching Pina, his eyes undressing her as he came round the car. He ignored Stella completely. Don Stefano said, "May I introduce Mr. Sean O'Brian?"

Pina inclined her head. She thought O'Brian would be about the same age as Carlo, as, hotly red, she endured his admiring gaze. He continued to look right through her dress.

"Delighted to have you know me, Miss Corrigan." His accent was brittle American. "I'm sure you and I are going to spend a few vurry pleasant days together! Capriotti, you old dog, why didn't you tell me that you had such a peach hidden away up here?" He returned to Pina.

"I figure from your name that you, like me, come from the Ould Sod." His Irish imitation was very poor. "Where would you be coming from, now, alannah?"

"My father was Irish," she said, thoroughly detesting this very brash self-confident young fellow who seemed to think that he was God's gift to all women. "I have never been to Ireland, but I believe that I have relatives in County Kildare."

"Begob, now, there's a coincidence! My folks from way back were from County Clare! We just gotta get together and talk a bit of bog Irish!"

Coldly she replied, "I have my duties here, Mr. O'Brian. I am a paid tutor, you must understand."

"Tutor nuttin'! Capriotti *did* mention that he had a governess up here, but he didn't say nuttin' about a doll like you! I guess he made you out to be one of the family!" Again his eyes devoured her.

"That's true," put in Don Stefano. "In my telephone chats with Stella I heard so much talk of 'Pina' that I could not fail to think of you as a member of the clan!"

Sandro came from the house and deftly caught the car keys that Don Stefano threw to him. "Unpack the car, please, Sandro, then have it filled up ready for the return journey - I may have to go at a moment's notice! I hope to be here for three days, but as things are in Roma, I can't guarantee even so short a stay as that!"

He helped Stella to manoeuvre the chair up the steps and into the hall. Pina, followed by O'Brian, also entered the house. The American's hot gaze on her back was almost palpable, and as soon as she reached the staircase, she escaped to her room. She decided that she did not like O'Brian. He was almost everything that she most abhorred - brash, bold, loud of voice, confident that money could buy everything, thinking that everything and everyone had a price. She wondered what on earth he could have in common with Don Stefano. It could never be friendship, she thought, for each man was the antithesis of the other.

Her thoughts were interrupted by Elsa telling her that she was wanted on the telephone. She went to find Carlo on the line. "How is mees today?" he asked. "Listen, can we dine tonight? I've found a place up in the hills where they do the most marvellous mushroom sauce!"

"I don't think I can tonight, Carlo. Don Stefano returned today with a house guest, and I think I may be needed to make up a dinner party. Luigi Passi warned me some time ago that I ought to hold myself in readiness for such an occasion, as there was no Donna Maria any longer to be hostess. But Don Stefano will be here for only three days. I will ring you later, when the house returns to normality, and then we shall be able to make a date."

"You shouldn't be required to act as hostess," he grumbled. "You're paid to teach Stella, not to grace your employer's table! But if you feel you must, then you must. Promise me that you'll ring me tomorrow, eh? Promise?"

"I promise, Carlo. Ciao!" She replaced the handset and stood for a moment or two, absorbed in thought. O'Brian came out of the office. As he passed her in the hall, he nipped her bottom with a sinewy thumb and forefinger. Involuntarily, she gave a small cry of pain. He grinned. "That's what all the gals in Italy expect and like, ain't it? I guess I been long enough here to learn that much Eye-talian!"

Pina turned and delivered at stinging slap to his cheek. He stood holding the place as it slowly reddened where her hand had connected. "A spitfire, is it? Well, that's the kind I like! We're gonna get along fine, baby, real fine!" He passed along the hall leaving her standing amazed and shocked, until at last she recovered sufficiently to return to her room and seek solace in writing a letter to Mama.

At four o'clock Elsa brought her a cup of coffee. "Luigi says you will be needed tonight, mees. It will be informal; a long skirt is not necessary unless you wish to wear one. We don't yet know about tomorrow night; Don Stefano may invite some of the neighbours to dine. Luigi hopes to know more later." She retired down the stairs, calling over her shoulder, "It's eight o'clock tonight, later than usual because that's the time Don Stefano likes to dine."

The gong sounded from the hall at five minutes to eight. Pina descended to the anteroom. She wore her only cocktail skirt, a wide flowing one of dark blue with a self-coloured belt. Her plain white blouse was tucked into the top of the skirt, and the outfit, when combined with the discreet make-up she allowed herself, gave her a very young and virginal appearance.

Don Stefano was standing before the fireplace, his foot resting on the fender as he talked with O'Brian. The pair had been engrossed in their conversation, but stopped talking as Pina entered the room. O'Brian looked at her boldly. He put his hand to his cheek. "No hard feelings, Miss Corrigan!"

His host looked at him in enquiry. O'Brian turned aside to answer the question before it was uttered. "A little private Irish joke, Capriotti," he explained.

"I see. But I don't understand it. I expect Pina will enjoy having a native English speaker, like herself, here for a few days."

"I don't think you would be justified in saying that, Capriotti. George B. Shaw said that the Americans and the English were two great nations divided by a common language. I figure the old s.o.b. was right - he wasn't nobody's fool, that Shaw." As far as Pina could recall, that was O'Brian's last contribution to the conversation that evening. Don Stefano was well-read and much travelled; he was interesting and witty, and the three younger people, for Stella had joined the company for the meal, were kept entertained throughout the entire evening,

Elsa, smart in her full grey livery, announced that dinner was served. The company took their places at the great table in the dining room. The napery was of a whiteness that dazzled the eye; silverware winked in the leaping flames of the fire and reflected the light of the candles in the ornate candelabra that were ranked along the centre of the table.

Don Stefano sat at the head of the table, with Stella at the foot.

Pina, eyes downcast throughout the meal, sat opposite O'Brian. During the length of the meal, she was aware of his questing foot searching and probing for hers beneath the table. In spite of the host's brilliant conversation, the meal seemed to go on for ever. Great was her relief when at last her employer took O'Brian to the study to discuss business affairs over coffee, liqueurs, and cigars.

With the departure of the two men, Stella remained in her place toying with a cup of coffee. "What do you think of Papa's guest?"

"I dislike him intensely," burst out Pina. "He seems to me to be the embodiment of everything that is detestable in a man!"

"I thought you did not like him much. You did not speak to him all through the meal - it was very noticeable!"

"And I don't care if I never speak to him, or see him, again!"

The girl looked at her in astonishment. "Why? What has he done to you, Pina?"

"Oh, nothing much. It's just that I consider him too big for his boots!"

When they had finished their coffee, Pina pushed Stella to her little cell, and helped her to undress. This was a long process, for the girl was excited and talkative about her father's visit. Eventually Pina was able to make her way to her room. Before getting into bed, she took the precaution of wedging a chair under the door knob, but there was nothing to alarm her during the night and in spite of her fears, she slept soundly.

She was able to avoid the American all the next morning. She took her breakfast with Elsa in the kitchen, as had become her custom, and then, working with Stella in the drawing room as they wrestled with the intricacies of the verb 'to be', she could hear those nasal tones as Don Stefano and he were talking about their business, whatever it might have been. She could not distinguish the words; O'Brian's speech was loud but not easily understood, while her employer's tones were so muted as to be almost inaudible. When lessons were over for the day, Pina went into the back yard, hoping to find sanctuary in Annibale's cell, but the old man was not there, and she had to retreat into the house again. She could not spend all her time in her bedroom, so in the hope that Don Stefano would keep O'Brian occupied, she decided to walk along the drive to the main road. Luck was not with her. *He* was sauntering towards the house, and there was no way that she could avoid him.

He approached and gripped her hands tightly in his own. "Gee, that sure is some wallop you pack in that right of yours! Would you believe that I hadda powder my face before I could go in to dinner?"

"You deserved it. It was despicable conduct. I don't know what sort of company you usually keep, but I am not employed by Don Stefano for his guests to take advantage of me!"

"Aw, shucks, honey, I didn't do nuttin' 'cept give you a friendly greeting between a man and a pretty gal with a nicely rounded derrière! Custom of the country, as you might say. I bet you've had the same treatment a zillion times since you've lived in Italy!"

"Whatever may, or may not, have happened elsewhere, such a thing had not been done to me in this house before you entered it!"

He looked keenly at her. "Gee, you're serious!" His amazement was genuine. "Look, hon, let's forget it, shall we? You're making a mountain outa a moleheap. It was all done in friendliness until you clonked me! Boy, what a smack!" He rubbed his cheek in admiration of the blow that she had delivered. Doing so, he released one of her hands, and with a quick twist she broke from his grasp on her other hand and stepped back a yard or so.

"If you mean that as an apology, and if it means that there will be no similar unpleasantness in future, then I accept the apology. But you will do well to remember that I am not one of those cheap - what is the word? Floozies. That's right - floozies that you seem to be used to!"

"OK, OK! I've said I'm sorry. Now let's forget it, why don't we?"

Pina looked at him icily. "All right," she said, after a long pause while he squirmed under her glance. "But to forgive you doesn't mean that I like you any the more!"

To change the subject, he said, "What's this tale the old man was spinning me about a spring of mineral water about here? That's what I came out to see. He's been on about it ever since I first met him in the Embassy in Rome."

"It's in there, behind the bushes. You can't see it from the drive."

He parted the undergrowth and went towards the fountain which was steadily gushing its apparently inexhaustible supply. Pina followed him just far enough to observe his actions. She did not trust him enough to enter right into the glade with him, in spite of his promise to behave himself. He leaned over the pool which lay under the waterspout, and cupping his hands, carried some of the water to his lips. As soon as he had tasted it, he spat it out with an expression of intense disgust.

"Hell's bells," he spluttered. "That's awful! It's absolutely vile! Get it into fancy bottles with a classy label, have some chemist certify that it will cure everything from ague to zymotic disease, and it'll sell a million bottles a month! There's a goldmine here if the marketing is done right!" He took another tentative sip, spat it out, and pulled a face. "That's why I'm here. Capriotti wants to raise a little mazuma, so he brung me in to assess the possibility of raising the needful from this here well. I'm into marketing and general development, as well as publicity, you see. Gee, this thing could be bigger'n Coke!"

He stood upright and looked through the undergrowth towards the church and the woods that gave the estate its name. "We could put a bottling plant up there, if we levelled the ground - about a coupla acres would be enough to start with for a bottling plant and a lorry park. We could always expand as necessary. Hell, we could practically mint our own money, I tell you! And if you're kind to little Sean, baby, you could get your cut of the gelt!"

"But that spells ruin for Tre Boschi!" As she uttered the words, Pina realised how much she had grown to love this place, and how much she would hate to see it despoiled. Certainly it seemed that O'Brian had no similar feelings; nothing mattered to him beyond money. That the peace and quiet of the estate would be ruined for ever by the comings and goings of heavy lorries, and by the noise created by a bottling plant weighed nothing in the balance for him. The only thing that really mattered was the fast buck.

He confirmed her reading of his character. "Money is the thing, honey! It's the only thing in life! Who the hell cares about a crummy old place like this when there's gonna be enough to replace it by a skyscraper once this hooch hits the market? That's why the British never have any real businessmen - you're all so sentimental about old things that have had their day, that are worn out and crying out to be replaced by something modern. Look ahead and think big, that's my motto! Boy, oh boy, will we clean up with this stuff!"

He made to back out of the bushes and she preceded him to the drive. Slowly they walked back to the house. Gone now, for the moment, was his interest in her or in any other woman. He was still enthusing about the fortune that awaited them as they reached the house.

Don Stefano was in the front court, talking with Passi. He turned as he heard their footsteps and smiled. "It's good to see that you have made friends! I expect you miss having young people about, Pina, and will be happy to talk with someone other than Stella." Plainly, like most of the rest of the staff, he was unaware of the existence of Carlo.

O'Brian began to enthuse about the spring. Don Stefano held up a steadying hand. "Patience, O'Brian," he counselled. "We have to talk to Stella about this, you know. She is my heiress, remember. And we must also consult the staff, all of whom are concerned. Don't count your britches before they are hatched!" Sometimes his metaphors got a little mixed, but the sense was there.

Pina entered the house. Her mind was busy with impossible schemes which involved enlisting the aid of anyone she could recruit to prevent the rape of Tre Boschi.

O'Brian

TEN

The next morning, immediately after breakfast, Don Stefano sent Elsa with a message to Pina, inviting her to go to the office. As she entered the room, she noted that the majordomo had been evicted from his place behind the great desk and had been relegated to a smaller table under the window. Behind the desk, her employer looked quite tiny. He stood up as Pina's entrance and motioned her to sit at a chair across the desk from him. For a few moments, he worked on the papers before him, then pushing them into a heap, he leaned back and regarded Pina with a friendly eye.

"I am pleased with the way that you have settled in here," he told her. "And I am more than satisfied with the way Stella has progressed since you have been teaching her. Her grasp of all her subjects has improved enormously, and her command of English has moved forward by leaps and bounds. In my considered view, before long, under your tuition, she will be speaking the tongue as well as I do myself, and perhaps even better than I do. I have tested her pretty thoroughly, and as I say, I am well satisfied with what I see. Luigi chose well when he told me, back in London, that he thought you would be a very suitable tutor and companion for the girl. Also I am happy with the way in which she has taken to you as a person. Plainly, she is quite fond of you. That is perhaps the reason that she works so well for and with you."

Pina thanked him, adding that she was fond of Stella. He accepted this remark with a quick fleeting smile, and continued, "That is the main reason why I asked you to see me this morning. A secondary reason is that I wish to ask a favour of you. I am going to be very busy about the estate all day, and tonight I intend to take Stella out to dine with a few friends. I shall be unable to take Mr. O'Brian with me; in the matter of the affairs of the estate, I think he would be bored, and in the matter of dining with my friends, since he has no Italian, he would be completely at a loss.

"Elsa has asked permission to attend a festa in her native village, and I have given that leave, since there will be no need for her services in cooking and serving tonight. Mr O'Brian has more than once expressed a wish to see how the local peasantry live and play, and I thought it might be nice for you to go and see a village festa, and act as interpreter for him. You might even get to know him a little better. Of course, I would not expect you to drive the seicento; Sandro will be ordered to take you in the Fiat."

Pina thought for a few moments. This was not a task she would have chosen for herself. She had no great desire to spend several hours in the company of the American, but of course, Elsa would be present. But Don Stefano has praised her work, and it might be politic to please him in such a small matter. Noting her hesitation, he added, "Of course, if there are any reasons why you cannot do this - perhaps you have made other arrangements - then I shall cast about for another method to amuse my guest. I rather hoped that perhaps you had not seen a festa, and it would be a novel experience not only for Mr O'Brian, but for you as well."

She hesitated a little longer. Then, reflecting that O'Brian had promised that there would be no repetition of his bad behaviour, she said, "Thank you, Don Stefano. I should certainly like to see a festa."

"No, thank *you*, Pina." He used her name quite naturally. "Luigi will give the necessary instructions to Elsa and to Sandro, and Elsa will inform you about times, etcetera. You should be home again soon after midnight. These jollifications tend to be rather long-drawn-out affairs, but with your interest in our region, I think it safe to promise you that you will not be bored!" He looked at her quizzingly. "You thought perhaps I didn't know that you had shown interest in the area? My dear girl, among my people, there is little you can do that is not general knowledge on the estate very quickly! To continue, however, as I say, you should not be bored, and with an interpreter like you, Mr O'Brian should not be bored either!"

At six o'clock, warmly dressed in a woollen dress and carrying a cardigan, for Elsa had warned her that the air could be cool up in the mountains where her family lived, Pina stood at the front door. The Fiat stood purring in the courtyard, almost as though it were looking forward to an evening of pleasure. At the wheel sat Sandro, muffled up as though for an Arctic expedition. Elsa came tripping out into the courtyard and took her place beside Sandro. Finally O'Brian made an appearance. Politely he saw Pina comfortably installed in the rear seat, and then took his place beside her. "Arrah, now, off we go, me bhoy!" he said.

Sandro turned to face his passengers. "Signori?" he queried.

"The signor says we are ready to go," translated Pina.

"OK," said Sandro, trotting the only word of American he knew, and the car glided smoothly down the drive.

The evening light was fading dramatically quickly. Remnants of the sunset lay on the clouds, tingeing them with red. Elsa, indicating the coloured sky, said to Pina, "Rossa del sera, bel' tempo si spera!"

"What's the dame saying?" asked O'Brian.

"She says 'Red in the evening, good weather, one hopes', or in plain English, 'Red sky at night, shepherd's delight,'" replied Pina.

"Well, I'll be a monkey's uncle! Now they've pinched our good ole American proverb!" He seemed to be astonished that the Italian saying should so closely resemble the saying he knew.

After some miles of travel along quiet country roads, Sandro turned on to a more important route. Here the traffic seemed to be welded into a solid immovable mass. The only movement was confined to the mopeds and small motorbikes which buzzed like little sawmills as the riders weaved their way through the packed ranks of the cars, able to find gaps where one would think not even a mouse could enter. Every driver of every car, whatever its size, was sitting with his thumb pressed firmly on the horn button, and the cacophony was deafening. Slowly, inch by noisy inch, the convoy moved along the road. Ahead, one, two, three maroons soared up into the now navy-blue sky to burst with crashes that sounded, even at that distance, like an artillery bombardment. Simultaneously with their explosions, the maroons gave out a bright light which hung in the air until it finally faded and was gone, leaving the spectators almost blinded by its glare.

Slowly, painfully slowly, the mass of transport approached the village. Even above the blaring of the cars' horns, Pina could hear the music of an electric organ being played at full decibels. Across the road, well above the height of anything that would pass below, clusters of lights shaped like stars were suspended, their brilliance somewhat diminished by the light of the moon, now fully risen. The road had narrowed at the entrance to the village, and its width was even more reduced by the cars that were parked, or maybe, abandoned would be the correct term, on each side of the carriage way. Children ran screaming up and down the street - the only street, as far as Pina could make out - holding in their hot little hands giant ice-cream cornets, which, without fear or favour, they wiped on the clothing of all whom they encountered. Older youths were armed with small fire-crackers which they lighted and threw indiscriminately into the crowd, each explosion eliciting a roar of disapproval from that section of the throng thus affected.

At the further end of the village, they came across a small fair, worked by what appeared to be a family of travellers. So slowly did the traffic move now that Pina was able to pick out each member of the troupe. Father was in charge of a rifle range where the village bloods, at a range of a full five metres, displayed their marksmanship while their admiring girl friends cheered them on. Mother worked the chairoplanes which whirled dangerously above the heads of spectators watching their friends pretending to enjoy the ride. A miniature roundabout, consisting of six assorted railway engines, cars, and motorcycles, intended to be ridden only by children, was controlled by a bored business woman of no more than ten years old, who stood in the centre of the machine, taking the fares, pulling the control switch, deciding when the clients had received a long enough ride to satisfy them, settled childish squabbles when two or more children decided to use the same conveyance, and did all these things with an air of having been similarly engaged since time began.

Sandro continued the slow drive up the hill. At a cry from Elsa, he turned the car across the traffic flow and drove into a narrow gate. Elsa leapt from her seat and was engulfed in embraces from a crowd of twenty people of all ages, each shouting greetings at the tops of their voices. Managing at last to disengage herself, the housekeeper came to the car door, and said, "Mees, would you please come to meet my family? They are all here, and everyone wants to meet you because I have told them so much about you!"

Pina alighted, closely followed by O'Brian. He seemed reluctant to be parted from his interpreter. They were then formally introduced to Elsa's grandparents on both sides, to a myriad of aunts and uncles, to brothers, sisters, nephews, nieces, first and second cousins without number. They all clustered round to shake Pina's hand, to exclaim in wonder at Pina's hair colour, her eyes, her fashion sense, her excellent shoes, and even, by one misguided grandparent, her taste in boy friends. Much of this had to be allowed to pass over O'Brian's head - there was no time for interpretation. He simply stood looking at the family reunion with an air of utter boredom.

At last all compliments had been paid, and Pina and O'Brian were conducted in triumph into the house. A long wooden table was waiting in the huge kitchen, laden with all the paraphernalia of eating. Wine was served in great tumblers - no tiny delicate wine glasses for these connoisseurs of the local brew! The tribe took their places at table, where Pina. who was, it appeared, to be treated as the guest of honour, was served first. O'Brian, seated beside her, waved away every dish that was presented to him, in spite of Pina's warning that he might cause offence by refusing food that had been cooked and was being served with such care. To all her persuasions, he shook his head glumly, saying, "I ain't gonna eat none of that hogwash! You seen that ole buzzard's hands?" It was true that Elsa's mother would never win any prize for having the best-kept hands, but the roast chicken which she had just torn to pieces with those same hands tasted delicious.

When she felt that she had eaten as much as courtesy demanded, Pina made her excuses and left the table, followed by O'Brian. She had seen that other guests had done the same, so was sure that such behaviour was the custom of the country, and would not give offence. They went out into the crowded street. To their left, up the hill, brightly illuminated stalls were doing a roaring trade in such delights as plastic toys, roasted peanuts, ice cream, and sticky sweets. A tiny piazza in front of the church was almost completely occupied by a bandstand with a space before it for dancers to exhibit their skills. The bandstand had enough lighting to furnish a small town - it dazzled the eye of every beholder, (to use a cliché). A group of five instrumentalists sat on chairs which had been borrowed from the church - the chairs were identifiable by the prayer book racks attached to their backs. Those racks now supported sheet music. Against a deafening background of noise, the players were trying to tune their instruments. The organ on the chairoplanes was blasting out hits of the previous year at full throttle; further up the hill, the proprietor of the village's only bar had dragged out his pride and joy, a juke box, and installed it on the terrace in front of his establishment, from where it sent out, at the maximum loudness, a repertoire of popular tunes, playing them over and over again without anyone having to insert a coin.

On the bandstand, a blowsy blonde was testing a microphone. "Uno, due, tre," she kept repeating at different sound levels ranging from forte to fortissimo and beyond. A group of children, armed with the plastic trumpets and saxophones that they had bought from one of the stalls, were assisting by blowing their new toys as hard as possible. Men stood watching, smoking and making coarse jokes about the blonde; they chewed peanuts and spat out the shells to be trodden underfoot by passers-by. One peanut shell makes very little noise when crushed by a stout shoe, but multiply the number by several thousand, and the noise is distinctly audible, even at a village festa. Young women, dressed in their Sunday-go-to-meeting finery, stood at one side of the piazza, studiously ignoring the admiring glances of the boys across the square. To put it all in a nutshell, it was festa time in Elsa's village.

O'Brian seized Pina's hand and dragged her away from the vortex of noise. He led her further up the hill, to where the road curved slightly and there were no more stalls. The bend of the road masked the sounds of revelry slightly, so that it was possible to talk in normal tones. Above, the bright moon lighted the valley on their right. He stopped and gazed downwards, where lights gleamed from the cottages of those who had decided to ignore the festa, or to join it later when things warmed up a little more.

"Gee!" exclaimed O'Brian, "I sure as hell would like to be back home right now, with a moon like that!"

"Why? Do you also have festas?" She knew that it was a silly question even as she asked.

"Nah. It's just that I miss my Mary-Lou. She's the gal I'm gonna marry soon's I can pull off this deal with Capriotti."

He was still holding her hand. Up here, in the shadow of the hills behind them, away from the crowd, Pina felt uncomfortable, "Let's go back," she suggested.

Grudgingly he assented. "OK. I guess I promised to be good, and I better keep my word. But I hoped that you might feel the romance of the night. I mean, what with the stars and the moon an' all that mush, we mighta done a little smooching. I reckon your life stuck out there with all those wop hicks on the farm, must be kinda short on romance." He grabbed her hand again.

"You won't get any romance from me!" She tore her hand from his grasp. "Come on, let's get back to the festa!"

"Running scared, eh?" he sneered. But as she started back down the hill, he followed her half a pace behind.

When they arrived at the piazza, the band had started to play for dancing. Some of the braver spirits among the village youth had taken the floor and were attempting the sort of steps that they had seen from time to time on the television or at the cinema. It was a poor imitation, and for some time O'Brian regarded their efforts with scorn. Then he seized Pina by the arm. "Aw, c'mon! Let's cut a rug and show them how!" He pulled her on to the dance floor and began to lead her. He certainly could dance well, and was easy for her to follow. Their feet fairly flew over the rough tarmac, and when the music stopped and they stood panting from their exertions, they were rewarded with a burst of applause from the onlookers, and cries of "Bis, bis!"

"What are they shouting?"

"They want an encore."

"OK, tell the man to play and let's get to it!"

The leader gathered his players together again, and they began to play a slow waltz. As Pina and O'Brian revolved alone in the centre of the circle of spectators, for there was nobody in the crowd who would dare to attempt to emulate such choreographic wizardry, he began to pull her closer to his body and to nuzzle her hair. Angrily she pulled herself away. Over the music and other noise, she cried, "You promised!"

"Sorry!" His grip relaxed slightly and she was held less closely to his gyrating body. But his hold was tight enough to preclude her from disengaging completely. In the hot atmosphere of the piazza, watched by a thousand eyes, they ended their dance and she pushed him angrily away, ignoring the cries for another repeat. She made her way towards Elsa's family house, while he followed, subdued and apparently penitent.

"Sorry. I guess I got carried away!"

"Well, I don't like it, and I won't have it!"

She walked on, head in air. Soon he caught up with her and handed her an enormous ice-cream cone, saying it was a peace offering. Relenting a little, she was sucking at the cool sweet mixture as they turned into the gateway and went up to the house.

In the patio, under the vine that made a mosaic of light and shade on the cement surface, coffee and wine were awaiting all who wished to partake. People sat on a variety of chairs, waving and shouting to the other folk passing ceaselessly up and down the street. Some of the walkers called out their congratulations to the couple they had recently seen dancing. Pina translated all their remarks and O'Brian swelled almost visibly with pride. "Aw, shucks, they ain't seen nuttin'. All we showed 'em was a few basic movements. Hell, they oughta be around when me and Mary-Lou really get goin'!" He continued to boast of his and Mary-Lou's talents and Pina drifted off into a reverie, just putting in a word now and then to make him think that she was listening. She thought how wonderful it would have been if Carlo had been her dance partner. Carlo! Her hand flew to her mouth. She had promised to ring him, and had completely forgotten that promise!

Elsa came laughing into the patio. She helped herself to wine, and said, "And what do the signori think of the festa in my village?"

"It's marvellous, Elsa. Quite different from anything I had imagined!"

"Yes, of its kind it is quite good. In fact, it is the best festa in the province! And why?" asked Elsa rhetorically. "Because my family are the organisers! They order the band, they organise the concertina competition which will be held tomorrow evening; they set off the maroons to mark the beginning and end of each day the festa runs. They do it all! Without my family, there would be no festa!"

Sandro came running into the yard, panting, he looked dishevelled, and under his left eye a dark bruise was forming rapidly. Elsa looked at him with concern. "What happened?"

"Those villagers of yours are too jealous! I barely spoke to the girl when I was set upon by four men and we had a battle! Mind you, I was attacked from behind!"

Elsa burst into a tinkling peal of laughter. "You mean, he hit you in the eye from behind? Come now, Sandro, not one of my villagers is that clever!"

"Well, there were seven or eight of them! Anyway, it was the girl's fault. She led me to believe..."

Again Elsa's tinkling peal of laughter rang out. "You know that they all do that at the festa! More fool you to be taken in. How old *was* the girl really?"

"She was quite sixteen, well, maybe fifteen then, but she knew what she was about. I want to go home. If that gang catch me, I'll be in no condition to drive you. Do you think the signori would like to return to Tre Boschi?"

Hearing the name of the house, probably the only words of Italian he knew, O'Brian pricked up his ears. "Say, does that wop say we're going back to the house?"

Pina replied that Sandro did indeed wish to get away. "It seems that a gang of youths are hunting him."

"OK then. What are we waiting for? I'm fed up of this dump anyhow!"

Pina translated a censored version for the benefit of Elsa and Sandro. Elsa was reluctant to leave her family so early in the proceedings, but was over-ruled by a majority vote. She made her goodbyes last as long as was humanly possible and then had to search for her handbag. At last, with infinite difficulty, Sandro got the car out on to the road, and by dint of nudging pedestrians with the car bumpers, they were able to leave the village and gain the side roads once again.

Elsa, still smarting because of the hurried move away from her family, was silent. She hated to lose a single moment of her festa. Such fairs are to the Italians what Christmas is to the British, a time when all the family foregather and the clans are once more united for a short time in the face of all the world.

Sandro was silent, sulking as he drove. He was highly indignant about the way in which he had been attacked. He thought darkly that maybe in a week or so, he would gather a few friends, return to that village, seek out the girl, and if there were not too many village men about, give her a beating similar to the one he had suffered.

O'Brian was silent. The dances with Pina had inflamed his desire. The proximity of her body, first as they had danced, and now as they sat together, was almost too much for him to bear.

And finally, Pina was silent. She was worried about Carlo, wondering if he would resent the fact that she had failed to keep her promise to ring him.

As usual, once they were clear of traffic, Sandro drove rapidly, and soon the car was sweeping along the drive to the house. They drew up before the front door, and O'Brian helped Pina to alight. With a brisk "Buona notte" from Elsa and Sandro, the car was driven away to the rear of the house where lay the garages and the servants' entrance. O'Brian roughly caught Pina and drew her to him. His hungry lips sought hers as she beat vainly with her little fists on his chest. His face was prickly with the stubble he had grown since his morning shave, and her cheeks were red and hot from the abrasion as well as from the effort of trying to resist him.

"Stop it!" she tried to utter through lips that were being pressed upon by his. But no sound came. She was unable to open her mouth against such fierce pressure.

She heard a voice from the shadow of the portico. "A touching scene!" said Carlo, in English.

O'Brian released Pina, who almost fell at the sudden relaxing of embrace, "Carlo!" she breathed.

"Shut up!" he ordered roughly. "I had thought you were different, but I see you are exactly like all the others!"

O'Brian stepped up to Carlo. "That's enough of that!" he commanded. "I dunno who you are, and I don't give a hoot in hell. But you can hightail it outa here just as fast as you like, or you might regret it!" Carlo drew back his right arm. His fist seemed hardly to move, but O'Brian fell to the ground as though pole-axed.

"Carlo!" cried Pina piteously. It was a cry from the heart. He ignored her. Turning on his heel, he disappeared into the darkness as Pina struggled to drag the inert form of O'Brian into the house. She heard the sound of Carlo's car as he departed rapidly from Tre Boschi.

ELEVEN

Pina was seated at the little table in her room, trying to compose a letter to Carlo. Repeated telephone calls to his hotel had served only to elicit the response that the signore di Felippo was not in. The receptionist did not know when he might return. Certainly a message would be passed to him, asking him to ring; a note to that effect would be placed in his pigeon-hole immediately. Several calls made afterwards had all had the same reply - the message was still in his pigeon-hole; it had not been picked up by him. Now she was trying to explain in writing those things that it appeared she was not going to be allowed to say on the phone.

After she had pulled the still unconscious O'Brian into the hall, she had passed the rest of the night in thinking of ways by which she could put things right between herself and Carlo. She had made her first telephone call as early as possible, just after seven o'clock, in fact, and other calls had been made at intervals of fifteen minutes right up to the breakfast time. When she entered the kitchen, Elsa had exclaimed at her appearance. Her eyes were red and swollen from crying and lack of sleep. She had not taken Elsa into her confidence. Coffee had been drunk in funereal silence and she had refused food. Elsa was talkative, but it was with total lack of interest that Pina learned that O'Brian had been taken by Sandro to Teramo station to catch a train back to Rome. Aloud, Elsa wondered what had gone amiss. In her uncomplicated mind, the guest's sudden departure and Pina's woe-begone looks had a common cause.

As O'Brian had left the house, refusing coffee and breakfast, a cardinal sin in Elsa's eyes, his coat collar was pulled well up to cover his face. He had had difficulty in speaking. Not that that made a great difference, added Elsa, for he spoke only English and it was only with a great show of pantomime and gesticulation that he had been able to convey to her his pressing desire to leave Tre Boschi. Sandro had expressed his opinion that the Americano had forced his attentions on the mees, and she, trained in martial arts, had been compelled to show him the error of his ways. Elsa did not mention Sandro's thoughts - she merely said that it was a great pity that anyone should visit a country without ever learning a word of the native language. Did not the mees agree?

Pina replied automatically. She even forgot to thank Elsa for taking her to the festa; nor did she ask the housekeeper to convey her thanks to the family for their hospitality of the previous evening. Elsa thought this was quite out of character, and the more she considered the matter, the more she was convinced that the mees and the Americano had had a terrible quarrel after she and Sandro had left them at the front door last night. In the meantime, the most urgent matter was how she, the housekeeper, responsible for the comfort of guests, was going to tell Don Stefano that his guest had departed without a word of farewell or thanks. Her employer was small of stature, but Elsa was well aware that his temper had a very short fuse. He might easily lay the cause of the trouble at her door, thinking that it was some shortcoming of his staff that had been the root of the rupture. However, until that dread moment arrived, Elsa had the festa to look back on. That would sustain her for the time being.

Lessons that morning had been disastrous. Pina had been quite unable to catch and hold Stella's attention or interest, and the child had been as naughty as any child of her age could be, refusing to do any serious work until Pina, at the ragged outer edge of her patience, had packed the girl off to her room with the threat that if she did not mend her ways, she, Pina, would be looking for a new post, and Stella would be seeking a new tutor/companion. Now with the house all quiet, Pina was deep in the effort of composing her explanatory note to Carlo.

She had torn up at least seven false starts and they lay crumpled in the basket under the table. Some had been written in Italian; others in English for subsequent translation. She thought that a letter in English would receive no interest, but would be torn up by Carlo before he would bother to read it. This, her final effort, was being written in Italian, and it was little better than any of her previous efforts.

'Dear Carlo,' she had said, no longer caring about the wording, just anxious to get something down on paper. 'Things are not what they might seem to be. When you hit that hateful man last night, I was truly trying to fight him off, rather than, as you seem to think, enjoying his odious attentions. Truly I detest him. I am sorry I forgot to telephone you as I promised I would. Don Stefano asked me to take O'Brian to a festa and in the rush of getting away, I simply forgot. I apologise.' She re-read what she had written. It seemed very cold. She let her pen race along with her thoughts. 'Oh, Carlo, please let us be friends again! I miss you so much already! Carlo, I am pleading with you; I could not bear it if you hated me! You are the only friend I have in the world now. This morning I even quarrelled with Stella! Caro, Carlo, I am so miserable! Please ring me soon.' She signed the note, 'Your loving Pina.'

Envelope in hand, she went into the kitchen. There was nobody there, but from the scullery came the sounds of pots being scrubbed. Pina looked in, to see Rosa, as usual up to her elbows in suds as she laboured at the brown stone sink. She was singing softly to herself, evidently quite happy. Pina felt a small pang of envy.

"Rosa," she said timidly, "do you think I could get a letter delivered in Giulianova today, urgently?"

Rosa stopped her singing and turned to face mees. Now here was real life, she thought. Mees and her boy friend have quarrelled; she wants to make it up, and the Americano just doesn't want to know, just like in the film at the Roxy in Ascoli Piceno last week. Well, if Rosa could further the cause of true love, she was ready and willing to do her bit!

"It's my afternoon off, mees, just as soon as I've finished these few pots. I intended to go to Teramo on my moped, but I can get what I want in Giulianova just as easily. I could deliver a letter for you."

Thanking her warmly, Pina passed the letter over. How good, how very kind, the girl was! Ignorant and untutored she might be, but her heart was pure gold! With her red and rough hands, and her rustic complexion, a less likely messenger of peace and friendship could scarcely be imagined. Rosa tucked the note into her pocket and resumed her work. Thanking her again, Pina returned to her room.

She really ought to write to Mama, she thought. But in the given circumstances, it would be impossible to write a bright cheerful letter. If her tone was anything other than happy, Mama would inevitably sense that something was seriously amiss, and before Pina could do anything to stop him, zio Giglio would be telephoning from Firenze, and probing to unearth every little fact, relevant or irrelevant, to forward to his sister. Pina therefore lay on her cot and allowed herself the luxury of wallowing in misery. The events of last night insisted on passing and repassing through her mind. She wondered whether she had done the right thing in writing as she had done, to Carlo. Several times she almost returned to the scullery to take back the letter from Rosa. When at last she decided to do just that, it was too late. The scullery maid had left, and the letter had left with her.

Returning to her room, she passed her time in little tasks. She sorted out her clothing: she mended items that demanded the attentions of needle and thread; she washed her hair, as though to wash O'Brian out of her life, then sat before the window to dry it in the breeze. She took her shoes out of the closet, lined them up, inspected them, then replaced them. She dusted the already speckless furniture, an action that would have shaken Elsa to her very foundations, should she ever learn what Pina had done. She washed out her duster in the hand basin. Then at long last, it was time for supper, and she descended into the dining room.

Elsa had laid covers for only two. Pina wondered who was to eat with her. Would it be Don Stefano, whom she did not particularly wish to meet that evening? It would almost certainly not be O'Brian. Or would it? He might easily have altered his mind and returned to press his plans about the fountain. Her doubts were resolved when Stella came through the door.

"Oh, darling Peppina!" she cried. "Please say you don't hate me, and that you will stay at Tre Boschi for ever and ever! I am so sorry that I was bad this morning. I don't know what made me behave so abominably! And then this afternoon I learned that Papa had been called back urgently to Roma. Perhaps I just had a premonition. But please don't say you really truly hate me!"

Pina bent and put her arms round the tin shoulders. "No, I will not leave you, Stellina. I have been upset, too, but it's all right now. We are friends again, and I really do love you!"

Elsa brought in the supper, and the pair ate, Stella chattering away happily now that she was assured that Pina was no longer annoyed with her. There was much to be happy about, she said. First and foremost, Papa had been home for two whole days, and had told her much about Paris and Roma and London, and even New York. She has been told about the plans for the fountain, and had scotched them with a firm refusal to allow any such thing as O'Brian contemplated, and on reflection, Papa had agreed with her. Of course, it would have brought in an awful lot of money, but Tre Boschi would have been ruined forever as a beautiful estate. The only fly in Stella's ointment was that Papa had been called away at such short notice, but even that was compensated for by her return to Pina's good books.

Listening to the child's happy prattling, Pina wished that her own troubles could be so easily remedied.

Elsa cleared away the debris of the meal and in the absence of Rosa, took Stella away to her room, after a huge wet kiss had been bestowed on Pina's cheek. Alone in the dining room, Pina sat in front of the fire. She was having a bad fit of the 'blackers' as Daddy used to say when he suffered an occasional fit of melancholy. She was brought back to the present by the insistent ringing of the telephone in the hall. There seemed to be no one to answer its imperious summons, so after allowing it to ring a dozen times or so, she went out to take the call. "Pronto!" she said as she lifted the receiver to her ear.

Her heart leapt when she heard Carlo's voice. "Carlo!" she almost shouted. "Oh, how happy I am to hear you again!" She felt almost suffocated with relief. "You received my note?"

"That's why I am calling now. I would have rung earlier. I had to return to Milano, but only for today. I've just got back. Oh, carina, I was so mad when I saw that man kissing you! Look, we've got to meet very soon. Then you can tell me all about it! But first, allow me to say it - I love you!"

"I love you, too," she responded, and stood aghast. Certainly she had intended to say no such thing. She merely wished to retain his friendship. What on earth was she thinking about?

"I'm coming straight over to see you!" he shouted. "Nothing and nobody can stop me! They had better not try! Say it again, Pinina, dearest one!"

"I love you," she said, and as she spoke, she knew it was the truth.

He made a kissing sound into the phone. "That will have to do for now, until I can give you a real kiss! Stay right there at Tre Boschi and meet me at the end of the drive in half an hour - no, in twenty minutes."

"Carlo, dear one, take care! You must not have an accident now!"

"Very well, I promise not to take more than forty minutes on the journey, because I just can't wait to kiss you!" He kissed into the phone once again. "I shall arrive on the wings of the wind - well, in the seicento, which shall be my chariot of Eros!"

They talked lovers' talk for a few minutes before ringing off. Pina went to her room and flung herself on the bed, bursting into torrents of tears. But these were tears of happiness.

Over what occurred when Carlo, true to his word, arrived forty minutes later, it is but decent to draw a veil. There are joys too deep for words. But when, much later, Pina went to her bed, her heart was full to bursting. Before she fell asleep, she remembered to send up a little prayer of gratitude to Sant'Antonio.

Il Padrone

TWELVE

The meal at the trattoria had been prepared and served by the padrone himself. Cooking and service were above reproach. Carlo had not been permitted to choose the wine, however. The padrone had argued that since all the food was of local provenance, carefully selected by himself, only he could be deemed to be qualified to say what wine went best with it. Pina and Carlo had arrived at that stage when the body is satisfied with the fare it has received, as far as actual hunger is concerned, but still emits a call for that little bit more of luxury that would change a good meal into a really celebratory banquet. The padrone had suggested that, to round off the evening, and to aid digestion, his clients should drink with their coffees a glass of the local liqueur - 'Cent' Erbe', the hundred herbs.

Somehow Carlo's chair had slipped round the table so that he was now seated next to her. He watched as she lifted the tiny glass, and let the candle flames play through the rich colour of the liquid. "You seem to have been a long time here in the Abruzzo, dear," she said. "Have your firm thought of calling you back to Milano? You were called back for a day, a week ago." She added hastily, "Perish the thought! I don't want anyone to take you from me now! It was just a black thought that struck me."

He selected a single large and luscious grape from the remnants of the bunch that still lay in the dish. Carefully, deliberately, he removed the stalk and with his fingers peeled the fruit. He then pushed the grape into Pina's unresisting lips.

"That is to quieten you," he smiled. "Such thoughts are best left unspoken - they could bring you bad luck if the local strega (witch) were to overhear them!"

She gave a little shudder, half serious, half mocking. "Such as...?"

"Such as the firm doing exactly what you have just thought of and calling me away before I have put a certain plan into operation."

"A plan? What are you scheming, caro?"

"A foolish thought, I suppose."

"This is a night for foolish thoughts, caro." She chewed upon her grape. "Here we have soft lights, a waning moon, and only we two left in the restaurant. All we need - and it would be perfection to have it - is a gypsy trio!"

"Darling Pina!" he cried. He raised her hand and covered it with kisses, then kissed her full upon the lips. "You make this and every night perfect for me! Look, I went shopping today."

He fumbled in his pocket and brought out a small box. Opening it, he displayed a diamond and sapphire ring, the stones winking in the candlelight.

"It's beautiful!" she gasped. Then, mockingly, "Am I to take this as a proposal, sir?"

"If you would accept it, and me, this would be the most wonderful night since the world began!"

"But, sir," she dimpled, "I hardly know you! Why, we haven't yet been properly introduced!"

He reached out and rang the little bell to summon the padrone. When he arrived, wiping his hands on a towel that he had snatched up as he left the kitchen, Carlo said, "See, my friend. This lady is the Signorina Corrigan. Can you say her name?"

"I think so, signore. Signorina Corrigan-a."

"Near enough. Now I am Carlo di Felippo. It is my wish that you introduce me to the signorina!"

The padrone stared at Carlo in astonishment. His eyes questioned the sanity of his client. Had not he spent the whole evening dining and wining with the young woman? Surely they knew each other well. "This is a joke, signore?"

"Do it, man. Don't waste time. Do it at once, subito!"

The padrone began to walk away. His was a respectable business, and he was not accustomed to the jokey ways of people who, by their accents, came from far away. Carlo gripped his coat tails and hauled him back to the table.

"Introduce us, please, maestro!"

Once again the man inspected Carlo closely. He decided that his client could not possibly be drunk on a bottle and a half of his best wine, plus a Fernet Branca and a Cent'Erbe. And to be called "Maestro" showed that the signore had a true appreciation of the art of the chef. It was arrant flattery, but who could resist it? He would do as the client said.

"Signorina," he mumbled, "Allow me to introduce to you the Signore Carlo di Felippo. Signore, this is the signorina... what was that foreign name again?"

"Corrigan, Signorina Pina Corrigan. Cor-rig-an"

"Ah, si. Signorina Pina Corrigan-a."

Carlo rose, and made a small bow in the direction of Pina. "Piacere," he said. He removed from his wallet a five-thousand lire note, and handed it to the padrone. "For the bambini," he explained. The padrone shuffled away, shaking his head at the odd ways of young people these days.

Carlo went down on one knee. "Pina, if I may so address you now that we have been introduced, will you marry me?"

"Oh sir," she dimpled. "This is so sudden! You will have to write to Mama before you pay your addresses to me!" For answer he pulled her to himself, fiercely, hungrily, and she let herself go to him, burying her head against the smooth texture of his dinner jacket. He put a finger under her chin, gently lifting her face, and kissed her, first on her eyes, wet with tears of happiness, then on the tip of her nose, and finally on the mouth where they clung together for a long ecstatic time. They broke apart, panting.

"Carlo, my love!"

"Pina, my dearest one!" Again they kissed. "I love you," he said. "I love you! My own adorable Pina! How soon can we get married?"

"Carlo, I am a working girl. I cannot marry at the drop of a hat! My employer will need a term of notice. I don't think Don Stefano will be very happy to have his daughter's companion wishing to relinquish her post so soon after he had paid her fare to Tre Boschi from London! No, Carlo, don't! The padrone is watching us! Yes, I will marry you, but a girl needs time to get used to the idea! Perhaps you don't know it, but there are a thousand things a girl has to do before she can walk down the aisle!"

"But I want you *now*! I will go and rouse the parish priest and he can marry us within the next hour!"

She laid a soft finger on his mouth. "You're shouting, dearest. And you know that what you suggest is out of the question. Let's be sensible. I love you, and I know that you love me. I want a proper white wedding, with all of our families in the church. I couldn't disappoint Mama with a hole and corner affair. You have to consult your family; I have to think about Mama and my brother and all the relations in both Italy and England. Time will not alter my feelings - will it change yours?"

"Yes, it will! I know that I shall go on loving you more and more with every day that passes. I know that every hour from now until the hour we marry will be endless; I know that I am mad for the love of you, and if you do not marry me soon, they will have to shoot me as they would a mad dog!" Once again he kissed her and she responded with all the love that her heart could hold for him.

The padrone broke up their embrace. He stood by the table, coughing loudly. "Would the signori desire something else?" With difficulty he stifled a yawn.

Carlo looked at his watch. "Dio mio, it's gone half past two! Woman, you have seduced me from my bed! You have caused me to break my resolve to get you to Tre Boschi by midnight!" He threw the padrone a bundle of bank notes. "Keep the change, my friend. It is a gift from a very happy man, one who apologises for keeping you from your wife and bed for so long after your other clients have gone."

The man rushed to bring their coats. They left the trattoria in a haze of happiness that spread like an aura around them, touching everything with its gladdening light. The beaming padrone was waving to them long after they were out of his sight, and then he turned into the restaurant humming a love ditty of forty years ago.

Carlo drove sedately to Tre Boschi, swearing a great oath that never would he, by reckless driving, endanger Pina's existence. From time to time, he would lean over to kiss her, so that she was compelled to remind him of his vow not to put her in peril on the road. He drove right up to the house and only after many kisses did he permit her to alight and enter her home. As she walked up the stairs to her room, Pina felt that she was walking on air. She felt so grateful to Fate for having brought Carlo into her life. Another little prayer went up to Sant'Antonio before she fell asleep.

THIRTEEN

In spite of being so late to bed, Pina awoke at her usual hour. For the first time since the days of Kevin, she found herself singing as she bathed. Her dreams of the transformation of Miss Pina Corrigan into the signora di Felippo were interrupted by someone knocking on the bathroom door and the voice of Rosa shouting that she was needed on the telephone. Hastily throwing a bathrobe over her still damp body, she rushed into the hall. To her disappointment, it was not Carlo who was calling. The voice of a strange woman asked, "Signorina Corrigan? Ah, si. I am to tell you that the Signor di Felippo had to go out early this morning. He said he would be out most of the day, and that he would not call you himself for fear of rousing you too early. He asked me to tell you that he would be at La Poltrona this afternoon at four thirty, and hopes to meet you there. He also hopes that he will be able to meet Stella at the same time." In answer to Pina's query, the woman continued, "No, he did not say when he would be back. Yes, should he come in, I'll tell him that you have received his message. Grazie e arrivederci, signorina." The woman hung up and the telephone crackled in Pina's ear.

Lessons for Stella that morning were somewhat perfunctory, and absent-mindedly delivered. Pina was full of her own affairs and could not devote her attention wholly to the matters in hand. Stella could not fail to notice her tutor's abstraction. She said, "I think, dear Pina, that something has excited you too much for you to teach me properly today! Have you had good news from your family? No? Oh well. I can't make a lot of sense of much that you have been trying to teach me. Let's stop now, and I will rest before lunch. Then when we have eaten, we can go out in the seicento and perhaps blow away these megrims that are affecting you!" Pina was only too ready to agree.

After lunch, while Stella was preparing herself for the outing, Pina went in search of Annibale, to inform him of their plans. The old man was not to be found anywhere. His gun hung on the rack in its usual place, but of the man himself, there was no trace. Returning to the house, Pina found Rosa at her normal duties. She told Pina that Luigi, Sandro and Annibale had had to go to Teramo to see a notary about some business; she thought it might be to do with the old man's wages. However, in view of the fact that Carlo was to meet them at La Poltrona, Pina decided that there would be little danger of this once if they went out without their bodyguard. She did decide to try to ring Carlo and inform him of their unprotected condition, but each time she got through to the hotel, she was told that he was out, and had not said when he would return.

She called Stella, and in the little car they drove sedately by a roundabout route to La Poltrona. Stella was happy that they could be together, for the first time in some days, without the presence of Annibale. She had found the man's constant attendance very restricting. She chattered away merrily as they mounted the steep slope that led to the "Armchair".

Pina had given some thought to telling Stella of her engagement to Carlo, but had decided to hug the secret to her breast for a little while longer; it was too new, too precious, at this early stage to be shared with anybody. Though it tore at her heart to do so, she had removed his ring from her finger and it now reposed in a drawer in her dressing table, concealed under her handkerchiefs.

It was a quarter past four when they arrived at the lay-by near La Poltrona. No other vehicle was in sight, and there was no sound of a car approaching. They might have been the last persons left alive in all the world, so quiet was it in this season. They decided to walk a little, with Stella using her crutches; they had been unable to load her wheelchair into the car by themselves. Stella was full of excitement at their new-found freedom from Annibale's presence, saying how pleasant it was to be able to talk without him listening, for though he said he did not understand English, yet he always seemed to know exactly what subject was under discussion,

They looked for wild flowers for ten minutes or so. So late in the year, only few blooms were to be found, and Stella held only a small posy of wilting flowers when Pina suggested that they ought to be returning to the car. Glancing at her watch, Pina saw that the time for her appointment had already passed by some five minutes. Plainly, Carlo had been delayed, or he would have hailed them when he arrived; they had not been out of sight from the road at any time. Slowly, and in the case of Stella, with some difficulty, they made their way back to where the little car was parked in the lay-by. As they descended the small hill that formed one arm of La Poltrona, Pina saw a bright red car climbing rapidly up the hill. By the time the girls had reached the road, it was parked tightly in front of their car. Pina's heart skipped a beat, for some reason she could not fathom, when she saw that the man standing by the car was Fronti. As they neared the parked vehicles, he raised his hat in a theatrical gesture, a mockery of politeness.

"Good afternoon, young ladies! It is indeed a good afternoon for me when I meet such beautiful signorine in such a pleasant place! Please do me the honour of stepping into my car - you will find it much more commodious than this roller-skate you are using." As Pina demurred, his tone hardened. "You had better accede to my request, mees. You see, I have a strong argument for obedience in this little toy of mine!" He produced from the waistband of his trousers a small handgun, which he waved negligently before them. "I have no desire to harm you, either of you, but if you prove unwilling..." Standing with the pistol hanging from his hand, he added, "Oh yes, mees, and please harbour no false hope of assistance from Signor di Felippo; he knows nothing of this assignation! One of my people made that telephone call to you, mees, after we had ensured that he would be in Pescara for most of the day! That's right. This appointment was made solely for my pleasure, mees." He bared his teeth in a wolfish grin. "You will do well to obey my every command, ladies! I do not accept with good grace disobedience from anyone!"

FOURTEEN

It was customary for Stella and Pina to work in either the dining room or in Stella's bedroom, and so it was not until some three hours after their departure that their absence was noted. Elsa had peeped into the dining room and finding it unoccupied, had decided that they were using the girl's bedroom, but had not checked, seeing no occasion to do so. Thus it was not until the dinner gong had been sounded and had failed to produce diners, that concern was aroused. Luigi Passi, who with his companions had returned from Teramo an hour after the girls' departure, wasted no further time before setting up a search of the house and immediate grounds, but soon called off the hunters when Sandro disclosed that the seicento was missing. A wider search was immediately instituted, and all farm workers were sent out to comb the more distant parts of the estate. Sandro was despatched in the big Fiat to scour the roads, in case the seicento had broken down far from a telephone.

By eleven o'clock that night, all the searchers were gathered in the office. The men were grim-faced and silent, the women weeping. Passi told them, "It is apparent that something more than a mere breakdown has occurred. I must now telephone Don Stefano and inform him. I shall also inform the carabinieri at both Teramo and Fortalezza del Tronto. As for you, there is nothing more that you can do tonight. We have searched every likely place; tomorrow we must look in the unlikely places. I now advise that you all eat, and then get some rest. We shall need all our energies tomorrow, which looks like being a long, tiring, and busy day!"

The party dispersed as Passi reached for the telephone. Don Stefano was justifiably worried when he heard the news. He held an important position in a government already shaky - a government whose enemies would not hesitate to use an abduction, if not actual assassination to gain their ends. In spite of the lateness of the hour, and the many duties he would have to leave undone, he told Passi that he would leave Rome forthwith to travel to Tre Boschi through the night. He would arrive, he hoped in the early hours of the morning, well before dawn.

The carabinieri were also concerned and worried. There had been a spate of abductions and ransom demands in the country, although so far, the Abruzzi had escaped any political crimes. The capo at Fortalezza was convinced that the kidnapping, for he was convinced that such was the reason for the disappearance of the girls, was a politically motivated crime. He was prepared to admit that it might be a merely cash-orientated offence, but was not prepared to bet on that thought. Whatever the reasons, he did not care for such occurrences in his parish. Neither he nor the men in his force had experience in such matters. The capo at Teramo yawned, and said that he would take notice, but was not prepared to do more; the crime, if crime it was, had not happened in his area.

Don Stefano arrived as he had promised. The dawn was just tingeing the eastern sky with yellow that foretold a fine day. He burst into the office. "What is going on? What has happened to my daughter? Surely the Englishwoman must have given her some protection? She must have been completely useless in a crisis! Why did she remove Stella from the security of the house? D'ye think she may be in league with a gang of kidnappers - if Stella has been kidnapped, that is?" He beat upon the desktop with a white-knuckled clenched fist.

Passi tried to calm him. "Nobody at this stage can apportion any blame, signore. Certainly not to the mees, who is devoted to the Signorina Stella. In any case, we are not yet sure that anything wrong has occurred. All we can be sure of is that the two young ladies went out in the seicento, and they have not yet returned. No trace has been found of the ladies, nor of the car. We have, to the best of our ability, searched round the whole estate, and also Sandro had been on the roads they might have used. I have informed the Capi of Carabinieri at both Teramo and Fortalezza; the latter informs me that no stone will be left unturned to discover some clue as to the whereabouts of the young ladies."

Don Stefano groaned. "It is too much! First my wife, too young and too beautiful to die, and now my little crippled daughter! God grant that we shall soon find her safe and well! I should never have left Stella here without adequate protection, but I felt that she would be safer here than in Roma. Of course, you are right, Luigi. Miss Corrigan was not engaged as a bodyguard and could not be expected to act as one. But what can have happened if this is not a kidnap? People do not just disappear off the face of the earth! I haven't an enemy in the world, as far as I know, and even my political opponents cannot be capable of attacking me through Stella - at least, I don't think they could! My belief is that they have had an accident, and the car is lying hidden in the roadside bushes somewhere. God grant that it is not a quarry or something similar! God, I feel so helpless! Why don't those filthy carabinieri come?"

Luigi rang his bell. Early as it was, Elsa was up and about. She entered the room and curtsied to Don Stefano. Luigi ordered coffee for the master. When the senator demurred, he said, "You need a stimulant after your long drive." Again Don Stefano protested that he could not and would not drink coffee, but when Elsa returned bearing a tray loaded with cups and a steaming pot of rich aromatic coffee, he had to admit that his majordomo was right. He *did* need something hot after the night drive. He gulped down the scalding liquid and began to pace about the office, impatient for action, any action, so long as something was happening, even though he knew that little could be done before full daylight had arrived and the search could be resumed.

When at last the sun peeped over the horizon and the morning mists began to disperse, Don Stefano leapt into action. All staff were ordered to report to the office immediately. Farm personnel were sent about their normal daily routine of attending to the animals. When their tasks had been performed, then they would be allocated areas of search. Sandro was sent out in the Fiat to search every road, large or small, for twenty kilometres around. Annibale was ordered to scour the woods surrounding the estate. Passi would remain in the office to answer the telephone and attend to other duties. Elsa and Rosa were to continue their normal duties, so that when search parties returned, hungry and thirsty after their long traipsing over the rough terrain, their hunger and thirst could receive attention. Don Stefano would deal with the carabinieri when they arrived. He might also be able to lead them to places where perhaps Stella had fallen and the tutor had been unable to lift her to her feet again.

At nine o'clock two carabinieri cars roared up to the house. The grey-green livery of the cars was covered in dust, which gave mute testimony to the fact that the crews of them had been searching through the night for the missing girls. Chins were unshaven and eyes bloodshot as the men alighted from the cars, and their capo was ushered by Elsa into the office. Don Stefano and the capo conferred alone in the office for a few moments, and when they emerged, the officer was shaking his head and saying, "No, senatore, there cannot have been an accident, or we would have heard about it; nor has there been any report filed of a vehicle running off the road with consequent admission to a hospital. My men have been out all night, but you will appreciate that in the present state of financial stringency," - the capo could not resist the opportunity of a dig at a prominent member of the Government even at such a time as this - "I am severely undermanned and cannot spare men for extra duties for long periods. My men are fully occupied at all times. You would be surprised to know how much crime is committed even in such a peaceful rural area as this. But rest assured that I will do all in my power, and will ensure that the men do all they can, too, to find your daughter and the Englishwoman. But in my heart, I am certain that soon you will receive a demand for ransom from the Brigate Rosse or some similar organisation."

Don Stefano's face was grey and drawn, his eyes screwed up from lack of sleep and the bright morning light. His suit was crushed and his tie hung limply from a wilting collar. The two men passed along the corridor and out of the house. The carabinieri were gathered in a small group, smoking and chatting as they waited for their commander. Crisply, he ordered them to search the shrubbery that bordered the drive. Don Stefano protested that a thorough search had already been conducted there.

"Senatore, you will forgive me, but my men are trained in the art of searching such places. They might well - indeed, I would expect them to - spot a clue that amateurs would overlook; one small but vital link that points to the perpetrators of this outrage, for I am positive it is an abduction. With the greatest respect, I request that you allow me to conduct this inquiry in the regulation manner!"

In obedience to their chief's commands, the carabinieri threw away their cigarettes and disappeared into the shrubbery, from where Don Stefano could hear them calling to each other as they trampled down the bushes. They had, thought the senator grimly, very little hope of preserving any clues that might exist. It was obvious that the capo was making a gesture to show that he was in control of the situation.

The Fiat tore down the drive followed by a dense cloud of dust. As it came to a stop with a shrieking of the brakes, Sandro leapt from behind the wheel. "Don Stefano, I have found the seicento! It was in the bushes by the roadside near La Poltrona. No one but I could have discovered it; it was well concealed!" In answer to a query from the capo, he said, scornfully, "No, of course I didn't touch anything. I've seen lots of films about crimes, and I know all about fingerprints Signor Commandante!"

The policeman shrugged. He raised a silver whistle to his lips and blew a piercing blast. His men emerged from the bushes, dusting down their uniforms. They clustered in loose formation about their leader. "Well, men, we have a lead. I have found the little car!"

Sandro looked at him in disgust, but a quick word from his employer stifled his indignant protest.

The capo continued, "Take one of the cars, Antonio, and you, Armando and Paolo, accompany him. This boy will lead you to where the car lies. You know the drill."

The named men got into the car and Sandro led the little convoy from the house in yet another cloud of dust. The capo and the rest of his men remained in the drive, lighting the inevitable cigarettes. Don Stefano said, "Pray God we find that all is well! Perhaps the girls are trapped, unhurt, in the car!"

The policeman shook his head. "My experience of these affairs is not vast," he admitted, "but as your honour realises, we are kept informed of the modus operandi of kidnappers, and this present affair begins to assume all the classic features of abduction. Soon, I think, you will receive either a demand for money, or for some service that the gang think you are powerful enough to render them. There is nothing we can do now, save to wait until my men return."

"I suppose you are right, capo. While we wait, shall I have coffee brought out to your men?"

"No, I thank you, senatore. I will send them about their business, and will myself remain here. Personally, I would not refuse the offer of a glass of something warming, but I do not permit my men to accept anything, not even a cup of coffee, while they are on duty." He turned to the three unfortunates whose faces had lit up at the mention of coffee, but had fallen when they heard that their superior had rejected the offer, and issued rapid orders to them to return to barracks and resume normal work. The three departed in the remaining car, and the senator and the capo entered the house. On Don Stefano's orders, Elsa produced a pair of tumblers and a bottle of grappa. They sat in the office, silently absorbed in their own thoughts as they drank the fiery grappa.

The shrilling of the telephone roused them from their meditations. Don Stefano reached out to pick up the instrument, but the capo stayed his hand and took the call himself. "Bianchi, capo of Carabinieri. No, she is not here. I do not know when she will return. No, I cannot take a message. What? Oh, that's different, sir! Yes, sir. May I suggest that you come here as soon as possible? Something has cropped up, and I may be glad of your help, although I think I have everything under control. What? Yes. I *do* think it may be an abduction. Eh? Yes, that's right, Bianchi, Chief of Carabinieri, Fortalezza del Tronto. No, I was not informed that you would be operating in my parish. Of course they keep your kind of operation rather dark, don't they? Yes, sir. In about three quarters of an hour then. Arrivederci, signore!" He replaced the receivers in its cradle.

"As you are a member of the Government, senatore, I may tell you, but please do not let anyone else know about it. It's highly sensitive and confidential. One of the narcotics squad is apparently working under cover in my district. He seems to be interested in Miss Corrigan-a. You heard what I told him. He is coming out to help in any way he can. He seems to be pretty senior in the squad, too. Of course, he did not say all this in plain terms, but we professionals have a code for such matters. It will do him good to see how real policemen work! I wonder how he came to know your Englishwoman, and what connection there may be there? But then, these undercover chaps have all sorts of weird and wonderful ways of going about things. Well, those who live longest see most!"

FIFTEEN

The pistol brandished by Fronti allowed for no argument. Pina ceased her protests and assisted Stella to get into the back seat of the car and then, urged on by the waving firearm, laid the girl's crutches beside her. Before taking her place in the car beside Fronti, as he was directing her to do, she took Stella's hand and squeezed it tightly. In English, she said, "Don't let him see that we are afraid. Soon we shall be missed and someone will come in search of us."

Fronti growled. "You will do well to stop your gabble, mees. I strongly advise that you keep tight hold on that tongue of yours. If, however, you *must* speak, then let it be loudly and in Italian so that I can hear and understand."

Pina glared at him. "I was only telling her not to be scared. Do you suppose that she can accept abduction as an everyday occurrence? What do you propose to do with us?"

"You will know soon enough. When my friends arrive, you will be taken to a comfortable place where you will stay for a few days. Then when we have allowed Capriotto sufficient time to get really worried about his brat, we shall find out how highly he values her. Would you consider five hundred million excessive? Well, we shall see. Naturally we shall try peacefully to persuade him to cough up, but if he turns nasty and uncooperative, it may be found necessary to send him one of Stella's ears, or perhaps a finger or two, to show him that we are in earnest. As for you, you have no value at all for us. It would therefore behove you to be civil to us at all times. None of us would be worried if this little toy went 'Bang', purely by accident, you understand. If, at the same time, it happened to be pointing at your head, that would be so much the worse for you, and also possibly for Stella, who might need a female companion while we are entertaining her. I'm happy to tell you that where you are going, there will be no women other than yourselves, and certainly my men do not know how to tend a girl who is crippled."

"You are a devil, mister Fronti! You must know that you will never get away with this! Any moment now my friend will be coming here to meet us!"

"I rather doubt that, mees. You see, it was one of my girls who telephoned after we had discovered that di Felippo had gone out for the day. It was simple for her to pretend to be the hotel receptionist. We only had to take the small risk that he might not be absent for most of the day, and that you might not follow instructions to bring the girl with you when you came up to this deserted spot. As you now know, the gamble came off, and here we are, cosily together, chatting away like old friends!"

Fronti lighted a cigarette and tossed the match, still burning, into Pina's lap. While she struggled wildly to save her skirt from complete incineration, he continued, "Your arguments lack logic, mees. At this moment, nobody is in the least concerned about you and the girl. Nor will they be for at least another hour. By that time, we shall be well away from the sphere of Capriotti's influence. But never fear. You will be permitted to rejoin your friends when the ransom money is in our hands. Little harm will come to you if you only obey orders at all times."

"You scoundrel! To think that I thought you were friendly when I met you at the shop! You... you... you reptile!"

"Please, mees, not so free with the insults! I am noted for my patience, but my capacity for taking rudeness is limited! Ah, here come the friends for whom we have been waiting. You will both sit very still and be silent, ladies." He waved the firearm at them.

Two men alighted from the car that drew up alongside the Alfa. One of them was tall and sallow of complexion, with long black sideburns that almost met at the point of his chin; his hands, which he waved a lot as he talked, were long and predatory with fingers heavily stained by nicotine. The other man was shorter, of more healthy appearance. Both were dressed in nondescript denim coats and trousers, and their shirts, of a similar material, were open almost to the waist, revealing thick matted hair on their chests.

"Ciao, Matteo! These are the goods?"

"Yes. You know the drill."

The pasty-faced man nodded as Fronti slipped out of the driving seat and walked round the front of the car. He motioned to Pina to get out of the front passenger seat, and into the rear one beside Stella. The man then got into the car behind the wheel while Fronti sat beside him. The shorter man, after favouring Pina with a leer that made her pull her skirt hastily over her knees, returned to the car in which the pair had arrived. Both cars moved away from the lay-by. Fronti turned and waved the gun at Pina so that involuntarily she drew back.

"You will attempt no tricks, mees, no heroics! In your own interests, I beg of you not to make things difficult for all of us!"

She cowered back against the upholstery. Pressed close to her body, she could feel the trembling of Stella's frail form. Once again she gave the child's hand a squeeze of encouragement. "Coraggio, piccola!" she whispered. "I know we shall get out of this horrible mess - I just know it!"

Fronti turned to the driver. "The seicento will be looked after?"

The man contented himself with a nod. "I hope that it will not be too well concealed," continued Fronti. "While it must not be discovered tonight, there must be no difficulty for them to find it in daylight tomorrow."

"Perbacco, you worry too much, Matteo! The boys know exactly what to do, and they will do it properly. You just do your part, and let the others get on with theirs! Now shut up, and let me drive!"

Daylight was fading rapidly. As the two cars turned off the metalled road on to one of the many 'white' roads that were a feature of the region, night had already fallen. Using only sidelights, the little convoy bumped uncomfortably along the rutted road, the driver making no concessions to his passengers as he mounted the steep slope at an angle and a pace that Pina would not have dared to use in broad daylight. He was plainly well acquainted with the route they were following.

Gazing out of the windscreen between the heads of the men in the front seats, Pina was totally unable to discern any feature of the land about them. She hoped that she could, at some later date, help to retrace the way, but the search for clues was hopeless. She gave up the attempt, and held Stella tightly in the vain hope of protecting her from the wild tossing and bumping of the car as it leapt, like some mountain goat, from rut to rut to ridge in the surface of the unmade road. Fronti, in deference to the admonition of the driver, was silent and still, save when he turned to look at the girls and wave his gun in warning.

After about an hour of this most uncomfortable travel, the car emerged on to a paved surface and the leaping and bucking ceased. The driver now put on his headlights, and was able to make good progress without rattling his passengers about in their seats. Very soon they pulled into another lay-by, and the other car drew up behind them. Both drivers turned off their lights. The pasty-faced man lit a cigarette and began to amuse himself by drumming an elusive and infuriating rhythm on the steering wheel until Fronti snarled at him to desist. A window was lowered to clear the air of smoke, and then Pina could hear from outside, the noises of the night. In the nearby undergrowth, something scuffled noisily, and from far away, a fox screamed eerily. Across what seemed to be a valley, the lights of cars flashed briefly; they were seen, and then gone almost immediately.

In vain Pina tried to locate their position. There simply was nothing by which she could identify the spot. She felt certain that they were fairly high in the Gran' Sasso, but how high, or where, she was completely unable to form an opinion. How she wished Carlo would come riding up to their rescue, like a knight in shining armour! But that was a hopeless dream! She and Stella were totally dependent on themselves, and Pina was forced to admit that they were woefully short of resourcefulness at that moment.

Fronti stirred. "Here they come," he muttered. There was a flashing of lights as a vehicle mounted the slope behind them, and the sound of an engine protesting at the way in which it was being driven. The vehicle drew to a halt in the lay-by. With a brief injunction to the driver to keep an eye on the captives, Fronti got out of the car and walked up to the newly-arrived vehicle. After a short time, he returned. He told the driver of the Alfa to put on the interior lights. "Out!" he commanded, waving his gun. Stiffly, Pina eased her aching limbs from the cramped back seat and assisted Stella to alight. When the girl was safely supported on her crutches, standing beside the car, Fronti said, urgently, "Over to the van, and get into the back!"

They obeyed. A man pushed them roughly up a high step of a large van. The interior was fitted with thinly upholstered seats that ran the length of the van on each side. In response to a gesture from Fronti, they took places on one of the seats while he sat opposite them. The engine roared and the van moved away rapidly. There were no windows in the sides of the van; they were completely blind now. The van raced on into the night. Stella began to weep softly, silently, her thin shoulders heaving with the intensity of her sobbing. Pina tried to comfort her, putting her arms about the child, but she was herself so close to weeping that she was not able to help much. In the dim interior of the vehicle, a dimness which was intensified by the small lamp in the roof, Fronti smoked and looked at them sardonically, "Nice little van, isn't it."

After what seemed to be an age of high-speed travel, the van turned on to yet another rough track, bouncing the passengers about cruelly. Pina stole a glance at her wristwatch, and was surprised to see that it was almost four hours since they had been accosted by Fronti at La Poltrona. The van lurched sickeningly, recovered itself, went on a little further and lurched again before coming to a standstill. The door was flung open from the outside. The air, tainted by Fronti's incessant smoking, was suddenly purified by a fresh cold blast as a voice outside invited them, in impolite terms, to alight. Fronti, his gun still very such in evidence, leapt from the van to be followed more slowly and painfully by Pina and Stella. The night was clear and crisp. There was no moon, but by the faint light of the stars Pina could see that they were high in the mountains, for a snowbank close by reflected the glimmering light. Breath steamed in the thin frosty air. Both girls shuddered with cold, for they were wearing only the thin dresses that were suited to the lower altitude of Tre Boschi. Stella's teeth chattered, and momentarily she whimpered a little - perhaps from fear, or perhaps from cold, or even perhaps from a mix of both sensations.

A man they had not seen before stood beside the van. He did not speak, but with a gesture ordered the girls to take a rough track that led yet higher up a steep slope. Pina protested. "Have a little consideration, I implore you! This child could never walk up there with her disability!"

The man emitted an oath. "Porca Madonna!" He seized Stella and flung her on to his shoulder like a sack of corn. She squealed in fright. "Zitto! Shut up!" he ordered, and stalked away up the hill. "You're not going to be hurt yet, and maybe not at all if your father is sensible and obedient!"

Fronti indicated with a wave of his gun that Pina was to follow. She stooped and picked up the crutches that Stella had dropped when she was so unceremoniously lifted on to the man's shoulder. In single file, the party moved on up the slope. As they climbed, Pina heard the van backing and turning away. Stealing a backward glance, she saw the tail lights receding down the steep gradient.

The climb was gruelling and hard. The cold air was thin, searing the lungs as they gasped for oxygen. Pina was now quite certain that this was the Gran' Sasso. Remote and impersonal, the stars winked frostily down on the party. No one wasted breath in talking. Stella sobbed spasmodically as she was borne upwards. Her carrier must have been an immensely strong man, thought Pina, for at that altitude, even Stella's light weight would have been burdensome. Fronti was making heavy weather of the climb. Behind her, Pina could hear his hoarse rasping breathing as he sought to obtain sufficient oxygen from the rarefied air. Pina hoped that he was in really deep distress. Things were bad enough for her, but she was young and fairly fit, and perhaps in better circumstances might even have enjoyed this starlit walk up the mountain.

The ascent continued at a steady pace, the leader never stopping nor seeming to alter his rate of progress. Looking to her left, Pina could see, dimly, a dizzy drop into a valley. Far below, at the bottom of the valley, a light gleamed fitfully at first as it was obscured by the branches of trees, and then more steadily as it was allowed to reach up to her when the breeze stirred the branches of the pines. At some point on the way, the mass of the mountain was silhouetted against the velvet backdrop of the navy-blue sky, now dappled with stars that seemed to glow brighter than Pina had ever thought possible. At other times, thick growths of pines hid the peaks. Here and there they had to traverse deep gullies in which snow lay deep enough to reach their knees as they struggled through it. Unable to read her watch, Pina guessed that they had been climbing for about an hour when their guide turned along a rough and stony path that was fairly level. The surface was still difficult to walk on, and cruel to her feet through her thin shoes, which were never intended to be worn in such conditions.

Finally the guide turned into a narrow slit that led them down an equally narrow passage. After some twenty paces, during which the way was lighted by a hand torch which the guide passed to Stella to shine on the ground behind him, they entered a large cave. It seemed to Pina to be as big as any cathedral. The light of a fire that burned in the darkness was not strong enough to allow her to see the roof of the cave, nor could she see the walls, even when a man rose from before the fire and threw some logs to it to make it flare up.

"You've been longer than I thought you would be," he said.

Fronti's breath was still coming in strangled gasps. He had difficulty in speaking. "It is not an easy path for a man of my age. And Angelo had to carry the girl."

Angelo, none too gently, laid his burden beside the fire and stood massaging his arms. Beside the child, Pina laid the crutches that she had managed to carry throughout the upward clamber. Fronti, now beginning to breathe more easily, said, "Welcome to your new hotel, my dears!" His teeth showed red in the dancing flames. I hope that you will find your quarters comfortable."

The other man sniggered. "We even have running water - down the walls!"

Fronti continued, ignoring the interruption, "You will find a smaller cave opening out from this one. It is over there." He pointed vaguely into the surrounding blackness. "A spring flows from the wall there, giving a constant supply of fresh pure water. That small cave will be your kitchen and also your lavatory - the water disappears down a hole in the floor to go God knows where. Giorgio has brought in a supply of fir branches for your bedding. There is a certain amount of food, and you, mees, will cook it as we order. Meanwhile, Giorgio has made hot soup, which we all need after our exertions. After we have drunk, we will sleep. Tomorrow, or rather, later this morning, we will discuss our arrangements more fully."

Giorgio produced a tin mug which he filled with some steaming liquid from a huge black kettle that was suspended over the fire. He handed the mug to Stella. Between half-stifled sobs, she took a few sips, then passed the mug to Pina. The soup proved to be quite palatable, though very greasy. In spite of Pina's pleas, Stella refused to drink any more, and Pina finished the soup, then placed the mug on the ground beside her.

Fronti snorted. "That will not do, mees! There's no Rosa to wait on you up here! Go and wash your mug in the kitchen, and take the others' mugs to wash also!"

Stifling a tart response, Pina dully took up the used utensils. Angelo handed her the torch and she moved to the small cave that Fronti had indicated. As he had said, there was a small freshet that sang happily to itself as it spurted from the wall and disappeared down a hole, about a foot in diameter, that yawned in the floor. Fronti had followed her into the 'kitchen'. Pointing to the hole, he said, "That's your lavatory, mees. Not every hostage has as much luxury as you are enjoying!" He laughed coarsely and sauntered back to the main cave, and the warmth of the fire.

Pina washed the utensils as he had ordered, and returned to the main cave. Around the fire, the men were stretched out, feet towards the warmth. Stella lay curled up. She, too, was asleep, but crying softly as she slept. Giorgio stirred at Pina's entrance. He looked up at her. "There's a bit of blanket you can have for the youngster. Sorry there isn't one for you."

Tenderly Pina wrapped the filthy rag round Stella, and then huddled close to her, so that they might gain some comfort from each other's proximity. The cave was silent except for an occasional snore from one or other of the men and the crackling of the fire. Try as she might, Pina could not bring herself to think coherently. At the back of her mind was the thought that with all the men sleeping, this might be a chance to escape. But she was too tired to take any decisive action, too tired to think, too... tired...

She sank into a deep sleep, her aching legs twitching from time to time as they complained about the unaccustomed exercise she had been compelled to give them, and about the poor quality of the bed she was sleeping on.

138

Capitano Bianchi, Carabinieri. Il Capo.

SIXTEEN

A brooding silence, almost palpable, hung over Tre Boschi. Rosa no longer sang at her work in the scullery, the sound of Annibale's circular saw was no longer heard; he was out with the search parties. Even the animals seemed to sense that something was amiss, and the small bleatings that they emitted from time to time seemed to be muted to suit the sad times that had fallen upon the house of Don Stefano. The silence was broken by the arrival of Sandro in the Fiat and the policemen in their smaller, but equally fast, car. The party was followed a cloud of white dust that hung on the morning air, undisturbed by any wind.

Sandro leapt from the Fiat and dashed into the house by the front door. He was closely followed by the policemen. They ran into the office. The capo was still there with the senator, their empty glasses before them on the desk. Passi was at work at the smaller desk.

The taller of the two carabinieri flourished a scrap of paper. "Read, Capo!" he cried, passing the note to his chief. A frown crept over Bianchi's face as he read, and then he passed the paper to Don Stefano. The note was typed on a rough piece of paper such as may be bought at any stationer's shop, and the message was brief. There was no salutation and no signature. "We hold your daughter and the Englishwoman. You will hear from us in due course. If our demands are not satisfied in full, then so much the worse for those whom we hold." Don Stefano read the message aloud.

"It is as we feared!" he whispered, almost to himself. "My poor little Stellina!" He lay his head on his arms as they rested on the desktop and his frame was racked by sobs. Awkwardly, for he was not a demonstrative man, the capo touched him lightly on the shoulder. He barked at the two carabinieri, "Where was this note found?"

"It was attached to the steering wheel of the seicento, capo. We found the car pushed into the bushes as the chauffeur had said, and the three of us manhandled it back into a lay-by. We have left it there, locked. Then we hastened to inform you."

"Well done! Now get on the radio and tell the fingerprint boys to get there quickly. Get yourselves out there to meet them. When they have done, bring the car back here, and see that it is locked away in the motor shed. I must ask that nobody use the vehicle again until I give it clearance. I intend that it shall be thoroughly checked over by my experts."

Passi looked up from his work. "I will attend to the security of the car." The capo gave him a bleak smile.

"Good. Now off you go, you two. Don Stefano, please accept my advice that you retire to your bed for an hour or so. We are now sure that the signorine have been abducted and we can be equally certain that nothing harmful will happen to them before we receive another message. Until we *do* receive a message, our only course is one of patiently waiting. When the message does come, we shall need all our faculties. That is why I counsel rest at this time."

The senator lifted his head from his arms. His appearance shocked the capo. In the past few hours he had aged ten years. He rose and walked stiffly to the door. There he turned and holding the crystal doorknob for support, he said, "Capo, I want your promise that you will have me roused as soon as anything comes in - the least, the most minute piece of information, I mean. Please make this house your headquarters for as long a time as you need to do so. I must be told immediately of any developments whatsoever. I beseech you to spare no efforts, or expense, to track down these scellerati, these scoundrels, and to get them behind bars and my daughter restored to me with the minimum delay."

Bianchi gave him the same cold smile that he had earlier given Passi. "You have my word, senatore. Remember that I have a great interest in this case. It is the first kidnapping that has occurred on my patch. If I can nip this one in the bud, others will perhaps be less eager to follow the example of these gangsters."

After the door had closed behind Don Stefano, Passi said, "What are the odds?"

"Speaking as a policeman, I ought to say that we can, and we will, eventually arrest the criminals. But, like you, I am also a man of common sense. I therefore can only tell you, in strictest confidence, that I believe that your employer will have to meet whatever demands the abductors may make, and hope that they retain sufficient shreds of honour left to them to return the child and her governess alive when the cash is paid over to them. And I find it hard to believe that kidnappers ever have any honour at all. No, my friend, I do not delude myself with the hope that we shall see these ladies alive again, and I would not be prepared to bet that we shall even see their dead bodies! But as I said, that is in the strictest confidence within these four walls."

Bianchi sat on a chair and hoisted his immaculately polished jackboots to rest his heels on an antique table, staring at his reflection in his toecaps as though in them lay the solution to all the problems that this case was presenting. He was engrossed in this exercise when a knock at the door interrupted his meditation.

"Come!" Passi called after a questioning look at him. Elsa entered, and hard upon her heels came the tall figure of Carlo. He made a slight bow in the direction of Bianchi, who scrambled to his feet.

"May I introduce myself? Di Felippo. We spoke an hour or so ago." He held out his hand and Bianchi shook it warmly. He seemed impressed by the appearance of Carlo.

"Bianchi, capo of Carabinieri at Fortalezza. I am happy to meet you. We are in the process of dealing with an abduction and although everything is under complete control, we may yet be glad of your assistance."

Carlo started. "An abduction?"

Rapidly Bianchi recounted the events of the past eighteen hours as far as he knew them, while Carlo took notes. At the end of the recital, he asked, "May I see the note?"

The paper passed over, and Carlo studied it intently. "H'm. Typed on an Olivetti 32, of which there cannot be more than a few million in the country. The 's' is slightly misaligned, which cuts the odds by about a half. Capo, we can glean little from this! Was there anything in the car to give a lead?"

"I don't yet know. My fingerprint boys are working on it now, and when they have done their stuff, it will be driven here for detailed investigation. It should be here in an hour."

Carlo turned to Passi. "I take it that you are Luigi Passi, the majordomo?"

"That's correct, sir. I am he. I manage the estate when Don Stefano is absent."

"I see. Tell me, would you say all the staff are trustworthy?"

"I can vouch for all of them, sir. There is, of course, an Englishwoman, a new governess, whom I do not know well, but she always seemed honest enough, and in any case, she appears to be a victim of the outrage."

"I can speak for her," replied Carlo. His voice was calm and apparently untroubled, the completely official tones masking the turmoil of thought that ran seething in the lower levels of his mind. Deep down, he wanted to thrash somebody to within a centimetre of that person's life, but all his training taught him to remain cool and seemingly detached. Aloud, he said, "What of the driver - what's his name - Sandro?"

"He's a good boy at heart, but a little bit stupid and too talkative. His father works on the estate, and I've known the lad since his birth."

"Why was Annibale not with the girls when they went out?"

Passi did not show his surprise that Carlo should know Annibale. He replied, "He had to go with me to Teramo; Sandro drove us, which accounts for all three of us being absent yesterday afternoon. I was aware that the mees had enlisted Annibale as a sort of bodyguard, and I permitted it, but why it was thought that a bodyguard was needed, or by whom, I do not know."

"It was on my advice. I knew that something funny was going on, and I half expected an attempted snatch such as this, I had hoped that the presence of the old man would prevent it happening." He paused for a moment, then, "May I speak to him?"

"Of course. Shall I have him called? He is probably resting in his room now, after being up most of the night searching the woods and other parts of the estate."

"No. I would prefer to see him in his room."

From his seat at the table, which he had assumed after his brief talk with Carlo, Bianchi said plaintively, "I wish someone would tell me what is going on!"

Carlo threw him a warning glance. "That will wait, Capo. Now, how do I get to see Annibale?"

Passi rapidly gave directions and Carlo left the office. He found Annibale resting, as Passi had predicted, exhausted by the effort he had put into his search. His age showed in his lined and worried face, and Carlo was shocked at his appearance. Where last he had seen a bright and sprightly veteran soldier, he now looked at a hollow-cheeked and gaunt old man. As Carlo entered the door, Annibale rose to greet him. His clothing hung loosely on his frame, and he raised a weary hand in greeting. "Good morning, Signor Carlo! Well, I failed you and the signorine, didn't I? If only I had known that they were going out... if only I had not gone to Teramo! I would think we were back here a matter of only half an hour after they had left!"

Despite his fears for Pina, Carlo could not help feeling sorry for the old soldier. "It is no fault of yours, Annibale! The girls were remiss in not waiting for you to return. I expect that they did not intend to go far, and thought that no danger could come to them if they stayed close to the house."

"If only there was something I could do! I feel so helpless! I must have been round the whole estate, but they appear to have vanished into thin air!"

"Of course, you would not know this, but a note has been found attached to the wheel of the seicento."

"O Dio! Then you were right. It's just as you told me it might be when we met down there by the fountain!"

"That's right. Now we can do little more than wait for a second note from the brigands which will give us more instructions." Carlo put a comforting hand on the old man's shoulder. "Bear up, Annibale. We shall bring this to a satisfactory conclusion, I hope. Keep your eyes and ears open. If you should get to know anything that seems to have a bearing on this matter, telephone me at my hotel." He scribbled a number on the bottom of the portrait of Stalin, and left.

In the courtyard, he stood in thought for a moment. His fiancée was in the hands of a band of brigands and was being held God only knew where. He vowed that should any harm befall her, he would exact fearful revenge. Pina, he considered, was in greater danger than Stella, for if the younger girl were harmed, the gang would be throwing away their strongest card. Pina, however, had little value for them. Carlo knew only too well the ways of the men with whom he had to deal, when they held captive a woman for whom they had little respect as a money-raising asset. He resolved to bring into play, as far as he was able, the total resources of his department in order to bring this case to a speedy and successful conclusion.

He returned to the office to take his leave of Passi and the capo. The officer accompanied him to his car. "Now, Signor di Felippo, may I ask just what you are doing on my patch?"

"It just so happens that my department is interested in your 'patch', with particular reference to the coastal strip, because some excellent high quality heroin is filtering into the country. We've picked up a lot of the stuff in Milan and in Piacenza, and the analysts are pretty sure that it comes from Albania. I have got a number of agents working all along the coast from Ancona to Pescara. We managed to pick up a member of the Red Brigades and after we had exercised a little persuasion on him, he sang loud and clear. Not only did he sing about the drug-smuggling we were interested in, but he also gave us an area about a possible snatch in this region. He couldn't give details, although we... er... leaned on him pretty hard. All he could say was that someone was talking about an incredibly rich man who had a crippled daughter and had recently engaged a bodyguard for her. There was a lot of chat about it among the local bad lads, he said. The bodyguard was reputed to be a black belt or something of high degree in martial arts who could kill a man with one hand while she picked off a fly on the wing with her handgun at fifty metres. Quite a lady, in short; very talented.

"As it happened, quite by accident, I met a young woman on the train as I was coming down here. I talked to her a lot and she fitted the description our canary had given us. But she was no bodyguard, nor anything like it. She was just a teacher of English, engaged to be a tutor and companion to the young Stella. I liked the Englishwoman, and she and I have been out together several times. So, you see, I have a vested interest in your kidnapping.

"Now you and I and everyone know who the great chatterbox might be. It was, of course, that braggart Sandro. He meant no harm, of course. He merely wanted to bask in the reflected glory of his employer's wealth and influence. He was overheard talking to a German girl in one of the bars last summer and again in early spring he was talking loudly to his cronies in another bar. From his baseless boasting all this to-do has been born! Boys like him should be strangled at birth! It is ironic that Don Capriotti is not wealthy at all. Oh, yes, he owns a lot of land, but I would guess that he has less ready cash than you or I! All his riches lie in property and very little in negotiable currency.

"Ah well! Keep me informed of developments. Annibale knows my number, and he will give it to Passi if needed. If I happen to be out when you make a call, leave a guarded message."

He entered his car, started the engine, and drove quickly down the drive, as the capo saluted him with a very proper military salute.

SEVENTEEN

This was to be the longest and coldest night that Pina had ever experienced. While the men slept, the fire had died down; Fronti apparently saw no need to mount a guard, and everyone was tired after the long and arduous climb up the steep side of the mountain. Eventually Giorgio awoke and stirred the fire into life. Angelo was shaken into grumbling wakefulness and sent to guard the cave entrance; in daylight hours, there was every possibility of mountain walkers using the track that ran in front of the cave. Those remaining in the cave began to feel the welcome warmth envelop their frigid bodies. Pina sat hugging her knees and bathing in the heat until she saw Stella moving beneath the filthy blanket, and heard the child moan as she came to realisation of her plight. Then Pina drew the child to her, taking Stella into her arms and crooning small words of comfort.

"Don't cry, cara. Soon Papa will find us, and then he will see that these scellerati receive their just deserts. Don't allow them the pleasure of seeing that they are making us miserable! Put on a proud appearance!" Deep within herself she wished very much that she could follow her own advice.

Giorgio put the blackened kettle on the fire and with a sort of slapdash dexterity made some coffee. He passed a mugful to Stella. She cradled the hot mug in her hands. The lid of a billycan was served to Pina with her ration of the hot drink. Giorgio took the base of the billycan and seemed to drain the almost boiling coffee at a gulp. Across the top of the billy, he grinned at Pina, and said, "My mother always said that I had a tin gullet!"

She gave him a weak tremulous smile in response to the sally. Of the trio who held them captive, he seemed by far the most human and the most humane. Fronti woke when the smell of the coffee penetrated his sleep and he took the refilled billy from Giorgio. Angelo came into the cave, attracted by the aroma, and Pina's billy lid was filled for him. Fronti went out, apparently to relieve Angelo at guard duty.

Angelo and Giorgio talked in dialect. "Dio, I could do with a woman!" Angelo said.

Giorgio nodded. "Me too. What wouldn't I give to have my Nita up here under a blanket!"

"Any woman would suit me - yonder Englishwoman, per esempio. I reckon she'd serve a turn. I'll probably try her before we set her free!"

"You'd be a fool, Angelo. You know people won't pay for damaged goods. What makes you think Capriotti would pay the full ransom if he knew that you had raped one of the women?"

"He couldn't know until all was over. Then it would be too late to complain about the fruit being speckled. I'm young, healthy. Any woman would do for me, young, old, willing, unwilling, as long as she had the right equipment! I can subdue the ones who are reluctant, and then I do believe they like it even better! A little bit of knocking about seems to make them want me more, and they certainly get me worked up when they struggle!" He leered across the fire at Pina, and she trembled.

"You be careful, Angelo. You know what Sandro told us about her. She could kill you with one blow of her hand! I can tell you that I think we were very fortunate that she did not put up a fight when we took them. You've got to give Fronti credit for the way he planned the snatch, and then for the way he carried out his plan. Personally, I intend to be as kind as I can to that woman, so that if ever she does get really angry, she will be easy on me! And as for taking liberties with her, well, I'm a very religious man, and would have to give the matter a lot of thought before I moved in on her!"

"Religious? You? What the devil are you talking about?"

"I mean that I'm a devout and practising coward, that's all!"

"It's as well that she doesn't understand the dialect. If they are forewarned, I find it takes a little of the enjoyment off the struggle, indeed it does. But I promise you that before we part company, I shall have the Englishwoman at least once and possibly more! If you promise to behave yourself, I'll let you stand and watch an expert on the job!" With which promise he coiled himself into a ball before the fire, and began to snore.

By straining her ears, Pina discovered that she could catch and understand the greater part of the conversation, and her blood ran cold as she viewed the prospect presented by Angelo. Stella had obviously not understood the purport of the talk between the men, and Pina was grateful for that small mercy. She could only hope that the child would be safe from Angelo's attentions. She resolved that as far as possible, she would try to keep the fire between herself and Angelo, and with that thought in her mind, she began to edge round the fire, taking Stella with her until they were diametrically opposite the two men. She also resolved to try to make a friend of Giorgio, so that if need should arise, she might be able to call on him for protection.

From her new position, Pina could see a little way along the passage that led to the outside world. There was very little to see, in fact, except for a slight lessening of the general darkness. She could not even see the path along which they had walked in the final metres of their journey to the cave. There was no sign of life anywhere save for the movements of their gaolers, when from time to time Giorgio replenished the fire, or Angelo stirred in his sleep. Despite all the efforts of Giorgio, the fire was not a really efficient means of heating the cave, as most of the warmth was dissipated in the blackness of the roof.

Neither of the girls was adequately dressed for the conditions. Stella wore a thin white woollen cardigan over a light cotton frock, and Pina was dressed in a thin silk skirt and matching top. When they had left Tre Boschi, the weather had been fine and warm, but people on the farms had begun to dress in winter gear, and, indeed, in the towns Pina had noticed a number of fashion-conscious young women wearing thick skirts and high boots. She wished devoutly that she and Stella had been similarly dressed. Riding in the car and then in the van, followed by the tramp up the mountain paths, had done little to enhance the appearance of either of them. They were grubby and unkempt. Their hair hung in knots about their ears, and they had not a comb between them to untangle their tresses. So far they had not availed themselves of the facilities afforded by the smaller cave.

Fronti came into the cave and stood by the fire, blowing on his hands and stamping his feet. "Dio, it's cold out there! What about some hot coffee?"

Georgia pushed a billycan over to him and he took a sip. "Bah, this stuff's stone cold!"

Giorgio shrugged. "Well," he retorted, "put it on the fire for a few moments. I'm not here to wait on you; we're all equals in this game!"

"I'm not getting at you. But with two women in the place, you'd think there would be a cup of hot coffee for a cold man!" He turned to Pina. "Here, you, mees. Make this drink warm!"

Pina seemed to be a little slow in obeying him. He drew his pistol and pointed it at her. "I shall not shoot you dead, mees. What I shall do is put a bullet through your ankle. You will still able to hop about and attend to domestic duties like putting a billy on a fire. So! I shall count to three. Uno. Due..."

Before he could arrive at "Tre", Pina had the billycan set on the fire. The coffee quickly reached a drinkable temperature, and Fronti smiled approval. "Now, that's a good girl! I see that we shall make a cave woman of you yet." He sipped the drink with relish.

Giorgio said, in dialect, touching Angelo with his foot, "You ought to watch this one here. He's beginning to get ideas about her. That's a scrap I shall keep out of. What with his strength and her skills, someone could get hurt and I intend to make damn sure that that someone is not me!"

"Angelo had better behave. He well knows that we shall not get paid for damaged goods. I know I threatened her a few moments ago, but I only wanted to frighten her. And don't you fret about martial arts skills. She hasn't any. As usual, Sandro was drawing a long bow when he shot off his mouth about her being a bodyguard. But you can tell Angelo when he wakes, that I am not going to be cheated out of all that I have planned for by a young fool who cannot control his animal nature. It will only be for a few weeks at most that he, and you, will be living here. I've already had a signal that Capriotti has received our first love note."

Fronti turned to Pina, and spoke in Italian. "I was telling Giorgio that our affair's beginning to take shape. Capriotti has found your car and with it, a note that we left for him. Now he will get a request for a tiny donation. It is our earnest hope that he will not keep us hanging about too long before he sees reason. I dislike being up here in these conditions as much as you do. I like my bodily comfort. Please forgive us for talking in dialect from time to time. We tend to forget that you are unacquainted with the speech. We have no desire to give greater offence than is strictly needful. On the contrary, when you leave here, we hope that you will recommend our establishment to other possible guests." His teeth gleamed in the firelight with that strange red appearance that she had noticed earlier whenever he was either angry or satirical.

Giorgio said, "When you got the message from down there, did they say that there would be food for us?"

"Yes. It will be concealed in the arranged place. You and Angelo can go and pick it up whenever you like. There should be rations for four or five days in the package."

Giorgio grunted. "I hope there's something decent in the pack. One thing I miss up here is good grub!"

"When you and Angelo have toted it up here, the mees will make it almost as good a table as you have at home, won't you mees?" Fronti again bestowed on Pina that peculiar red smile.

Angelo stirred and Fronti prodded him with none too gentle a foot. "Rouse yourself, boy! Time to go with your comrade here to collect the rations. I suppose you do like to eat sometimes? Eh?"

With an oath, Angelo rose and stretched himself. "Why must it always be me and Giorgio? Why not you and him? I had to tote the cripple all the way up here last night! She may look small to you, but I tell you, after the first half hour or so, she gets damn heavy! You go with Giorgio, and I'll stay here on guard. Look, I'm still tired; I need more rest. You two go. Go on!"

Fronti put his hand on the handgun in his waistband. "I say that you two go!" he snarled. "You're both younger than I am. So what I say is, if you want to eat, you go for the grub! Me, I can manage without food for several days yet. The only time I shall go down that path is when I am called from below. Let me remind you that I am in charge up here, and I say that you two go for food. Anyway," he continued, "if you think I would be fool enough to leave you - you, of all people - up here with two females, you should think again! I haven't known you all your life without gleaning some idea of your appetites, let me tell you. Now quit fooling and get down that path before you and our guests die of starvation!"

Angelo quailed at the scorn in his voice and at the overt threat of the pistol. He dropped his eyes and slouched out of the cave, followed by Giorgio. Fronti said, "Mees, if you have trouble - you know what I mean - with that young stallion, let me know. I am well aware that all his brains are in a peculiar part of his anatomy. While I am present, the only fear you have of that kind of trouble could come if Capriotti decides not to pay up. Until that happens, - and I would not like to see it happen - you will both be under my protection. Of course, should the money not be forthcoming, I should have to stand back and let Angelo enjoy himself. But I believe you need have little fear of that happening.

"I advise you, while the young men are away, to heat some water in the billycan and attend to your toilettes as best you can. You need not fear that I shall peep or anything of that nature. I gave up such ideas many years ago!"

He sat before the fire, gazing into its depths as though he could read the future in the red embers, while Stella and Pina crept about making hot water and attending to their cleanliness in the inner cave.

EIGHTEEN

Immediately on arrival back at Giulianova, Carlo telephoned his Head of Department to explain the state of affairs at Tre Boschi. He reported that it was his belief that the abduction was to some extent connected with the drug smugglers; it was something he felt by instinct, but was not able to prove. He told the Chief of his meeting with Pina on the train, of their subsequent closer acquaintance, and his eventual proposal and acceptance by her. The name of Don Stefano was a powerful lever, and after some initial hesitation, the Chief agreed that Carlo might run the two cases in parallel. There was no point in drafting in another agent to deal with the smugglers, and as Carlo had broken his cover to the Carabinieri, he would have to suffer the consequences, if there were any. The Chief stressed that Carlo was an anti-narcotics agent, and not a kidnapping expert, and had better not forget that fact. His priorities were to be kept in mind at all times.

Carlo then rang Records, from whom he requested information on known kidnappers' methods of operation. This case did not appear to conform to any modus operandi used previously, and Records agreed with Carlo that this was probably a band of petty villains trying to emulate hoodlums who were more expert at the game. They tended to agree that it was possible that it might well be a band of drug smugglers trying to make a small fortune before ceasing to ply their trade. Before Carlo got off the line, the Chief came on again. "We'll give you what aid we can, but don't expect too much from us," he said. "Mostly you'll have to work on your own with the local law. In my opinion, much depends on whether Senatore Capriotti can raise whatever cash is demanded. You don't need me to remind you that everyone down there is related in some degree to everyone else! They may know exactly what's going on, but the family honour, the 'omerta', is as strong as it is in the Mafia, and if nothing else will keep mouths shut, fear will certainly do so. Your most valuable card is the daughter. For her, there will be much sympathy, and you might be able to play on that. For the Englishwoman, there will be no feeling at all; she means nothing to anyone save you. I wish you well in the task you have set yourself. You said you have spoken to the Carabinieri at Fortalezza, but I'll make it official with a letter. Keep me informed, and don't go and get yourself killed too dead! Ciao!" He rang off.

Carlo sat for half an hour after that call, deep in thought. He mulled over all the scanty details known to him. He then shook his head to clear it of the fog that seemed to envelop it, and dowsed himself in the washbasin in the vain hope of furthering the process of clearing his mind. He then decided to return to Tre Boschi on the off-chance that he might learn something new there.

Sandro was washing the Rolls. He was quite willing to stop work and indulge in a little gossip. "This is a dreadful thing! Little did I think when I picked up mees at the station that she would be soon kidnapped by a gang of merciless and rapacious criminals! And the poor signorina Stella, too. My heart bleeds for them both. But there it is, that's this modern world for you! My aunts say that things were better when they were young. People had less money, but there was a lot less crime and everybody worked harder than they do today. They tell me that I have an easy life. Easy life, indeed!" He kicked the fat tyre of the car. "They should try washing and polishing this brute of a car! Zia Mina says that she and zia Maria are going to give up the shop and buy a little farm. They will find farming a lot harder work than chopping off a few metres of cloth!"

Carlo stopped the flow of words. "Did the mees ever meet your aunts?"

"Yes, I took her to Bellante one afternoon. I hoped that she would buy something from the shop. But they never got as far as talking business because my Cousin Fronti came in. I'm not too fond of him. He drives me mad! He's a cattle dealer and travels all over the country. He wanted me to join in some scheme he was hatching, but the aunts talked him out of the deal. I wouldn't have minded being in it; I'd have liked to travel, even if it meant that I had to endure Fronti! But in a way, I'm happy enough here, where I get to play with cars and that. Except that I don't like having to wash and polish the damn things. Before the mees came, I used to take out signorina Stella sometimes, but I didn't mind losing that chore, because she was always telling me to slow down so that she could look at a view. What's a view, really? I am very fond of the view from the belvedere at Bellante, but when you've seen one view, you've seen the lot! Anyway, Elsa says that Stella was better off with another woman to go out with her. Not that that did a lot of good either. I hear that they've just been kidnapped. No, if *I* had been there when the criminals struck..."

Carlo felt his gorge rise at the unvoiced criticism of Pina, but he checked the angry words that sprang to his lips. "D'you think I could visit your aunts? As far as possible, I want to meet everyone the mees met since she arrived here."

"Are you a detective?" asked the boy, his eyes widening.

"Not really."

"Dio, I'd love to be a 'tec! I'd shoot all those villains down without a second thought! Bang, bang! I wonder how you start to be a 'tec?"

"I think it's a long and complicated process. We'll have a chat about it one of these days. Tell me, what is the best time to visit your aunts?"

"Oh, you can see them any time. They keep a shop and work shop hours - you know, open at seven every morning, close at one, open again at half past three and close for the night at ten. Sundays, they only open from eight in the morning till noon."

Thanking him, Carlo left Sandro to complete his task. Somehow, he thought, if the boy did think he was a detective, he would not fail to get the news to the bandits. They, in turn, might try to eliminate the danger that he, as a suspected investigator, could be to their plans, and so, in a roundabout way, the gang might be flushed into the open.

He drove slowly to Bellante. He parked his car at a filling station. The attendant promised that the car would be safe in his care. He would also ensure that it was greased and replenishments made as necessary. While he waited, perhaps the signore would care to stroll up to the belvedere for which the town was justly famous. The signore was agreeable, and on receiving directions from the man, went to have a look at the valley. After ten minutes or so of viewing, he wended his way into the maze of narrow streets that made up the town's small business quarter. After several enquiries and a few false leads, he came upon the sisters' shop. Evidently the siesta period was over, for as he neared the door, a young woman emerged, calling her goodbyes over her shoulder as she stepped up into the street.

Carlo pushed aside the curtain and entered the shop. Behind the cluttered counter, an old and apparently feeble woman was straining to replace a bolt of fabric on a shelf. With a polite "Permesso", he relieved her of her load and slid the cloth into the space which the woman was trying to reach. As he did so, he glanced down the central cardboard tube. Something was inside it, obstructing the light. Releasing the bolt, he took a surreptitious sniff at the end of the tube. The old woman thanked him breathlessly.

"The signore desires...?"

"Before I make known my wants, allow me to help you to clear the counter." Deftly he rolled up one of the bolts on its tube. "Where does this one go?" She pointed out the correct place for it, and for all the other bolts as he picked them up. Each one, as he put it in its appointed position, was subjected to the inspection he had given to the first one. Some fifty per cent of the rolls were blocked off, and each one of those gave off that faint odour that he had detected with the first one. As he worked, the old woman delivered a wordy and somewhat breathless, diatribe on the shortcomings of the flighty flippertygibbets who hadn't the slightest idea of what they were seeking, and made old ladies drag out half the stock for inspection before they left the shop without spending a single lira.

When the counter was clear, and the racks tidy, she said, "You have been very kind. Will you take a little coffee to refresh yourself?"

He accepted the offer, and she motioned him to follow her through the curtain that separated shop from living quarters, calling, "Maria, we have a guest for coffee!" To Carlo she said, "My sister Maria likes to be warned that a visitor is coming into the house. She is a semi-invalid after suffering a stroke, and cannot talk well - in fact, very few can understand her at all. But she is always happy to see a new face and to hear a fresh voice. She will understand everything you say to her, for although she has had that stroke, her brain is still active; she is by no means simple."

Maria was seated at the table, exactly as she had been when Pina called. The other old woman filled the coffee machine and put it on the gas. The flame flared round the base of the pot, and she said, "My nephew Sandro is everlastingly scolding me for allowing the flame to rise so high, but I maintain that to make proper coffee the water must boil fiercely. But you would not know Sandro, signore."

"Ah, but I do! It was he who told me of this delightful little shop, when I met him in a bar somewhere - I forget where exactly. He would make a very good salesman!"

Hearing Sandro's name mentioned, Maria nodded her head and

Carlo was irresistibly reminded of those toys with the ceaselessly bobbing heads that he had owned as a child.

Minute cups of coffee were poured when the mocha machine boiled, and a carton of sweet biscuits was produced. Carlo took a biscuit and dipped it into his coffee under the approving eye of Maria's sister who plainly appreciated a man who knew how to behave himself in an Abruzzese kitchen. He said, "I saw Sandro quite recently. He was very proud that he had brought an Englishwoman to your shop."

"That's right. We thought her a strange girl, but quite pleasant for a foreigner. She seemed not to be quite used to our ways, but he was very good. She had spent a lot of time in Roma or Napoli or somewhere, where the customs are very different from ours. I remember that she left quite abruptly when our cousin Matteo Fronti came in to say goodbye before he left on one of his business trips."

"That would be the cattle dealer that Sandro mentioned."

"That's right. He's been all over Italy, and even to Roma! He always comes to say 'Goodbye', and again when he returns and so we get to know of the wicked ways of the world outside Bellante. We don't think we would care to live in that world! There's too much crime for old women like us!" She smiled a fleeting smile that did not touch her eyes, while Maria kept nodding away.

"I think I would like to meet Signor Fronti," said Carlo, sipping his coffee. "He is evidently a man of the world. We might even have met the same people at some time or other. I know a few cattle dealers, but not many Italians in the trade. Most of the cattlemen that I know seem to be Albanians." He noticed a quick exchange of glances between the sisters.

"This is a beautiful little town," he continued. "If I lived here, I would pass a lot of time - too much time, I guess - up there on the belvedere."

"Yes, it is beautiful. When we buy our little farm, it will be just below the belvedere, so that we shall be able to look out over the valley all the time."

"You are going to buy a farm? With all respect, are you not a little, may I say it, old, to make such a drastic alteration to your way of life?"

Maria made a strangled noise. "What does she say?" asked Carlo.

"She says that we will certainly have our farm and that very soon

now. We know that a lot of money is coming our way, and when it
arrives, we shall put a manager in the shop. Sandro will be our farm
manager. We are beginning to find it rather cramped here; we would
like to breathe more easily, as it were."
    "Have you won the Pescara lottery, then?"
    "As good as. If you stay in the district, you shall see!" She put an
end to the conversation by rising and hobbling towards the shop.
"Now, signore, what was it you came to buy?"
    "Oh it was only a couple of handkerchiefs."
    In the shop she showed him a selection, and he made a choice and
left, thanking her for the coffee, and assuring her that he would call
again. In his car, he made a few notes before starting out to call
again at Tre Boschi.
    Sandro was still languidly washing the Rolls when he entered the
yard. He waved his wash leather to Carlo as he alighted and rang the
house bell. Elsa conducted him to the office where Passi sat behind
his small desk, immersed as always in a sea of paperwork. "Can I
help?"
    "What do you know about the two old biddies, Sandro's aunts,
who keep the shop in Bellante?"
    "Oh, they're harmless enough. Somehow they scratch a living
from their trade, but only the good Lord knows how! Lately they've
been talking about buying a farm and having Sandro to run it for
them. They'd be idiots to take on anything like that at their age, even
with Sandro's help. Work and Sandro are but poor bedfellows and
you cannot run a farm of any size without a lot of really hard
slogging!" He fiddled with the papers before him, plainly anxious to
proceed with his task.
    As he left the office, Carlo thought that Passi had made a very fair
assessment of Sandro's character. The boy was still working on the
car, without a great deal of interest. He was wringing out his wash
leather, a task which he was performing painstakingly, making it last
as long as possible. Carlo went towards him.
    "Did you see my aunts?"
    "Yes. They gave me coffee. We talked a little."
    "Why did you want to meet then?"
    "I like to see how people live. It's always interesting to me.
Well, I must get back to town. Ciao!"
    He drove slowly back to Giulianova. His thoughts were centred

on Pina. He had no doubt that she and Stella were in great danger. He wished devoutly that he could do more, but he could do no more than poke about like this, until such time as the kidnappers made their next move. In sheer frustration, he thumped the steering wheel with a clenched fist. His whole body ached with the desire to bring this affair to a rapid and successful close. He wanted to hold Pina close in his arms again.

As he passed Bellante, a conversation was proceeding in the shop. Maria was berating Mina. "You are a fool, sister! I tell you that fellow is dangerous! He is dangerous to all our people. I smell the aroma of an agent about him. Did you let him handle the bolts?"

Mina, lying stoutly, replied, "Certainly not! I know better than to permit any stranger to touch our stock!"

"I do not like that tizio - that fellow," grumbled Maria. "And you, Mina, are suffering from Sandro's disease - you talk too much! You should never have let him think we are coming into money. I don't like it at all. I fear the man. No innocent stranger would come out here to buy a handkerchief or two from us when he could get them cheaper in town. We must get in touch with Matteo and see if he can put this man down permanently! He could ruin everything for us!"

NINETEEN

Don Stefano sat in the office of the Capo at Fortalezza. That great man sat on the opposite side of the desk facing the senator. The full ashtray before the elder man testified to the state of his nerves. He would light a cigarette, take two or three nervous puffs at it, then crush it in the ashtray, only to light another immediately. His face was grey and drawn; his shoulders drooped in dejection. Even the tough policeman felt pity for the man.

"In the name of God, can't you do something other than just sit there, polishing your chair with the seat of your breeches? This inactivity is killing me!"

The Capo shook his head. "My men are on constant patrol, senatore. All our usual sources of information have been tapped, sadly without us gaining one iota of useful ideas about this crime. Every vigile urbano - town policeman - is on the alert. But we are in the hands of the criminals - we cannot do a thing until we hear from them, and they will only contact you when they think the time is ripe to do so. I regret to tell you that they usually like to let their victims suffer a little, in the hope, to put it cruelly, that they will soften up. When they judge that your powers of resistance are at breaking point, they will pounce. All I ask is that when they do, you will let me know immediately. Meantime, I can only counsel patience, which is, I own, poor consolation for anyone in your position."

Lighting yet another cigarette, Don Stefano took his leave of the Capo. Outside the barracks, Sandro was waiting in the Rolls, with an admiring crowd around him and the sleek car. Seeing his master approach, the boy leapt from his seat behind the wheel and pushed through the throng to meet the senator. "Is there any news, signore?"

Sadly the senator shook his head. He slumped heavily into the front seat of the car and Sandro closed the door quietly and walked round to take his place in the driving seat. Don Stefano stared into space, heedless of the crowd around him. "Where to, signore?"

"To Tre Boschi. Maybe there will be news awaiting us there."

The car glided away from the kerb, scattering the throng clustered about it. For once, Sandro had the sense not to talk, and Don Stefano, his chin sunk upon his chest, was allowed silence to think as he was wafted towards his home. He had done much thinking in the past few hours. Unfortunately every line of thought had led to the same inescapable conclusion - there was nothing to do save wait, hope, and pray. The Rolls drew to a stop at his front door. Before Sandro could leap from the car and rush round to open the door for his master, Don Stefano was almost sprinting along the corridor to the office. "Any news?" he demanded of Passi.

"Nothing, signore. Of course, it is early days yet. From press reports of similar outrages, we know that these people are not good communicators."

The senator flung himself into a low chair and lighted another cigarette. Passi returned to his work, seeking comfort in his endless calculations. He glanced at times in pity at his employer. The stillness of the room was broken by the whirr of a helicopter passing over the house, and both men realised that the Capo was perhaps doing his best and the search was continuing relentlessly. The sound died away. The implication was that the machine was not going to land this time, and therefore that the police were no wiser than was Don Stefano himself.

"May I suggest that you go to your bed, signore? You have had scarcely any sleep since you arrived here from Roma. When the time comes, you will need all your wits about you. Please, I beseech you, go to your room and I will send Elsa with a tisane to help you to sleep."

"Perhaps you are right, Luigi. I *shall* need all my faculties. Yes. Do I have your promise that you will rouse me should even the least snippet of news come in?"

"But of course, signore. You need have no fear that I would not awaken you."

The senator tottered from the room as Passi pulled the bell to summon Elsa and issue the necessary orders for a tisane. Elsa was a past mistress at the preparation of such herbal concoctions, and her skills did not fail her on this occasion. The potion worked its healing magic with complete success and the senator was able to sleep for four hours before waking perfectly naturally. Opening his eyes, he wondered for a moment what on earth he was doing here at Tre Boschi when he ought to be in his office in Roma. Then hastily donning his jacket, the only garment he had removed when he fell on to his bed, he hastened to the office. Here his unspoken question was met by a shake of the head from Passi. The majordomo rang the bell and Elsa appeared with a bowl of steaming coffee. Don Stefano drank the coffee with relish. He had not realised how dry his mouth was, after the tisane and the heavy sleep it had induced. From the silver box on the table, he selected a cigarette, lighted it, and inhaled deeply.

Passi looked up. "You will do yourself no good if you smoke so heavily all the time, signore," he observed.

"But it is such a comfort to me, old friend!" He drew deeply again as though to demonstrate how much the action and the acrid taste of the smoke solaced him. "And, moreover, it gives me something to do during these empty hours when I must merely await others' convenience!"

Passi shook his head. "They are unpleasant things, cigarettes. But I suppose if you must have them, then you must!"

Both men jumped as the telephone shrilled with an urgent imperious summons. Passi picked up the instrument, listened for a few moments, then passed it to Don Stefano. He heard the voice of a man. "Capriotti?"

"Pronto. Chi parle?"

"Never mind who is speaking. Just listen carefully. If you want to see your daughter again, as well as the young Englishwoman, you will follow these instructions to the letter. Just be quiet and listen. You will put four hundred million lire into a suitcase. The money will be in used one hundred thousand lire notes. Tomorrow night at precisely seven o'clock, you will bring that money with you in your Fiat. You will travel alone. You will come up the hill from Pietracamela towards Prati di Tivo. At two kilometres along that road, there is a white road leading off to the right. At three hundred metres along the white road, there is a culvert. You will put the suitcase with the money in it in the mouth of the culvert on the left hand side of the road. Without further delay, you will turn your car round and return to your house.

You will NOT tell the police of this message - if you do, your daughter will die! You will not bring anyone with you to the place you drop the cash, nor will you permit anyone from your household to follow you for any part of the journey. You will not loiter about after you have put the cash in the required place. You will not see anyone at the spot, but we shall be there watching you to see that our commands are obeyed. You will not attempt to trace this call." There was a click as the caller rang off, and in spite of Don Stefano's frantic jiggling of the switch, only the dialling tone was to be heard on the instrument.

Swiftly, he told Passi the burden of the message, and the majordomo took notes in his jotter so that there should be no mistake made when they tried to obey the orders given by the abductors. The two men then discussed how they might raise the cash demanded. Four hundred million lire is a great sum - in English, something of the order of £250,000.

Passi was glum. "This will bleed us white!" he declared. "We shall have to pledge everything we possess to raise anything like that amount! Certainly it cannot be raised at a moment's notice, as these rogues seem to think it can. Frankly, signore, I don't see how we can succeed at all in raising such a vast sum! We simply do not have the resources. Somehow, we must play for time. You will, of course, inform the capo of this call?"

"Never! I dare not imperil Stella by so doing. Listen. You ring round all my friends. Implore them to lend me what they can, but without divulging the reason for the request. Ask them for one hundred thousand lire notes. You could say that the cash is needed for urgent business reasons. Wait a moment - I have an idea. What was the number of that fellow who said he was a friend of Miss Corrigan? Ah, here it is! Now, you get ringing all my friends while I go to the public phonebox and call this di Felippo fellow. Now at long last, we can do something positive! Come on, get that phone busy! We've only thirty hours and a hell of a lot to do!" He dashed from the office as Passi began to make the first of the many calls that demanded his attention now.

In the callbox, Don Stefano was tapping impatiently on the coin holder as the staff at the Albergo Victoria Regine went in search of Carlo. After a wait that seemed endless, the thin metallic voice came through. "Chi parla?"

"Capriotti. There is news."

"What news, senatore?"

"I cannot tell you over the phone. Come to Tre Boschi urgently."

"I am already on my way!"

Slightly relieved that he now had an ally in addition to the staff at the house, Don Stefano returned to the office. Passi, with the telephone at his ear, greeted him with a grimace. He turned down his thumb. At the conclusion of the call he was making, he said, "We are not having a lot of luck, signore! So many of your friends seem to be away from their homes. Including our own available resources, I have so far managed to raise only half of the sum we need. And speaking as your manager and financial adviser, there is not time to sell anything. I fear that the gang will not be satisfied with what I have gathered in so far."

"I have the same fear, Luigi. These vampires will want their full bucket of blood, and anything less will certainly not satisfy them, of that you may be sure. My poor little Stellina!" He buried his face in hands as Passi came round his desk to lay a comforting arm on his master's heaving shoulders.

Elsa ushered in di Felippo, who had made record time on the journey to Tre Boschi. "What news have you, senator?"

Passi told him the contents of the message they had received, referring to his notes to ensure that no important detail was omitted in his recital.

"Now we shall see some action! Tell me, senatore, shall you be able to raise the sum required?"

"I very much doubt it. Even if we could contact all my friends - and we cannot - we could never amass such a sum in so short a time. To borrow from the bank would take too much time, while to get them to move more rapidly would entail explaining why I need so much cash, and that I dare not do for fear of imperilling Stella even more. And, of course, your fiancée also."

"I agree. The girls are in danger enough as things are. Nothing would be gained by breaking the gang's conditions and revealing the reason for needing cash. There would also be little to be gained, at this stage, by informing the Capo of events. Much as I respect the man himself, I regret that I have doubts about his staff. No, for the time being, we are on our own. Tell me, how much will the shortfall be, as far as you can see?"

"Luigi deals with all the financial matters of the estate. He reckons we shall find about half the money by the deadline the ruffians have set. Frankly, di Felippo, I am at my wits' end! I had hoped earnestly that you would be able to come up with a contribution."

"I am not a wealthy man, senatore, but of course I will make available what I have. The fact that the gang have made such an exorbitant demands indicates that we are dealing with dilettanti, mere amateurs. Professionals would have made it their business to discover to a soldo what you could stand." He paused for a moment to collect his thoughts. "Might I suggest that this is what we do? You follow their orders to the letter, except that with the cash we can raise between us, you enclose a note saying that this is all you can raise at short notice, that you are pressing on with your efforts to raise the rest, and asking them to contact you again in say, three days' time. Meanwhile, I will go to Pietracamela and do some reconnaissance. If you hear nothing from me in forty-eight hours, then get in touch with the Capo, and tell him everything."

"The gang won't be happy about that," put in Passi.

"They'll have to accept it."

"Whatever you do, di Felippo, remember that on the outcome of this affair rests all my future happiness!" said Don Stefano.

"So does mine, senatore!" Carlo left the office.

The senator turned to Passi. "God grant that he is successful in whatever he intends to do! Now, have you tried the Ganci? They're not such close friends, but they may be willing to assist me."

Annibale was not in his room when Carlo went in search of him, but the scream of the saw led the searcher to the woodshed. "Can you get away for a short time, Annibale?"

"Why?"

"I need someone for the next twenty-four hours on whom I can rely totally."

"If it's to do with this kidnapping, then I'm your man, even if it means losing my place here! I will be very happy to help. Although I am old, yet all this chopping and sawing has kept my arm strong. Do I bring my gun?"

"Yes, and plenty of shells! You do not fear being shot at?"

"Signore, I am an old cavalryman!" There was deep reproach in his voice and in his eyes. "Also towards the end of the war, I fought over mountains and valleys with the partisans. I know this terrain as well as any man living!"

"Good! Then collect your arms and join me at my car in front of the house!"

When they were travelling along the Teramo road, Carlo said, "I am making for Pietracamela. It is a small winter holiday resort above the valley of the Vomano river. Maybe six hundred people dwell there permanently. You shall pretend to be my manservant, so hide your gun in the back of the car. Manservants don't normally travel armed to the teeth!"

"Signor di Felippo, I know Pietracamela well! It was our headquarters at one time, when I was a partigiano! We could stay at the house of my friend Baldini..."

"No!" Carlo interrupted him fiercely, "On no account are you to make contact with anyone who may have known you in the past! Your Baldini may be as honest as the day; equally, he could be in league with the gang of abductors! When we arrive, you must keep quiet about ever having even seen the village before this time. If anyone says he recognises you, you must deny all knowledge of both place and people! From here on, you are Annibal Brambilla, and like me, you come from Cremona. I doubt if anyone up there ever heard of the place, let alone visited the city. If you don't talk too much, your Italian accent will not betray you. But for heaven's sake, don't lapse into Abruzzese!"

Carlo drove fast through the evening air. Within a couple of hours, they were climbing the steep rise to the village. Most of the hotels, they found, were not yet opened; they would remain shuttered until the snows permitted skiing to begin. Eventually Carlo discovered a small guest house which had remained in business all through the summer, and which had rooms to let; it was completely empty of guests. After agreeing terms and arranging dinner, he and Annibale went out again in the car, Carlo explaining to the padrona that, as an artist, he wanted to see the effect of the waning light on the hilltops. He particularly wanted to see the land before the darkness closed in, so that he could finalise a plan which was lurking at the back of his mind.

He had no difficulty in locating the white road which the telephone caller had mentioned. A short step up the hill there was a small passing place and below it was the culvert that had been mentioned. Carlo pulled into the passing place and parked the car. He walked a hundred metres or so up the slope, and the same distance downhill. The gradient was very steep, and he had to stop several times to recover his breath. During these short halts, he inspected the lie of the land. As the two men approached their car, he said, in a loud voice, "I'm sorry, Brambilla. I can't go any further. This gradient is too much of a strain on my heart! I must return to the hotel." They got into the car, and Carlo drove slowly back to their guest house. He spent some time in conversation with the padrona, explaining that he was an artist who was interested in the local mountainous scenery, but had a heart condition which was worsened by altitude. On her part, she was pleased to have guests in her house at a dull time of year, when summer guests had gone and winter visitors were still awaited. She promised to prepare him a dinner of local recipes that he would long remember. When Carlo had finished his chat, he and Annibale went to their room.

"Now, Annibale, this is what I think will happen. Don Stefano will come at the right time to the appointed place with the ransom, and will deposit it in the method ordered by the kidnappers. I must admit that they have chosen a good spot - just the spot I would have chosen myself for the purpose. Early tomorrow afternoon, I shall go for a walk alone. I shall walk slowly because of my weak heart, and when I am quite certain that there is nobody about to watch what I am up to, I shall conceal myself in a spot I noticed up the hill from the culvert, from where I shall be able to keep it under observation. I shall also be able to see the road in either direction for about fifty metres. I intend to remain there until I see the ransom picked up; I hope that somehow I shall be able to see who does the picking up.

"You will remain here. If I have not returned by midnight, come and seek me. Stroll along the road like a drunken peasant, singing at the top of your voice. When I hear you, I shall wait until you reach the end of the verse you are singing, and I shall then whistle like this." He pursed his lips and gave a distinctive whistle. "If, however, I do not respond to your melodious voice, pass on up the hill for about a hundred metres, then stop and listen. If you still hear nothing from me, return here and wait till dawn. Then come again and search for me. If you still do not find me, telephone Don Stefano immediately and ask him to inform the Capo of all that has happened. You understand?"

"Might you not need help, signore? Can't I lay up with you? I could have my gun!"

"No. If I get into bother, someone will have to run for help. By all means carry your gun when you come singing up the road, but remember that your first duty is to back me up, not to provoke any trouble. On no account make any move before midnight. I believe that the gang will make no attempt to pick up the ransom before nine or ten o'clock. They will ensure that Don Stefano is well away from the scene before they appear on it."

"Understood signore. But I must admit that my greatest hope is that I may draw a bead on the villains who have taken the signorina Stella and the mees!"

"I sincerely hope that you will get that opportunity! Now let us go and see if the padrona is as good at cooking food as she is at talking about it!"

After a meal that proved to be all that had been promised, they retired to their room. It was early by Italian standards. They went to stroll about the village, and discovered that it appeared to have died by ten o'clock. This was important - anyone moving outside after that hour might well be seen or heard by a villager, which could lead to unpleasant consequences.

They spent the next morning sitting in a quiet spot while Carlo tried to make a few sketches on a pad he had remembered to bring along to support his artistic claims. He worked until lunch time, and was pleased to note that none of the passers-by appeared to recognise Annibale. If the old man were to be accosted by an ex-comrade, much of Carlo's planning would fall apart at the seams. Together they partook of a meal, described by the padrona as a light mid-day snack; it was a repast that would have satisfied half a dozen healthy young appetites, and their failure to eat all that was put on the table caused the padrona to lament their lack of appetite, which she attributed to Carlo's poor health and his servant's age. They then retired to their room to rest in readiness for the work that lay before them that evening.

At five o'clock Carlo began his preparation when the gong sounded for dinner. Annibale was to make excuses for his 'master', saying that he was unwell and had no appetite. Annibale was to inform the padrona that Carlo often suffered such attacks, and if this one followed the usual course, he would be confined to his room for twenty-four hours, after which time the attack should have passed off. In the meantime, while they awaited the summons to table, the pair went over their roles once more, until Carlo was certain that everything was as well-prepared as possible.

At five thirty, Carlo slipped quietly out of the room without, he hoped, being observed. On arriving at his selected lookout point, he searched all round. There appeared to be no living soul other than himself for many kilometres around. He moved rapidly to the place which he had earlier marked out for his concealment. As he had thought, there was a small hollow there in which he made himself comfortable. There was in fact a similar hollow lower down the slope, but he felt that perhaps that one was reserved by the ransom collectors. With a pair of night glasses, he scanned the countryside as far as he could see. He had been worried lest he could be seen from above, but was relieved to see that the steep slope above was scree which offered no concealment to anything, not even to a marmot, of which there were so many in these hills. He also saw with satisfaction that the culvert below him was in full view. He congratulated himself on dressing warmly; at this altitude, the evening air struck chill already and it would be much colder as the night advanced.

He could have been a thousand light years from any other human presence. No traffic seemed to be moving; indeed, if there had been any movement on the main road, the sound of it would have been completely screened by the groves of trees and undergrowth all about the place. A few birds called as they settled for the night. In the undergrowth he could hear faint rustlings as small creatures of the darkness began to go about their business of finding food. The eerie cry of a rabbit, hunted perhaps by a stoat or some other predator, rang out across the valley, clear as crystal in the still air. He found it difficult to remain wakeful - only the thought of Pina and the suffering that she might be undergoing helped him to keep his eyes open.

An owl hooted. Another rabbit uttered a squeal of terror. Something, he knew not what, slithered lightly over his bare flesh between the top of his sock and the bottom of his trouser leg. He shuddered slightly. This was work for which he had not been trained. He was much more at home in streets than in wild uncultivated places like this. He dare not move lest some slight sound, not in keeping with nature, betrayed the fact that there was an alien presence on the hillside.

A car moved slowly up the hill from Pietracamela. It halted by the culvert. The luminous hands of Carlo's watch told him that it needed a few minutes to seven o'clock. By the light of the car's side lights, he saw a shadowy figure creeping into the end of the culvert, and knew that it was Don Stefano. He watched the dim figure struggle with a heavy suitcase down the slope to the mouth of the pipe, then return to the car and drive it away further up the hill where the white lane rejoined the main road. He resumed his vigil. Nothing happened anywhere in the world. All was still and silent again.

At ten minutes past eleven o'clock, another car climbed up the white lane. The car stopped and a man alighted and shone a torch down the slope to the mouth of the pipe. A second man remonstrated, saying that a flashing torch here and now might get them all gaoled. The first man, in somewhat impolite language, told his companion to shut up. A light was essential if he, the first man, was to clamber safely down the slope in this darkness. He did not want to break his neck. Then, with a mighty explosion of oaths, the man slid down to the pipe mouth. He returned carrying a suitcase - a heavy one, thought Carlo, to judge by the difficulty the man was having in clambering up the slope to the roadway. Don Stefano must be a fitter man than he appeared to be, although of course, it would have been much easier for him to descend with the heavy case than it was to ascend the steep slope with a similar burden.

In the light of the headlights, switched on for the purpose, the men opened the case. This action, mused Carlo, was yet another indication of their amateur status. Professionals would have got well clear of the dropping place before they took any such action. The first man swore again. "Here's a fine thing! Capriotti says he can't raise all the cash, so he's sent only some of the mazuma! What do we do now? Take it up to the cave?"

"No. If we carry it up there, we'll only have to cart it down again. And anyway, I don't fancy meeting Fronti with only half the loot! He'll go berserk! We'll take it to the Prati and make a signal that we want to see him. Let Fronti decide what he wants to do!"

Carlo fumbled with his glasses, trying to get a better view of the men. He must have disturbed a pebble, for with a shattering sound breaking the silence, the stone rolled down the slope. One of the men drew a pistol. "Come out!" he cried. "I can see you! Come out or I'll shoot!" Carlo remained silent and unmoving.

"Ah, there's no one there!" said the other man. "It was probably some animal that disturbed a stone. Come on, let's make tracks. I don't like hanging about like this!"

Still flourishing his pistol, his comrade said, "That wasn't no animal. No animal would disturb a stone like that when there are humans nearby. You go up there and have a sniff round while I cover you."

"I say there's nobody there!"

"And I say, get on up there and have a look round. Draw your gun, and shoot first. We'll ask questions afterwards."

With a marked lack of enthusiasm, the man began to mount the hill towards the hollow. Slowly, carefully, Carlo drew his own little Beretta and cocked it. The slight click made by the action sounded loud in the stillness. The man fired blindly in the direction of the sound. It was a lucky shot. The last thing Carlo remembered was a searing pain in his head. Then everything went black.

The man lumbered about in the bushes for a few moments longer. "There's no one here," he called to his companion. "Definitely nothing and nobody." He stamped about, breaking branches off bushes with a crackling that sounded like fire.

From below his companion called, "If there's anyone within a kilometre, that shot will have roused them! Come on down, and let's get the hell out of here!" The searcher scrambled down the slope and got into the car. Rapidly it was turned round, the tyres scrabbling for hold on the dusty surface and sped away down the hill.

In his hollow, Carlo lay inert, blood pouring from a wound in his head.

Angelo and Giorgio

TWENTY

Fronti had refused categorically Pina's pleas that she be allowed to carry on with any of Stella's lessons, particularly the tuition in English. "How are we to know that you are not plotting?" he demanded. "None here understand your barbarous tongue. We should never know what you are saying." She bit back a sharp retort that when he and the other men spoke in dialect, she was in a like position. There was nothing to be gained from angering him, and so far, the girls had not been badly treated - that is, insofar as kidnap victims could be said not to be maltreated.

Both of the girls were beginning to feel the lack of really adequate personal cleanliness. They felt, with some justice, that they were dirty and unkempt; they believed that their bodies smelled of all manner of things unpleasant. Their clothing was badly soiled and crushed. Their teeth, when they ran their tongues over them, felt sorely in need of the attentions of a good brush. Their hands were no longer soft, and Pina was sure that if they could be inspected in daylight rather than by the dim red light of the fire in the cave, they would be revealed as being black with ingrained filth.

Stella was bearing the captivity with a stoicism that astonished Pina, who had not expected that frail body to support such a spartan existence for any prolonged period. But the child had inherited the spirit of her father, together with his strength of character, and while she must have suffered inevitably and severely from her present mode of life, somehow it seemed that it was she who gave strength to Pina rather than the other way about.

While they were not dozing, for true sleep was not possible in the conditions applying in the cave, or when Pina was not engaged in cooking, as Fronti insisted that she should be, in spite of her lamentable lack of culinary skills, Pina and Stella talked much about their future lives. Pina had disclosed the secret of her engagement to Carlo. There were many opportunities to dream aloud as they made plans for Stella to be chief bridesmaid at the wedding, and when Pina and Carlo were settled in their new home, wherever it might be, for Stella to pay visits. According to Stella, there would be many reciprocal visits to Tre Boschi, where, Stella assured her, there would always be a welcome for her and for Carlo. Stella was certain that the first-born of the marriage would be a girl; she ordained that she should be godmother to the child, and that it was to be named Stella. Such confidences had perforce to be exchanged when the men were outside the cave; as soon as their captors returned, the chatter would cease, and in silence Stella would huddle close to Pina before the fire,

Refuelling the fire was never carried out consistently, being subject to the whims and attitude of whichever of the men was on guard at any given time. Giorgio was good, and throughout his night duty hours, the fire burned bright and clear. Angelo, on the other hand, refused to make any effort during his night time duties, and often the fire was permitted to die down almost to the point of extinction. Fronti would never replenish the fire; he was the boss and it was beneath his dignity to perform such manual functions. As he refused to allow the captives to leave the vicinity of the fire, save to visit the small cave when necessary, Pina was not permitted to fetch wood from the far end of the cave. At times, when cold struck home most bitterly and the fire was dying, Pina was most pessimistic about their chances of survival and ultimate release. At such times, the noise of the falling water in the inner cave seemed to be louder and more threatening than ever it was when the flames were leaping and dancing and casting their ruddy glow over everything within five or six metres radius.

The lecture that Fronti had read to Angelo, when Giorgio had mentioned that worthy's intentions towards Pina, seemed to have had the desired effect. Now, when they all sat round the fire, Angelo treated Pina with a studied disdain. When Fronti was in the cave, no one spoke to the captives save he himself. It was he who issued instructions to both guards and prisoners alike. Pina felt sure that, providing all went according to his plans, she and Stella had but little to fear from him. He was a strange mixture of harshness and moderation, and it was never possible to predict with certainty how he would react in any given circumstances. On the whole, Pina felt inclined to place trust in his assertion that as a cattle dealer, he never sold, wittingly, any unhealthy animals, and she could but hope that as far as she and Stella were concerned, his principles would hold true. On the other hand, however, since both she and Stella knew his name and origins, she sometimes felt that when he had received the ransom money he seemed so sure of obtaining, he would have no compunction in throwing the pair of them to the wolves and then shooting them out of hand; the wolves, of course, being Angelo and any of the band who had similar tastes. She knew little about kidnappers and their ways, but even to her, it seemed impossible that any kidnapper who intended to free his victims unharmed would have allowed them such intimate knowledge about himself. Perhaps, she told herself, Fronti was not a professional abductor; perhaps he did mean to free them, and escape the law by disappearing to some place where he could not easily be traced.

Giorgio was completely different from Fronti and Angelo. He had a simple, easy-going nature. His manner was lumbering, not unlike that of a puppy, anxious to please everyone, and this manner extended to Stella and Pina. The latter felt for him almost a warmth, and she was always glad when he was the only one of their gaolers in the cave with them. On the other hand, there was about Angelo a dark brooding malignity that repelled. Pina was certain that if the gang's plans did not work out, she and Stella would be in grave danger; that Angelo would not have the slightest compunction about killing the pair of them after he had had his way with them both. There could, Pina felt, be certain preliminary events before their deaths, very unpleasant in a personal sense, before a merciful, if prolonged and tortured, death intervened.

She racked her brains trying to recall the advice that she had read from time to time in womens' magazines when they were offering tips on what action to take if a sexual attack appeared to be imminent. Such advice did not seem to take cognisance of the intended victim being in some sort of incarceration, and being denied liberty of action. 'Do not resist', most of the articles warned. 'To do so could well inflame an attacker, and so make things worse for you. Scream loud and long - that often has a delaying effect on the would-be rapist.' But there would be little profit in screaming up here! Unless, of course, Fronti was at hand, or maybe Giorgio, but there could be but little certainty of either of them helping in certain circumstances. Then, quite possibly, they might stand idly by as mere spectators, as indeed Angelo had suggested to Giorgio during their conversation only a few days ago.

Pina thought long about what little she knew of self-defence. The quick knee into the groin might deter the rapist, said some authorities, as might also a finger jabbed into the eye. The side of the hand brought sharply into contact with the underside of the nostrils was effective in some cases, she had read. A stiletto heel brought down hard on the instep might work. None of these so-called expert tricks was going to help her a lot, she thought, but certainly she would put up a terrific struggle before Angelo overcame her resistance, of that she was resolved.

Then she would shrug off these black thoughts and try to fix her mind on a future in which Carlo played an important role. She could not envisage exactly what work he did, but she was fully aware that he was not the lawyer he had told her he was. Well, when they were married, she would find out! When they were married! She entered a private world of daydreams concerning that beautiful but rather nebulous future. Her visions served to mask the hideous conditions of her present surroundings and the worries she entertained for Stella and herself.

Once, when there was no one in the cave but themselves, and they were not sure who was on guard outside, she and Stella had tried to creep to the mouth of the tunnel to look out and perhaps glean some idea of the site of their prison. Unfortunately, Stella's crutch had knocked against one of the many loose stones that littered the floor and the noise had brought Fronti storming into the cave before they had covered a couple of metres. He had given them both a severe tongue-lashing, warning them of the direst consequences should they be so ill-advised as to attempt to escape. His diatribe had been punctuated by the waving of his pistol under Pina's nose, and, crest-fallen, they had crept back into the cave, to resume their places before the fire.

At infrequent and irregular intervals, Fronti produced food. Sometimes there would be a rabbit or a hare, which he would throw to Pina with orders to paunch and skin it and prepare some dish from the carcass. She had never tackled this distasteful task before, but somehow, gagging, she would rip off the pelt and disembowel the animal, her face screwed up in an expression of utter disgust, as she prepared it for the pot. Sometimes there would be pasta, coupled with a firm admonition from Fronti to 'cook it properly this time'. The men's comments on her cooking were scathing, and she had difficulty in restraining her tears as they criticised a dish she had cooked for them.

There were times when she was floundering in deep waters with some unfamiliar task, that Giorgio would take pity on her, as he did when a fawn was produced for her to butcher. Stella had wept many tears, too, over the fawn, which had been brought in while the body was still warm. It was Giorgio who showed Pina how to pluck and draw a bird, and how to break free from the monotonous diet of stew which was all she seemed able to cook. He showed her how to impale joints on sticks and set them before the fire to roast after a fashion. Perspiration would stream down her face to mingle with her tears as she endeavoured to get their food ready at the times ordained by Fronti, and the heat would sear her arms and hands. She felt a fellow-feeling for the cave-women of pre-history who had to overcome almost identical conditions to those under which she now laboured, perhaps in this very cave. She often thought that the hour or so before a meal was the worst part of the captivity she had so far experienced.

The meals that she prepared were eaten without benefit of plates or cutlery. Each member of the party would dip into the pot with bare hands, often unwashed, and then tear at the food with his teeth. Juices were scooped up in billycans or mugs, and then the washing-up was simple - the vessels would be held under the freshet in the inner cave until they were approximately clean. On those rare occasions when hands were washed, similar action would be taken, and then the hands were dried by the heat of the fire.

On what Pina judged to be the fourth day of their captivity, Fronti sent Angelo away on some message. He told Giorgio to get on guard, despite the man's protest that he had just completed a long spell of that duty. His appeals were vain; he was over-ruled and grumbling, left the cave. Fronti then told the captives that he was going to town. Pina could glean no information about either the name or the size of the town; he had used the term 'paese', which could mean anything from a whole country to a small village. He told Giorgio that he would return well before nightfall. He then departed, giving the girls a warning look as he left the cave. As soon as he was gone, Giorgio returned to the cave, and sat on his bed of branches, supporting his chin in his hand as he gazed into the depths of the fire.

He was clearly smarting from a sense of great injustice. He sat in silence, and Pina and Stella respected his taciturnity and spoke to each other in whispers. Finally, he said, "Today I will cook! I am sick of your poor attempts to produce good Italian food, so I ask you to watch me carefully and try to learn something!" He went to their larder, the niche in the cave wall where food was stored, and emitted a howl of frustration. "That unmentionable Fronti! He has left us without a mouthful of grub!" He kicked at a stone like a small petulant boy. "Well, I suppose we shall just have to starve until Angelo comes up with a parcel!" Sullenly, he threw himself back on his bed and lapsed into a brooding silence.

Pina judged that an hour passed before he spoke again. "I'm starving! It's no good! Fronti or no Fronti, I've got to eat. I'm a growing lad and I must keep my strength up!" He stalked about like a hungry lion just before feeding time at a zoo. Finally he moved towards the tunnel. "I'm going out. I've got some traps set not too far away. Don't get any funny ideas, because I shall be in sight of the cave all the time. Any move you make would be dangerous for you, anyway. There's only a narrow path and then there's a hundred metres sheer drop. Just be good girls and in a few minutes, I'll be back with some grub!" He slipped away along the tunnel. They listened to his footsteps retreating until silence reigned again.

Pina put her fingers to her lips. Stella nodded to indicate that she understood that she had to be silent as Pina crept along the adit that led to the outside world. Slowly, with infinite caution, she emerged into daylight. Her eyes, accustomed to the dimness she had just left, hurt when the glare of the sunlight struck them. She approached the cave mouth on hands and knees.

As Giorgio had said, the adit led to a narrow path, less than a metre wide. She crawled to the further edge, and looked over. Her head swam. Far below, she could see the tops of some pine trees swaying in the light breeze. Further down the precipice some sort of bush with bright shiny leaves winked and glimmered in the light. Yet further down, she could make out thin plumes of smoke rising from the chimneys of tiny houses, so distant that they looked like dolls' houses in a toy village. It was plain that even if they had the opportunity, she and Stella would never be able to make their way along such a dangerous path which might, or might not, lead to safety and freedom.

She returned to the dimness of the cave, which seemed very dark after that tantalising glimpse of the outside world. She could hardly distinguish the form of Stella as she lay before the fire, now burning very low and in need of refuelling. "It's no good," she gasped. "We'd never be able to make our way along that ledge without guidance! I was dizzy even though I was down on my stomach! To attempt to walk along it would be tantamount to suicide!"

"Could you see much of the countryside?"

Pina described as best she could the view from the ledge.

"I believe that we are in the Gran'Sasso," said Stella. "From what you say, I think this cave is high in the side of either the Corno Grande or the Corno Piccolo. I know such caves exist because Annibale has often spoken about them when he was telling how he had been a partisan and his band of patriots were hiding from the Germans. I think the little town you saw would be either Prato Selva or Prati di Tivo - it might even be Pietracamela. All those places he mentioned when he was telling me about his adventures. I wish he was here now! He would be able to guide us away from this dreadful place!" She sniffed and in the gloom, Pina thought she might be crying.

"We certainly would never get away without help," said Pina. "Whatever happens, I simply dare not walk along that path, and even if you had a head for heights, you could not get along it with your crutches!"

"I know. We shall just have to sit here and wait for Papa to rescue us!"

"I fear so. Pray God we do not have to wait too long!"

"Amen to that," said Stella, crossing herself.

They were silent for a spell. A step in the adit broke the silence. Both looked up, expecting Giorgio. Angelo entered, bearing a sack. He was blinking as he tried to adjust his eyes to the gloom after being so long out in the sunshine. "Where's Giorgio?" he asked.

"He went out on guard. And he said he would try to get some food for us because he was hungry."

"*I* was sent for food. Where's Fronti?"

"He said he had to go to town. That's why Giorgio is in charge."

"Oh." A long pause ensued. "How long since Giorgio went out?"

"A long time, a very long time. He should be just outside the tunnel."

"Well, he ain't! I bet he's gone to look at those precious traps of his. There's nobody on guard here at all!" He looked at Pina with hot eyes. She gazed back, trying to stare him down, but at last her eyes dropped before his bold and lustful gaze. He dropped the sack of food and slowly removed the denim jacket he was wearing, exposing a barrel chest covered in matted coarse black hair, still heaving from the exertions of his climb up the mountain. Pina rose to her feet. Stella edged anxiously away from her, away from the fire to a far corner of the cave. He advanced slowly and deliberately on Pina.

"So! Nobody on guard, and still you decided not to run away! Do I read something into that? Something you would prefer not to put into words? Like, for instance, that you are too interested in one of us strong and lusty Italians? In Giorgio, maybe? No, never in him. He is too young, too callow. Then perhaps in Fronti? No, not him, either. He is too old, too dry, all his sap used up. So then I must be the magnet that detains you, that anchors you to this place!"

"No!" breathed Pina. "No!"

"I say 'Yes'," he corrected her. "That is only reasonable." He moved close to her, his bare chest almost touching her breast. She could smell the hot animal odour of his body mingled with the rank aroma of cheap wine, garlic, and tobacco on his breath. She backed away. He followed. Step for step, they circled the fire. Then his hand shot out and he pulled her roughly towards himself.

Her puny struggles were vain against his enormous strength as he dragged her resisting form nearer. Hungrily his mouth sought hers, finally to clamp his lips on hers in a fierce kiss. She felt the stubble on his cheek rasp over her face. With a superhuman effort, she tore herself free and delivered a stinging blow to his left cheek.

"Ah, a little English tigress, is it? I like my women all the more if they struggle! Then the victory tastes all the sweeter when it comes, as come it must!" He gripped her in a bear hug that threatened to crack her ribs. She was faintly aware of Stella behind her, as hand to mouth she emitted a thin wailing scream.

Pina strove to bring her knee up into his groin, but he was waiting for just such a move and twisted agilely away from the threat. His mouth was still pressed to hers, his questing tongue seeking to force its way between her teeth. She opened her lower jaw slightly and allowed him to enter her mouth. Nausea rose in her throat as she bit hard and tasted hot salt blood. He pulled his face away and gave her a slap on her jaw that almost stunned her. She went limp in his arms as he fumbled with her clothing. Again his bloody lips sought hers as he kissed her. Almost fainting, she managed to pull away from him again, but only slightly. She tried to poke a finger into his eye, but he was holding her too close for the ploy to be successful. Her breath was almost gone. She felt that she was fainting. Behind her, Stella continued to scream.

Under the pressure that he was exerting, Pina sank to the floor. She gave herself up for lost; she no longer possessed any power to resist him. Supine on the hard uneven floor, she made a last convulsive effort to extricate herself from his weight above her. It was in vain. He rolled on top of her once again. His left arm held her securely while his right hand sought that which he so much desired. Once again, she managed to tug herself free, fear lending her a strength she did not know that she possessed. The cave was filled with noise now. Pina's gasping sobs mingled with Angelo's fevered panting, while Stella's thin screams lent a descant to the symphony of rape.

Pina was struggling ever more weakly against the powerful onslaught of Angelo. She felt that very soon now she would have to cease her battling and submit. She made one more gigantic effort to throw off the dead weight of the man now pinning her down, pressing hard on her supine body while his hands sought to do unmentionable things to her. She had almost reached the point of fainting completely away when she heard the voice of Fronti, "What the hell are you at? Let her go, you ape, let her go, I tell you!"

Obsessed, possessed by his lust, Angelo ignored the command, if indeed he heard it at all, and persisted in his attempt to force Pina's submission. Coolly, Fronti drew his pistol from the waistband of his trousers, and holding it by the barrel, awaited the opportunity that would surely come. When the writhing forms on the floor presented him with the chance he sought, he brought the butt of the weapon hard down, just behind Angelo's left ear. The struggle ceased abruptly. Angelo lay unconscious on the rock-strewn floor, breathing heavily. He was on his back, with blood running from his face, where Pina had left a legacy of scratch marks, and also from the back of his head, from his encounter with Fronti's handgun. In the ruddy firelight, he presented a gory sight.

Pina was in little better case. Her face was covered in Angelo's blood. Her skirt had been pulled high above her waist and her underwear pulled down and torn to shreds by Angelo. She sobbed and gasped, as with her ribs bruised and aching from the pressure they had undergone, she dragged herself to her feet. Every fibre of her complaining frame was trembling. As she adjusted her dress, she panted, "Thank you, oh, thank you, Signore Fronti! I had almost lost the fight! You couldn't have made a more timely arrival!"

He gave her a bleak smile. "Please do not delude yourself that I struck Angelo merely to save your honour, my girl. I did it rather to preserve my own honour. I am of Capriotti descent, and therefore a man of principle. I told your friend the senator that on payment of your ransom, both you and his daughter would be restored to him, sound in mind and limb. I like to keep my word. In a way, my sympathy goes to Angelo. I really think that he was winning, and it must be hard to have one's fun interrupted in such a violent manner. But he is strong; he will survive to fight other jousts in the lists of 'amore', aye, and win them, too, I would imagine, from the way in which he was getting the better of you!"

Stella had ceased her hysterical screaming, and had subsided into quiet sobbing. Slowly, Pina recovered herself. Her tortured breathing had returned to a more normal rate. On the floor, Angelo still lay, groaning a little from time to time. Fronti glanced down at him. "He will be quiet for at least an hour; when I hit them, they stay hit! Now, where is that cretino Giorgio?"

Between sobs, Stella said, "He went to see if there was anything in his snares. Then Angelo came in and began to fight Pina. I was scared!" Fronti looked at her quizzically. "Consider yourself fortunate that he didn't pick on you, my lady! Had I been the attacker, I should certainly have gone for the easier target! But then, regrettable as it is, I am past that sort of excitement. At least you are safe from me. Now, mees, you will do me the favour of cleaning yourself up and then set about preparing a meal for us from the stores that your young stallion carried up. Work will be for you a far better therapy than sitting and thinking of what might have been. And when young lord Giorgio returns, you shall have the inestimable pleasure of hearing me deliver a lecture that will make his hair curl!"

Trembling and weary beyond measure, Pina stumbled blindly about as she attempted to obey Fronti's orders. Stella's offers of help were frustrated by him brusquely ordering her to desist - Pina alone was to attend to the meal. When after what seemed to her to be an interminable period, he sat to eat the pasta she had cooked, Pina dragged her aching body to the inner cave and was violently sick. She returned to lay before the fire. Her ribs ached dully. Her face had been badly rasped by Angelo's beard and felt as though it was on fire.

It pained her every time she moved her jaw. Her legs were scratched and still oozing blood from ankle to upper thigh, thanks to the attentions of Angelo and the rocks that littered the floor of the cave. She was weary beyond all bounds. On her rough bedding, she collapsed into a shapeless sobbing heap.

Painfully, Stella crawled to Pina's side. Tenderly she wrapped her governess in the filthy piece of blanket, then, taking the elder woman into her arms, crooned over her until she slept.

TWENTY ONE

Annibale was worried and restless. At nine o'clock that night he had eaten his solitary dinner, and with the meal had finished a whole bottle of Montepulciano, having first ensured that the cost of the wine would go on Carlo's bill. He had followed this with a glass of grappa - well, if he were on oath, with four glasses of the fiery liquid, but even that could not lift his own spirits. Then he had gone back to their room and had meticulously cleaned and oiled his shotgun. That proved to be thirsty work, and he had descended to the small but well-stocked bar in the hall of the pensione, where another three or four glasses of grappa seemed to have but little effect on his worries. Grappa is a powerful potation to those unused to its properties. It is derived from the parts of the grape that are left over after the wine has been made, added to a distillation of the wine itself. Annibale's libations had had no visible effect on his wiry frame.

Inactivity irked him. Time dragged. From his service days, when he had been a corporal of cavalry, he recalled that war (and this *was* war) was ninety per cent boredom and ten per cent violent action, but his patience was out of practice. He had lost the art of resting, unthinking and motionless, awaiting the call to action and the stirring of blood in his veins. At half past eleven, he broke his gun and wrapped it in the piece of canvas which he kept for the purpose. With the package tucked inconspicuously under his arm, he had left the hotel, explaining to the padrona that he could not sleep, which was true, and that he was going for a walk in the cool night air, which was equally true. That good lady, nothing loth to get to her couch at a respectable hour, gave him a key to the front door, saying that as there were no other guests, he could let himself in whenever he decided to return but to be sure he locked up before retiring. Bidding her goodnight, he slipped out into the street, which was dimly lighted by half a dozen widely spaced street lamps which did little beyond enhancing the surrounding darkness.

Nobody was stirring. Here and there a house displayed a lighted window, but most dwellings were in complete darkness. Soon he had left the little community and was strolling easily along the road that led to the higher village of Prati di Tivo. Almost inaudibly he was whistling an old cavalry barrackroom song. He felt and heard the stones on the road crushing beneath his boots. In a manner almost boyish he took to the grass verge, and was happy to discover that his ancient skills in night stalking had not deserted him - he could still creep up on a sentry without the man being remotely aware of his approach, he was certain.

It lacked a few minutes of midnight when he arrived at the culvert. During his silent approach to the rendezvous, the tune that he had been whistling had undergone a subtle change. He smiled wryly to himself. It was hardly the most appropriate ditty for such an occasion as this. Years ago - could it really be almost sixty years past? - his mother was wont to sing as his younger sister gyrated before the fire during the long winter evenings, a little country carol called 'Ma come balli bene, bella bimba!' 'How well you dance, pretty girl!' It was this song he found himself humming now. Well, he was committed now, although the song was so unlikely. Like the peasant he was hoping to represent, he began to talk to himself. "You grow old, lad! You should sing a more manly song than that, lad! However, if it's all that comes to mind, then so be it, and have at it!" He raised his voice and sang the inane words loudly.

The steepness of the slope made him go more slowly. He grew a little breathless, but persevered with his serenade, and was in full voice when he reached the culvert. Pausing here to regain his breath, he seated himself on the low stone wall. The deep silence of the night was broken only by his own breathing. Then between his own deep-drawn breathing, a small sound stole softly through the gloom. It was faint, tenuous, almost inaudible. With a effort, he held his breath and listened intently. There it came again. It was a human, groaning!

He moved swiftly across the road, his breathlessness forgotten. With astonishing agility for a man of his years, he moved up to the place which Carlo had described to him as a possible hide-out. The young man was prone on the grass, and he groaned again even as Annibale neared him. Carlo's head was covered in blood, black in the starlight. Beside him lay his binoculars, also smeared liberally with blood.

Annibale grasped the shoulders of the wounded man and raised him to a sitting position. He moistened his handkerchief with spittle and wiped some of the blood from around Carlo's nostrils. He was able to distinguish that the source of the bleeding was in the head, in the hair. He guessed that the wound had been made by a bullet. He

184

had seen many such wounds before, when he and his comrades had known it as 'creasing'. It could be a painful wound, but was never fatal. In fact, it could best be described as a 'near miss'.

Leaving his shotgun beside the wounded man, Annibale made his way back down the hillside to the road, and then descended into the gully where the stream ran beneath the road. At this season, before the winter rains and snows began, no water ran in the bed of the stream, but here and there were small pools of stagnant stinking semi-liquid mud. He filled his hat with this nauseous mixture and returned to Carlo. He dashed the hatful of mud into the young man's face.

Carlo opened his eyes. He groaned again. "Oh Dio! Wha' happened? Santa Madonna, my skull is splitting!"

"You've been creased, signore. A centimetre lower - no, a millimetre lower - and you would have been killed! A millimetre higher, and the bullet would have missed you altogether! Whoever shot you was either a good marksman or an unlucky one. That is, good if he meant to crease you, and unlucky if he shot to kill!" He took the arm of the wounded man. "Can you rise now?"

Carlo rose shakily, despite the steadying hand of Annibale. After a short pause while he allowed his head to stop swimming, he said, "I think I might manage now. D'you think you can support me back to the hotel, Annibale?"

"No problem. Take it easy as you go down the slope to the road, and then it will be all plane sailing."

With infinite tender patience, the old man assisted Carlo to descend. While he went back for his gun and the binoculars, Carlo sat on the culvert wall. Then they set off on the slow trek to the hotel. The journey took far longer than it had done when Annibale came up and made the rescue, but eventually they arrived and were thankful that the place was in darkness. Neither of them wanted to try to invent an excuse for Carlo's bloodied condition. Annibale gently inserted the key into the lock of the front door and noiselessly opened it. He hung the key on the rack according to the padrona's instructions, and then half carried, half led, Carlo to their room.

Annibale locked the door as a precaution against anyone entering unexpectedly and then set about cleaning up his wounded 'master'. When all the dried blood had been washed from the wound, and Carlo's face and hair were quite clean, Annibale inspected the damaged area with a critical eye. "Nothing much to worry about," he said, cheerfully. "You'll have a scar for the rest of your days, so you'd better consider parting your hair on that side in future, for I assure you that no hair will ever grow there again! But you'll live! Now get your duds off and slip between the sheets. I'll nip down to the bar and get you something to help you to sleep." He left the room and Carlo began shakily to undress.

In a few minutes Annibale returned with a glassful of colourless liquid. "I can recommend this," he said. "I think the lady of the hotel distils her own grappa, and if this doesn't knock you out for the rest of the night, you're past redemption! I advise you to get it down and forget everything for a while." He removed the pillows from his own bed and arranged them round Carlo's shoulders, ignoring the protests from the wounded man. "If you want anything, I'll be in my bed, so just give me a cry. Now, good night."

The wound in his head throbbed and smarted, but the grappa sent a warm glow throughout his body, which had chilled during the time he had lain unconscious in the hollow. But in spite of his fears that sleep would elude him, he fell at first into a fitful doze from which he awoke every time he moved his head. Finally the strong liquor took effect and he went into a deep and restful slumber. His last conscious thought was for Pina. How he hoped that she was not being badly treated by her captors! He tried to send a telepathic message to her, bidding her to be brave. He would come soon to rescue her and Stella, he tried to tell her; of that he was quite certain.

He slept soundly at last, and when he awoke, disturbed by Annibale moving about the room, he was astonished to note that he had slept for eight hours. His mouth felt dry and sour - from the vast amount of grappa that Annibale had prescribed, he guessed. He rose and tottered to the hand basin where he put his mouth under the cold tap and drank deeply. Somehow, the water put strength into him, and he was able to walk more erectly back to the bedside. He took his clothing from the radiator where Annibale had laid it after washing the blood and other stains from it. It was fairly presentable, but he was vexed to see how much his expensive suit had suffered.

Dressing, he gave himself over to thought. It was a pity that he had not been able to catch a glimpse of the men who had picked up the ransom money. Had he been able to get a clear view of only one of them, he might have been able to furnish a description adequate for the Capo to work on, when, as inevitably would be the case, he was called in to continue the investigation. Carlo was certain that he had heard the name Fronti mentioned, and there had been talk of a cave. He would have to talk to Annibale about what he had seen and heard. The old man was nobody's fool; he had a clearer brain than many a man half his age.

The door opened and Annibale's head inserted itself. Seeing Carlo up and about, the rest of Annibale followed his head into the room. "Buon' di, signore! I have just been into the village to see if there was anything about last evening, but it seems that there is no gossiping at all! How do you find yourself?"

"Buon di, Annibale! I have felt better in my time, but then, I might be worse. Could you rustle up a cup of coffee, do you think?"

"Subito, at once, signore!" He left the room while Carlo completed his toilette. Within three minutes he reappeared with a small tray on which reposed a steaming cup of coffee. Carlo took a sip of the scalding beverage. "Dio, I needed that!" He patted the edge of the bed. "Come and sit here, Annibale. I think I can recall most of what occurred last night. And perhaps as I talk, other things will spring to mind."

Annibale took his seat on the bed, and Carlo began his recital. "I saw Don Stefano come up and drop a suitcase in the culvert - that would have been about seven o'clock. There was a long wait after that, until about eleven, or perhaps a little later. Two men then came in a dark coloured Alfa Romeo - I would say it was either black or dark blue. One of them, to judge by his voice, was youngish and I would think the other was rather older. I think he smokes a lot, because he is very hoarse. I looked at them through my glasses, but the light was too poor to see much. But they spoke loudly enough for me to hear almost every word they said. After they had picked up the suitcase, would you believe that they looked into it by the lights of the car? They also read a note that the senator had put in with the cash. The younger man asked if they should take the money up to the cave, or leave it at the Prati. The other said that he would not dare to take only half the cash up there, as Fronti would go berserk. Just then, as I squirmed about trying to get a better view, I managed to dislodge a pebble, and the younger man came up in search of me. I lay doggo, and I'm sure he did not see me. Then a shot was discharged in my direction and all the lights went out! The next thing I knew was that you were chucking filthy water in my face!" He reached out and shook Annibale's hand warmly. "But for you, I might have been up there still!"

"It was nothing, signore! At least your time wasn't wasted. Now we have something to work on. We know that there is a cave, and that Fronti is involved. Now, when the world was a little younger, and I with the world, a little more spry, I was fighting with the partisans. Fronti was also one of our band - a good fighter, but much given to planning and a little reckless. We used to lie up in a cave up above this very village. It was known to us as the Cave of the Black Madonnina. Not many know of the cave nowadays, because it is difficult to get to. You have to travel along a narrow dangerous path, a mere ledge, that creeps across the face of the Corno Piccolo. There is a tiny slit of a fissure that gives access to the cave, but once you get through that, you come to a place as big as the Duomo at Teramo. There is a spring which gives good water, and because of the difficult approach, the place is quite impregnable. Two determined men could hold it against an army! There's no way to attack it from below, and above it, the rock face is vertical for twenty metres! It would make an ideal place to hold anyone captive. Food could be carried along the path just as we used to do thirty years ago. The problem is, if the young ladies are being held there, how are we to free them? I can't, for the life of me, see how we could rush the cave. As I say, it is truly a fortress."

"H'm. You don't hold out a lot of cheer, do you? But in my experience, the place does not exist that cannot be successfully assaulted by a small band of determined men. So, let us go and tell Don Stefano what we have learned so far." He took out his wallet and handed it to Annibale. "Will you go and settle our bill, please? Tell the padrona that I apologise for leaving so precipitately, but my condition does not permit me to stay longer, not even to lunch at her table. Nor am I fit to take personal leave of her. Thank her prettily for her hospitality, and then we can slip out by the back stairs and away."

He walked over to inspect his features in the mirror as Annibale left the room. A chalk white face stared back at him. Above his pinched nostrils, two black eyes were rapidly acquiring a yellow and blue tinge. His hair was parted by the livid scar that the bullet had given him and as he peered more closely at the wound, he could appreciate the truth of Annibale's remark that he had had a very narrow escape from death. His chin was in sore need of the attentions of a razor, and the black stubble of his beard lent him a somewhat piratical look. He decided to forgo the frivolity of a shave for the moment. There would be plenty of time for that later.

Annibale returned with a receipted bill and regrets from the padrona that they would not be sampling the hare that even then was in the oven. Then, with the old man struggling with two suitcases and his shotgun tucked securely under one arm, the duo left the room and made their way down the steep back stairs. Carlo was grateful to his guardian angel that they met nobody as they were making their exit.

Once in the car and on the road, he began to feel stronger. The cool mountain air revived him after the vitiating atmosphere of his room with its central heating. With Annibale beside him cradling the gun between his knees, they began the descent of the valley of the Vomano. Feeling that with every passing minute he was gaining strength, Carlo steered a course for Tre Boschi and Don Stefano.

TWENTY TWO

Don Stefano had returned from depositing the ransom and was in black despair. Passi had found more and more difficulty in raising funds as he began to approach those people on the periphery of the senator's acquaintance, who were less likely to help, or less able to lend any appreciable amount. In addition, so many of his friends were absent from home, having left Italy to escape the rigours of the coming winter, as was their custom. At each abortive attempt of his majordomo, Don Stefano would cry, "Don't these so-called friends understand that it's my only daughter who is being held by these villains? Can't they understand that Stella may suffer unspeakable treatment at the hands of these rogues, if I cannot ransom her? How can people be so unfeeling as to leave Italy when I need their help so much?"

He railed against Carlo. "Why doesn't that fellow return with some news? Any news! God, doesn't he realise what the feelings of a father can be at a time like this? I bet he's carousing around in some sleazy bar! No, that's not fair - his involvement in the affair is almost as great as my own! But why, why does he not come? D'ye think the bandits have smoked him out and executed him?"

The majordomo, not knowing how to answer, took refuge in silence as his master beat upon the desktop with a clenched fist, as though the pain in his hand would in some way make things happen as he wished.

The senator had refused all food. All the cajoling of Elsa would not induce him to eat. A red-eyed Rosa had kept the coffee pot constantly replenished, and he smoked incessantly, lighting one cigarette from the half-consumed butt of the previous one. The office was foul with the stench of stale smoke; not even the open window could clear the air and restore it to its wonted purity. Desk and table were littered with scraps of paper, all covered with calculations or names of those who might be asked to advance the money so urgently required to swell the sum already raised by Passi's efforts.

At noon the telephone had rung, and Don Stefano leapt to answer its summons. But the caller was only the Capo, enquiring if any further information had been received. The senator was tempted to tell the policeman the whole truth, but the threat that he had received in the first message, coupled with the knowledge that di Felippo was working on the case, and was some sort of policeman himself, made him withhold the full facts. There was nothing new, he told the policeman.

At half past one, there was another call. This time it was that well-remembered voice, which, although he had heard it only once before, Don Stefano would never forget.

"You are naughty, Capriotti," the voice chided him. "You didn't obey your instructions, did you? Would you like us to send you one of the young Stella's ears, or would you prefer a finger, to remind you of the plight of your beloved daughter? Would that urge you to work a little faster and in accordance with our orders?"

"No! No!"

"Well, you know how to prevent such a calamity, my dear fellow! But because you have caused us some anxiety and delay in the completion of our plans, we find it necessary to increase the sum we require for your daughter's board and lodging. We therefore have to raise the sum to six hundred million. In our clemency, we will agree that you have passed us a third of the figure we ask, so now you have a mere four hundred million to produce. Otherwise...

"I will give you further instructions on how you are to get the cash to us. In generosity, we shall allow you - shall we say, forty-eight hours from now. Yes, I think that should be enough time for you. Allow me to add that this is your final opportunity! If no cash is forthcoming by our time limit, you will receive information as to where you will be able to find the bodies of the two signorine!"

"But you are bleeding me white! Already I have borrowed more than I shall ever be able to repay!"

The voice was curt, hard. "Your problem, Capriotti, your problem! You have much land. Sell some. You have forty-eight hours and if you are still disobedient after that time, we shall get very cross. And when we get cross, someone has to suffer! Four hundred million, Capriotti, and not a soldo less!" The line went dead.

With a shaking hand, Don Stefano replaced the receiver on its cradle. There was no mistaking the resolution in the tones of the caller; no doubt could be harboured by the most incorrigible optimist. These people were in deadly earnest. Quickly he told the majordomo the gist of the conversation.

Passi shook his head gravely. "It is useless, signore. You cannot possibly raise such a sum in so short a time. No man could. I am sorry to give you so little comfort. We can only hope that the gang will see the folly of such exorbitant demands, as well as the idiocy of their actions, and deliver up the Signorina Stella and the mees without further palaver. We cannot hope for more!"

Don Stefano glared at him with red-rimmed eyes. "These men are without all human feelings! But there's got to be a way! I shall ignore the so-called instructions and go to consult the Capo without further delay! Call Sandro to get the car out to take me to Fortalezza immediately!"

Sandro was shocked at his master's appearance when he took his seat in the car. He had not seen the senator for some hours and now had difficulty in recognising the man for whom he had worked all his life. As he started the engine, his master said, "To the Carabinieri barracks at Fortalezza, and drive as fast as you can!"

Sandro pressed his right foot hard on the pedal, and the car gathered speed, taking bends in the road with great lurchings of the heavy body. When they had completed the descent of the slopes, a long straight flat presented itself. With gritted teeth, Sandro crouched behind the wheel, impelling the car to yet greater speed by rocking his body to and fro on his seat. The straight at last ended, and Sandro was compelled to moderate his speed to negotiate the bends that he knew were approaching. On a short piece of straight between two sharp bends, a small car hurtled towards them from the opposite direction. Recognition was mutual. In the same instant that Sandro became aware of Annibale sitting beside the driver of the smaller car, Carlo noted the driver of the Rolls. Both cars came to a halt with a squeal of brakes. Carlo hurriedly backed to stop beside the senator's car and leapt out to speak to him.

"Tell me your news quickly, di Felippo! I must hasten to the Carabinieri!"

"We believe that we know where the girls are held!"

"What?"

"We think - no, we are sure that we know where the girls are!"

"You are not absolutely certain!" Don Stefano was plainly not too happy with a statement that appeared to hold the least suspicion of doubt.

"Look," urged Carlo, "Turn your car round. Then Sandro can drive my car back to Tre Boschi and Annibale and I will ride with you and tell you all our news."

Much to Sandro's disgust, he was ordered to do as Carlo suggested. Then with Don Stefano at the wheel, the Rolls retraced its tyre marks back along the route which it had just travelled at such breakneck speed. Carlo recounted all that had occurred, and the senator told him all that had happened in the house, including the details of the latest telephone call. By the time these recitals were over, the little convoy had arrived at Tre Boschi. As the trio entered the office, Passi looked up in surprise. "I thought you were going to see the Capo, signore."

"There are fresh developments. Listen to what di Felippo has to report."

Again Carlo told his story. At the conclusion, Passi said, "I agree that it seems very likely that the signorine are being held in the cave of the Black Madonnina. Although you were not overtly one of the partigiani, signore, you well know why that particular cave was chosen by us during the war. It was, simply, because it is quite impossible to attack and laughably easy to defend!"

"You are pessimistic about the chances of rescue," stated, rather than asked, the senator.

"No, signore, realistic would be a better term. For what it is worth, my opinion is that we should now tell the Carabinieri of what we believe to be the facts. They are a military unit, and with their resources could set up an attack that well might result in rescue. I do not believe that a private army such as we could muster would have any hope at all of success. We are not equipped for such a venture, and moreover, none of us is in a fit state of health for such an attempt."

Don Stefano, looking at the floor, said, "True, Luigi. But if we *do* inform the Capo, think how long it will take them, being, as they are, nearly all natives of other regions, to set up an assault! Remember that we have only forty-eight hours. Personally, I want to get up there now, and attack the beasts at this very moment!"

Carlo said, "Gentlemen, we go too fast. Allow me to make the point that we are by no means certain that the girls are being held in this particular cavern. There are undoubtedly many caves up there in the mountains, and they could be in any one of them! All we are doing now is surmising. The first requisite is a reconnaissance of the site to ensure that we do not waste time cracking an empty nut. We have, as Don Stefano says, forty-eight hours, or a little less, to make our play. The great question is, how do we obtain the information we need? Someone must make a search, quietly and secretly. I am the youngest here, and therefore although I am not familiar with the terrain, I volunteer to go up there alone and take a look and see."

Don Stefano looked at him. "You have been wounded, my friend. You are still weak from the ordeal. Additionally, as you say, you do not know the lie of the land. You would be at a grave disadvantage..."

"As far as that goes, I am well-enough rested. I can do it."

Sandro had slipped unobtrusively into the room and was listening to the discussion. Now, almost timidly, he raised his hand, much as he used to do as a schoolboy.

"Well, boy?" The senator's tone was testy. He wanted no time-wasting interruptions from this yokel boy.

"Signore, I am the youngest here by far, and with apologies to the Signor di Felippo, the most nimble. Let me go to find out what you need to know. I know the site of the cave; indeed, I have been to visit it when once I went up to find out if the tales my father told me were true!"

"You are a brave chap, Sandro," said Don Stefano, "but also you are very immature and extremely impetuous. I wonder if you realise that if you are discovered, you may well be killed, and not you alone, but also the signorine."

"I realise it fully, signore. But since I now feel that in some measure, I am responsible, through my boasting, for their predicament, perhaps I could make amends..."

Annibale said, "I think I ought to go. I was a soldier, and I know how to reconnoitre. True, my legs ain't as young as they were, and I can't move as fast as I could thirty years ago. But I will go if Don Stefano prefers me to Sandro, or anyone else."

Passi said, "I feel much the same as Annibale. And since Sandro says he has been up there before, I think that he should be the one to go, if anyone at all goes. Signor di Felippo is perhaps not as strong as he thinks he is, and also admits to ignorance of the terrain. However, I am prepared to go, if my lord so orders."

"Listen, my fiancée is being held up there in a cave! I want to go, and I ought to go!"

Don Stefano stroked his stubbly chin with a waxen hand. "I think, though it goes against the grain, that the boy is right. How do you propose to tackle your reconnaissance, Sandro?"

"There are many tracks along the face of the mountains. All summer long, there are young men walking those trails. I could wear a rucksack and pretend to be one of those."

"But you are well-known to Fronti, and therefore, perhaps to other members of the gang! Suppose you meet face to face?" asked Carlo.

"I hadn't thought of that," confessed Sandro. "Well, then, suppose I just go to Prati di Tivo and prowl about and ask questions?"

"No good," observed Passi. "With your well-known tact and diplomacy, for you to ask a few questions, as you put it, would be tantamount to telling all the world what you are about! Anyway, there isn't time for play-acting! Listen carefully to me, and remember what I am telling you, because your life, and those of the ladies, depend on your memory of these words.

"Go on your moped to the Prati. Leave it in the carpark, and take the seggiovia, the ski-lift. At the top station, go to your right and past the statue of the Black Madonnina. There the path divides. You take the upper one, the left hand one. That track runs about fifty metres above the path that leads to the cave in question. From the upper path, the slope is not so steep that you cannot get down to a point directly over the cave entrance, though there is a drop of some five or six metres anywhere near the adit. The ground between the two paths is well-covered by rocks that afford fair cover - although from below, nobody could possibly see you. If you approach the edge with care, you ought to be able to see if there is any guard below at the entrance to the adit. And if there *is* a guard, it means that there is something there to be guarded - that's axiomatic! However, we shall not even then be certain that whatever is being guarded is that which we seek. Listen carefully, and you may overhear some chitchat from below. After you have found out as much as you can, get back to the upper path carefully without dislodging any stones to give warning of your presence and make your way back here as fast as you can! Always, of course, making sure that you do not kill yourself on that moped of yours!"

Carlo, doodling on a piece of paper, said, "Of course, as Signor Passi says, the only way to be quite certain is for you to see or hear Fronti himself. I doubt if he would so demean himself as to stand guard, but you never can tell with these people. At best, you might hear his name mentioned. And if you do that, then we shall have to accept it as proof that the young ladies are being held in that particular cave, and formulate our plans accordingly."

Sandro stood and bowed to Don Stefano. Not for nothing had he spent so many hours at the cinemas at Ascoli Piceno and Giulianova, watching such great films as 'The Captive of Love'! "May I ask one favour, signore?"

"What is it?"

"That I be allowed to call on my aunts in Bellante on the way out. In case I don't get back, you understand, signor! Today is the day for my customary visit to them."

"That I totally forbid!" cried Carlo.

Don Stefano looked at him curiously. "Why, in heaven's name? I think the boy has every right to make such a request, providing he doesn't waste too much time."

"That, er, that was my very reason, signore! It would be wasting precious time that we cannot spare!"

Annibale intervened. "I think the signor di Felippo is perfectly correct. After the gangsters, time is our greatest enemy!" He winked at Carlo to show that he was supporting the objection although unaware of the reason for imposing the ban.

"Well, you are, I suppose, quite right." To Sandro the senator said, "Now off you go, lad. If your aunts want to know where you are, I will explain that you are away on business for me, and that you will pay them a visit as soon as you return. And if, God forbid, you are hurt on your mission, I will see that the old ladies are told everything and how you died a hero, if that drastic course proves needful!"

"Thank you, signore," said Sandro, and bowing, withdrew.

Don Stefano drew Carlo to one side. "Why were you so vehement about Sandro not visiting his aunts, even momentarily?"

"I have certain reservations about those old biddies. I have a gut feeling that they are somehow mixed up in this affair. Nothing definite, you understand, senator; say, a sort of blind instinct."

"Well, perhaps you know what you are talking about. Personally, I would have said that no more innocent old women ever existed. And they are relations of mine, you know; we share the family name!" He shrugged, and the incident was closed.

Elsa was called into the office and received instructions that Carlo was to be accommodated at Tre Boschi for the next two or three nights. As Don Stefano said, it was better that he be on immediate call if there was to be sudden urgent action. To Carlo, this was quite agreeable. He was pleasantly, though painfully, surprised when Elsa conducted him to what she said was Pina's room. Left alone there, he prowled about touching and looking at Pina's few possessions. Each thing that he touched, everything that he inspected, seemed to be part of the woman he loved and the presence of those articles served to deepen his affection for her. Faint and elusive, her perfume still hung about the room. To lay on the bed that she had so recently occupied was bitter-sweet pain and pleasure combined, and exquisite torture. To use the towels that Pina once had used; to see his face reflected in the mirrors that once showed her dear face - all these combined to steel his determination to rescue her and to ensure that her abductors were put behind bars like the feral animals that they were.

Without undressing, he threw himself on the bed. Everything, for the moment, was in the unsure and unreliable hands of Sandro; Carlo himself could do nothing. He abandoned himself to dreams of Pina. His head still throbbed from his wound. At last, he slept.

TWENTY THREE

Pina was roused from a troubled sleep by Fronti, who was applying the pointed toe of his shoe to her sore ribs. She looked up at him dully. Then, seeing the intense rage on his swarthy face, she came rapidly to full awareness and scrambled to her feet. The man was in a paroxysm of anger, and it seemed that in some way, she was to blame for whatever it was that had occasioned his loss of control.

"Read that!" he screamed, and thrust a paper beneath her nose. "Your precious employer says that he has not enough money to pay your paltry ransom! Would you, would anyone, believe it? Dammit, he's the richest man in the whole damn province! What kind of man can he be, to play such games with us who hold his daughter? Is he too stupid to realise that it is we who hold the whiphand? Or is he so mean that his property takes precedence over his daughter's life? And yours!"

He glared down at Stella, still, where she lay wrapped in the grubby blanket. "Be warned, girl! Your Babbo has forty-eight hours to ensure that you retain both your pretty shell-like ears! If Daddy insists on playing the comedian, then I shall let Angelo have a little fun with his knife! He will enjoy that!"

He snatched the note away from under Pina's eyes. She had been quite unable to read it because his hand was shaking so violently with rage, but from his words, she could easily guess its contents. She judged that those contents did not portend any amelioration of their current living conditions. "In the meantime, mees, get the breakfast made. Fortunately Angelo has made a complete recovery from the attacks you and I made upon his person. He will need sustenance before he undertakes the long walk down the mountain!"

Pina dragged her protesting body into action, and stirred the fire into life. She boiled water in the billycan and made coffee. Bread was put out to be broken by them as they needed it. Then Fronti called to them to come and break their fasts quickly. Time pressed, he told them. They all ate in silence. From time to time, Angelo favoured Pina with a malevolent glare that boded ill for her future relationship with him. Then, their breakfast completed, all three men left the cave.

Stella held out her hands to the comforting blaze. "Do you think he was in earnest when he threatened me?"

"I rather doubt it. You have heard him say many times that he does not deal in damaged goods, and as much as I hate him, I think he speaks the truth as far as that goes. I believe that neither of us stands in much danger from Fronti. I am not so sure... Her voice died away as she relived the experiences she had suffered at the hands of Angelo.

"I think they are all beasts. I thank God that Fronti came in to stop Angelo doing whatever it was that he was doing to you! I was terrified, and I couldn't help you at all! I think you were very brave and strong to fight him as you did."

Pina shuddered. "I was very lucky indeed that Fronti came in just then. My strength was almost gone!"

"Are you very sore, Pinina?"

"My legs are badly scratched, and my ribs hurt where Angelo held me so very tightly. Fronti did not make my chest any more comfortable when he kicked me awake just now. But on the whole, it's not too bad. Fortunately, I heal quickly. By tomorrow I expect I shall be as good as new. Now, as we are all alone, shall we do a little English? A lesson will take our minds off our plight, perhaps, and will help to pass the time."

Stella pouted, but obediently moved nearer to Pina. She seated herself and took the younger girl into her arms. Her heart was touched by the feel of the almost fleshless shoulders under the thin dress. Poor kid, she thought. Her life had been hard enough since her accident; she did not need this extra ordeal. If they came out of this alive, she vowed, Stella would never again want a friend while she lived! Captivity had brought them very close indeed.

Giorgio was making faint sounds at the end of the adit, Fronti's lecture had had its effect, and Giorgio was not going to roam far from his post today. He gave continual notice of his presence by a tuneless whistling that carried no melody that Pina could distinguish.

He came into the cave. "It is almost noon. Would you care to eat, signorina? I could prepare for you a recipe used often by mother. She lives in Val Castellana, whose women are famous for their cooking. She has a marvellous way of doing rabbit. Yesterday, I caught a rabbit, which went uneaten because of all the trouble I was in with Fronti!"

"You are very kind, Giorgio, but really I do not feel well enough to eat just now. But you go ahead," said Pina.

"I will." From the food recess he produced a large rabbit which he dextrously skinned and jointed. He stuffed the carcass with herbs, and dusted some of the same herbs over the legs of the rabbit. "These herbs grow wild in my village. I gathered some and put them in my pack for just such an occasion as this!" he told them.

From the firewood he selected a thick stick which he sharpened at one end. He impaled the stuffed carcass on it and then propped the stick on some stones before the fire. Now and again he turned the stick to present a fresh part of the rabbit to the flames, and soon a delicious fragrance began to steal through the cave. Despite themselves, the girls drooled at their mouths. It seemed ages since anything so savoury had assailed their nostrils. Pina's efforts in the kitchen left much to be desired!

In half an hour, Giorgio declared himself satisfied with the cookery. "It's done," he assured them. "Are you sure that you won't join me? The food will keep up your strength, and you must admit that up to now the menu hasn't been really of three-star quality! Aw, come on, be friendly! I hate to eat alone. It may be long before you get another chance of decent grub."

Stella clutched at Pina. "May I?" she breathed.

"Why not? After all, he seems to be the best one, and I am quite sure that he means us no harm. Yes, we will join him!" In Italian, she said, "Thank you. We accept your invitation!"

Grinning with pleasure, he tore the body of the rabbit into handily-sized pieces. "I apologise for the lack of fine linen on a table, and silver plates and that. But to relish the meat properly, you have to eat it anyway in the manner which my folks eat it - that is, with your hands. And if those hands are a little dirty, what of it? It will add savour to the meat!" He passed a hind leg to Stella, while Pina was presented with a thick lump of the back. In perfect accord the trio sat before the fire, chatting about inconsequentialities as they ate, for all the world as if they were the best and closest of friends.

When nothing was left of the rabbit but the bones, clean-picked, and a still appetising aroma, Giorgio produced from his pocket a piece of newspaper which he tossed to Stella. "Here you are, wipe your fingers on that!" He threw the debris of their meal on to the fire where it flared up in a crackling of brittle bones and fat. Stella passed the paper to Pina. She was just about to use it when she spotted the print. Hastily she tucked the paper into her bodice.

Giorgio said, "There! Thank you for your company at my meal.
We must do it again sometime! Now I must get outside and be a
conscientious guard like Fronti wants me to be! You won't tell him
about this feast. will you?" He rose and left the cave.

His footsteps died away and Pina produced the piece of newspaper
that she had concealed. By the firelight she was able to read through
the grease deposited by Stella, guessing at any words that were totally
illegible.

'There is as yet no news of the two missing women, one the
daughter of the Senatore Don Stefano Capriotti and the other her
English governess, who have been missing from their home at Tre
Boschi for five days now. It is understood by our reporter that the
carabinieri, under their gallant leader, the capitano Bianchi, have a
very strong clue which they believe will lead them to the unfortunate
duo within hours rather than days!' Pina did not read aloud any more
of the report, which proceeded to give masses of detail, mostly
invented, about Pina's history before she arrived at Tre Boschi, and
concluded with the observation, 'Without doubt, if the women have
indeed been kidnapped, the miscreants may even now be regretting
their choice of victims. Common report has it that the Signorina
Corrigan is an accomplished user and exponent of the art of kung-fu,
which will enable her to give a very good account of herself in a
rough and tumble!... The inhabitants of the whole region feel sorrow
and pity in their hearts for Don Stefano, who is a popular and well-
known representative for them in the Senate, and everyone is
determined and confident that under the relentless leadership of the
Capo of Carabinieri at Fortalezza, the missing pair will speedily be
brought out of their durance, if indeed they have been abducted, and
restored to the bosoms of their worried families. Capitano Leonardo
Bianchi is well-known to all our readers since it was he who...!' and
here followed a long and wordy encomium about the valorous Capo.

With the naiveté of the young, Stella seemed to be convinced that
all was going well, and that the police were hot on Fronti's trail. For
her part, Pina had to smile wryly at the report. She thought that
Bianchi, like so many of his kind, was simply trying to keep the press
quiet and himself in the public eye. She would rather trust in Carlo,
who, she was firmly convinced, was straining every nerve to discover
their hiding place.

She tossed the screwed-up paper on to the fire and watched it flare up and disappear. Perhaps it was wrong of her to have told Stella as much as she had done. Such reports could only serve to build up hopes in the mind of the child - hopes that could be foredoomed to disappointment. In a sudden access of affection, she seized the child and hugged her tightly. Fiercely she resolved that she would do all in her power to preserve this mite from harm, and to bring about their release. She had to admit, however, that if pressed on either of these points, she would have had great difficulty in describing exactly how she would achieve either part of her resolution. Wrapped in each other's arms, they sat and gazed into the fire, as though in its depths lay release, waiting only to be seized.

TWENTY FOUR

Sandro had pushed the tiny noisy engine of the moped to its limit. He had arrived at Prati di Tivo in record time. Hastily he stood the overheated machine in the carpark and hastened to the ticket office, where the woman who was in charge there tried hard to dissuade him from going up the mountain at such a late hour. Her frugal mind was shocked that anyone should be so foolish as to waste good money on what would be, in her opinion, only a rapid ascent and immediate descent, with no time to see anything in the area of the upper station, not even the sunset. She underlined her opposition to his will by reminding him that should he be compelled to make his descent in darkness, it would be on foot, and he would be in great peril - the path was ill-defined and beset with all sorts of traps into which the unwary or the ignorant could fall. He brushed aside all her objections. He was an artist, he told her, and it was of the greatest importance that he should see the sun descending behind Monte Gorzano. He had been commissioned to make a picture of that particular scene, and simply must have it, or he would be put to immense pecuniary loss. It was for him to decide whether he would risk descending by the path, and he was not to be swayed by any argument that she could produce to the contrary. As she took his cash, the woman tapped her head muttering, "Pazzo, pazzo - he is mad, mad!"

In a fever of impatience, Sandro leapt on the exiguous seat as it came swaying towards him where he stood in the centre of the blue circle that denoted the boarding point. He felt the satisfying thump of the hard edge of the wood as it contacted the back of his thighs. With trembling fingers he lowered the safety bar across his lap and was wafted away, swaying as he dangled from the thin cable above him. Each gantry seemed to approach him with agonising slowness. After what seemed to him to be an eternity - he was unaccustomed to the ways of the seggiovia, and in spite of his outward appearance of serenity, his heart was beating wildly - the upper station loomed before him. He lifted the safety bar with an audible sigh of relief and catapulted himself into the arms of the waiting attendant. Before him, the machinery creaked and groaned as it performed its ceaseless round. Handing his ticket to the man, Sandro accepted the warning that he had but a quarter of an hour before the last descent was made and the machinery stilled for the night hours.

He dismissed this information with a nonchalant wave of his grimy hand. If by some mischance he was not present when it was time to hush the noise of the great wheel that drove the cable, why, he would walk down! He knew what he was about, he informed the attendant. With that, he left the station and walked up the rough path that led to the shrine of the Black Madonnina. He stood before the statue in an attitude of prayer while the attendant disappeared into the little café which catered for the needs of travellers who made the journey up or down at more reasonable hours. Once he was quite satisfied that the man had no further interest in him, he vaulted lightly over the rickety handrail that assisted weaker folk in their trek up to the shrine, and made his way along the path that led to the west.

The red disc of the sun dipped below the shoulder of Monte Gorzano. Shadows mounted rapidly up the side of the mountains while to the east a thin crescent moon rose timidly over the seaward horizon. There was light enough for him to pick his way along the rough path without the need of other illumination. For this mercy, Sandro breathed a quiet prayer of thanks to his patron saint. After about twenty minutes of marching, none too easy at times, the path split at a Y-junction. The main way led straight on, and from his previous visit, Sandro was aware that that way led to the cave entrance. The smaller track led on yet higher up the face of the mountain. He knew, again from his earlier visit, that this path ran parallel to the main track and about fifty metres above it.

Beneath his feet the stones slipped and rolled. He congratulated himself on having the forethought to wear his heavy rubber-soled track shoes. Nearing the spot where he thought he might be exactly above the cave entrance, he increased his caution. Every step was felt carefully before he entrusted his full weight to his leading foot. How lucky he was, he thought, to have noted so carefully how film stars proceeded in the same conditions. Money paid over to the Ariston Cinema in Giulianova was well spent! Unfortunately this method of progression slowed him considerably and a walk that should have occupied a mere fifteen minutes took him over an hour to accomplish. He was pleased that he had met no person on the path. The only people, in fact, whom he might have encountered were the kidnappers themselves, from whom he could expect but short shrift.

He now left the path, turning to his right and moving gingerly over the ever more steep slope. The surface was covered in loose scree, and his every step seemed to create a small avalanche. With infinite caution he crept downwards, holding his breath at each slight movement of a pebble. His luck held, however, and no serious dislodgement occurred to betray his presence. At last he arrived at a sheer drop of five or six metres. Lying on his stomach, he peered over the edge. He was annoyed to see that he had not yet come far enough along the track. He lay still on the loose surface debating whether it would be better to get back on the path or try to make his way along the edge of the cliff. He decided that the upper track was the better course, and so crawled up to regain the track once more.

After a further ten minutes of careful progress, he began a fresh descent over the scree. A couple of metres before he reached the edge, he froze. Panic swept over him in waves and nausea rose into his throat. The sound of a cough came to his ears, and the evening air was tainted by the reek of a cheap cigarette. Conquering his revulsion at the task he had imposed upon himself, Sandro slowly wriggled towards the cliff edge once more. Not in vain had he watched Red Indians creeping up on unsuspecting palefaces!

At the very edge of the declivity he came to rest. Far below, he could see the lights of a small town, which he judged correctly to be Fano Adriano. Nearer, a thick screen of pines, black in the dimness, crept up the mountainside, to give up the struggle eventually when they attained the beginning of the hard unyielding rock face. For a good hundred metres above the treeline, the rock face was completely bare of any type of growth, and was also almost vertical, so that he could not see the first forty metres or so of the descent. Certainly such an approach forbade any frontal assault on the cave! The path by the cave entrance was narrow, barely a metre wide. Sandro thought that the partigiani of old had chosen well, considering their lack of knowledge to be gained without benefit of cinema effects. Not even he, the great Sandro, could have selected a better place.

Almost immediately below him he could see the figure of a man, presumably on guard. It was this man who was smoking the cigarette, and who coughed. From above, in the little daylight that remained, the man's features were not discernible. Even if Sandro had known him, he would have been quite unable to recognise him. Quivering with an exciting mixture of fear and elation, Sandro remained still and pondered the situation. The mere fact of a man standing outside a cave and smoking a Nazionale cigarette proved nothing, he told himself. The chap could easily be a path walker who intended to pass the night in the cave because it was now almost too dangerous to proceed further along the path. There was nothing to prove that the fellow was doing anything in the least nefarious. Of course, Sandro was suspicious, but his native cunning told him that suspicions were insufficient - proof was needed. At the same time, however, he felt that he ought not to stay too long in that perilous spot. He was in full view of anyone who might walk along the upper and safer path, even though from below he was completely invisible. Things were getting complicated, and Sandro was beginning to feel at a loss as to what to do next.

A glance at the Carro di Bööte (The Plough) revealed that he had been away from Tre Boschi far too long already, but he was reluctant to leave with the meagre facts he had so far gleaned. More, much more, was needed, but how was he to obtain more? People at Tre Boschi were waiting impatiently for information, but really he had not found out anything except that a man was smoking a cigarette on a narrow ledge outside the cave. He lay in motionless silence while he devoted himself to an unaccustomed exercise - thinking!

His dilemma was resolved by the sound of footsteps coming from his left, the westward side of the cave. Two men loomed out of the shadows. One of them called, "All well, Giorgio?" and with a shock Sandro thought he could recognise zio Matteo's voice. But reason informed him that this could not possibly be true; zio Matteo was away on one of his cattle dealing trips. But all doubt died when the guard replied, "All well, Fronti!"

The second arrival, speaking in dialect, asked, "Have you had a go at the mees, Giorgio?" and Sandro heard the other's indignant denial as he retorted that he was no rapist. The second man snorted, "You waste time, Giorgio! Had I been left alone with them all these hours, I'd have had another go at her. She owes me a little pleasure for what happened last time! In fact, I reckon I'd have had a go at both of them, even if one is a cripple. Come to think of it, I've never had a cripple yet. Now, that would be a novel experience!" All three men passed into the cave.

Sandro shuddered as the full import of the words penetrated his slow mind. With limitless care he began his withdrawal up the slope, remaining on his stomach, rather unnecessarily, until he had gained the comparative safety of the path. Once he could feel the worn surface beneath his hands, he stood for a moment, deep in thought. Then, heedless of any noise he might make, he ran along the path, believing that he was now safe from all possibility of discovery. He met nobody until he reached the ski-lift station, where he was gruffly informed that the machinery was shut down for the night, and would recommence operations tomorrow at eight o'clock. If the gentleman so wished, he could partake of the hospitality and shelter of the hut wherein the attendant planned to pass the night, Sandro made an obscene gesture, which happily the attendant could not see, and replied that he was going to make the descent on foot. The man told him that he was foolish, but wished him well none the less.

It was an agonising journey. Rocks, some of them as big as a house, blocked the trail and compelled him to make long detours. A cold stream babbled noisily across the track and in the dark beneath the shrub, he more than once tripped and measured his length in the bitterly cold water. At each detour he was forced to make his way back to the line of the ropeway that swayed above in the dim light, for only by this navigation could he be certain that he was moving in the right direction. It was a desperately uncomfortable, unhappy, cold Sandro who after an hour of struggle eventually gained the carpark and found his moped. His hands were shaking and his teeth chattering as he unlocked the safety chain and started the engine. He sped off down the hill, hugging to himself the knowledge that he, and nobody else other than the kidnappers, knew the whereabouts of the signorina Stella and the mees. Surely Don Stefano would reward him well for all that he had suffered this night! What was the phrase? 'Above and beyond the call of duty!' That was it. Were medals awarded by the Government in Roma for such devotion to a cause? And maybe, even, Don Stefano would award him the hand of Stella in marriage! Such thoughts kept him warm as he sped through the night air at breakneck speed, his trouser legs clinging clammily to his legs in he night air.

TWENTY FIVE

It was just after four in the morning when a frozen Sandro rode along the drive to Tre Boschi. The young moon had long since descended. To the east a faint green glow heralded the dawn. He felt as though he were the only person on earth still alive - some cataclysm had wiped out the whole of humanity save himself. That illusion was dispelled when he saw that every light in the house was burning brightly.

He did not stay to prop the moped on its stand, but dropped it on the gravel, where it lay leaking fuel and emitting a series of creaks as the overheated engine cooled. The front door of the house, as was customary, was not locked, and Sandro flung it open and ran along the corridor to the office. He entered without the formality of knocking. Passi was seated in his usual place behind his desk, but this time his head was cradled in his arms and he was sleeping soundly. In a large and commodious armchair, Don Stefano slept, his legs extended and hands clasped across his stomach. His head was thrown back and his mouth was half-open as he emitted a sound half grunt, half snore, with every breath. His beard showed blue against the pallor of his jaw. In no way did he resemble the well-groomed gentleman whom Sandro was used to driving around the countryside in an expensive car. Sandro thought that he looked very old; older even than his father, who was at least ten years older than the senator and had raised ten children as well.

The boy's entrance, unceremonious as it was, had failed to waken the sleepers. He stood by the door, uncertain what to do next. Then, greatly daring, he tiptoed to his master's side and gently shook him by the shoulder. Don Stefano awoke with a start. He rubbed red-rimmed eyes with the back of his hand, and peered up at Sandro.

"What brings you here, boy?" Then with full wakefulness came recollection. He leapt from his chair, knocking over the tall ashtray which stood beside him. The noise roused Passi. He too sat up and rubbed his eyes. "What news, boy?" demanded Don Stefano.

"I think I have - no, I *know* I have - found the hideout, signore! As I had suggested, the signorine are being held in the cave of the partisans up there in the Corno Piccolo. I saw three men. One of them was my zio Matteo Fronti, the cattle dealer. He hasn't been around for a few days, and we all thought that he was away on a dealing trip as he so often is. There was a young chap who seemed to be a sentry or guard. His name is Giorgio. The name of the third man was not mentioned. They all spoke in dialect, so they must be local men - I mean, the other two must be, because naturally zio Matteo is local, isn't he? Just as I am." At his master's impatient gesture, he continued, "I heard them mention two people - they were the mees and the cripple, begging your pardon, signore!" He made a quick bob in Don Stefano's direction as if to apologise for the brutal description of Stella. For a brief moment he pondered the advisability of reporting the whole of the conversation he had overheard. Equally quickly he decided that it might be kinder to forget that the third man had said that he had never had a cripple. Such information could do nothing but add to the senator's worries.

Passi had heard the report in silence. He now said, "I will have Signor di Felippo called. We had better have Annibale here too; he might be able to contribute something useful." He seized the bell pull and gave it a couple of hard jerks. Elsa must have been expecting such a summons for she was very quickly in the office, her night-clothes covered by a dressing gown and her feet bare. Sandro had never before seen her so attired; hitherto she had always been the cool efficient housekeeper, clad in grey livery. He thought she looked rather pretty, and decided it might be interesting to get to know her a whole lot better when all this to-do was behind them and life had reverted to normality. In obedience to Passi's commands, she rushed from the office to rouse Carlo while the majordomo stamped hard on the floor to waken Annibale. After a very short delay, the pair of them arrived in the office almost together, closely followed by Elsa bearing a steaming container of coffee.

"Now," said Don Stefano, when all were seated and sipping coffee. "Repeat all that you have told me, Sandro!"

Nothing loth at being the centre of attention, Sandro repeated his tale. At the end of his recital, and after a series of questions which he answered with commendable patience, since it seemed to him that they were making him go over ground he had already covered at least twice, there was silence while the little party waited for Don Stefano to address them. At last he said, "Now, di Felippo, advise me. You seem to know something about this sort of work and how to go about it. Shall I inform the Capo?"

"I think not. If you do, he will want to raise a small army to attack the cave. To do that, he would have to obtain authority from higher command. If I know the men we are dealing with, the kidnappers, I mean, they will have someone planted in the Capo's office who would lose no time in passing all such information to the bandits. They would then be quick to remove the girls to another hiding-place and we would be back to square one, with the added disability of the gang being aware that the Capo has been informed, which might lead them to carry out their threat to harm the captives."

Annibale said, "We know that the cave is to all intents and purposes impregnable. Only one man at a time can approach it from either side. Above and below it is guarded by a vertical slope which would make a mountain goat dizzy. If the bandits are armed, they could pick off, one by one, any person who came near them. Even if they are not armed, it would be extremely difficult to get anywhere near the cave, anyway." He nibbled at his nails as an aid to thought. The others remained silent in deference to his professional knowledge.

"There is," he said, "one faint chance that we might be able to storm the cave. It's a very slight chance, and a very dangerous task; more so, if the kidnappers are armed. Someone would have to go where Sandro was last night. Somehow, he would have to make his presence known and distract the attention of the scellerati while the rest of the party moved quickly along the path. It's perilous, but it is our only chance."

"Can you enlarge upon your plan?" asked the senator.

"We would have to split into two parties - three, if you count the person above the cave as a party. One party would approach the cave from the eastern side, the other from the west. I think, if he's willing, Sandro should be the decoy above the cave. He should be safe enough; it's difficult to hit a target above you, as any soldier knows, and I do not believe for one moment that our opponents will be good enough sharpshooters to pick him off. They might not even see him. I think he could perhaps throw rocks over the cliff edge, and while the gang is engaged with the attack from above, the other two parties could rush in. It wouldn't be easy - the path is only a metre or so wide at best."

"You say," said Don Stefano, "that even if the gang have no arms, it would still be dangerous. I don't follow that at all."

"I did not mean dangerous for the attackers, signore. I meant

210

dangerous for the captives. If the gang think that they are liable to be overcome, I fear that they might throw the signorine over the edge to their deaths. That is a powerful card, which they could well play as a last resort."

"Do you then think that there is the slightest chance of success? It would be dreadful if the gang grew so desperate that they would resort to such ploys!"

"Who can tell? But I can see no other way by which this projected attack can come to a successful conclusion!"

"It is a dreadful dilemma. We shall have to 'play it by ear'," said the senator.

"I think we have no alternative," replied Annibale. "It is the only plan I can work out. I thought of it while I was with the partisans, and we discussed it frequently, and that was the final answer any of us could come up with. Distractions from above and an onrush from each side simultaneously."

The senator sighed. "What must be, must be!" He turned to Sandro. "Would you be willing Sandro? I mean, perhaps to risk your life to save your young mistress?"

Sandro nodded. Already he had cast himself in the role of hero, daring all for his beloved mistress, who depended solely on him for her rescue. A parallel case had happened in the film he had seen only last month in Teramo. The heroine, held captive by a merciless gang, had gone through all sorts of suffering, admittedly without disturbing her coiffure, and with an hourly change of dress, before the hero had single-handedly foiled the machinations of the gang and had brought off a most unexpected and ingenious rescue. Her father had been so grateful and so amazed at the hero's resource and intrepidity that without bothering to ascertain his daughter's feelings on the subject, had without further ado married her to her rescuer. Sandro, seeing before him a dazzling future since Don Stefano had no son, drew himself up proudly. "I will play that part!" Much to his disappointment, Don Stefano did not seize his hand and cover it with kisses. Indeed, he seemed to think that no less could be expected of Sandro anyway. The talk in the office now reverted to tactics.

Carlo was all afire to get at the kidnappers and release Pina and Stella, but aware of the need for careful planning, managed to restrain his impatience. "I take it that since he knows the terrain better than any of us, Annibale will be in command?"

"I agree. Have you any further comments, Annibale?" asked Don Stefano.

"It will not be politic to rush matters. We should all go up the mountain by seggiovia; one party from Prati di Tivo and the other from Prato Selva. I think that the senator and Luigi should start from Prato Selva two hours before the rest of us. They have the longer distance to traverse. They have about two kilometres to walk to the last bend in the path before the cave entrance. Sandro should start an hour later, so that he can be in position where he was last night, by the time Signor di Felippo and I arrive at the bend on our side of the cave. It is now almost six o'clock. It will take two hours to get to Prati di Tivo or Prato Selva, then half an hour, a generous allowance, to arrive at the upper stations of the ropeways. Another hour, or let us, to be on the safe side, say an hour and a half should see all of us in position. If we depart from here at nine, we should all be in position by about one in the afternoon. That is good, because then the sun will be casting shadows on the track, and will be shining directly into the eyes of anyone looking upwards to where Sandro will be. So! We go into action at fourteen hundred hours! Gentlemen, will you please synchronise your watches."

Sandro's hand shot up. "Well, Sandro?" asked Annibale.

"I ain't got a watch!"

"I will lend you mine," said Don Stefano, removing from his wrist the expensive gold watch with its matching bracelet. He passed the watch to Sandro, who spent the rest of the conference in stealing surreptitious glances at his thick peasant's wrist adorned by the inappropriate ornament which represented more money than he had ever seen.

Watches were synchronised, and Annibale went on, "The signal for our assault to commence will be a shot from my gun. Let us hope that any shot heard by the bandits will be attributed by them to a hunter in the area." He fixed Sandro with a steely look. "You, young fellow, will be extremely careful that you make no move that might give us away before my signal. You will remember at all times that you are a key figure in this operation, and if you make a dog's breakfast of it, you could be the cause of every one of us getting killed and the whole exercise failing!" He looked round at the others. "Any questions, gentlemen?"

Like Carlo, Don Stefano was irked that having made a plan of action, they should have to wait to put it into operation, but was able to see the wisdom and sense of Annibale's timings. "As it is still early," he said, "would it not be as well if we all got some rest before we set out?"

"I agree, signore," replied Annibale. "Sandro especially needs rest after his busy night. He can use my cell where I shall be able to keep an eye on him! Let us all meet here at eight forty five. We shall not need to carry rations; if all goes well, we shall be home again in ample time to feast, and if it goes against us, none of us will be in fit condition to eat! But perhaps a little coffee and a crust of bread might be welcome before we set out. May Elsa have orders to that effect?"

"Will do!" said Passi laconically, and the party split up, Annibale, determined that Sandro should not leave his sight, shepherding the boy from the room. Carlo returned to Pina's room. He lay on the bed, and gazed about him, fixing every little detail in his mind, and trying to form an idea of what it might look like when, please God, Pina was again occupying it. Then he rose and began to check and recheck his pistol. In the courtyard below, he could see Annibale engaged on similar work. In the cell, Sandro was sleeping soundly - very soundly indeed. Carlo had never heard so young a man make so much noise while sleeping!

Things were going to happen now and he, Carlo, was going to play a leading role in ensuring that those things happened as he wanted them to happen! He just hoped that Sandro would not make a hash of things. He almost whistled as he worked on the vicious little automatic.

TWENTY SIX

Stella had developed a cold. She was hot and flushed; a harsh cough racked her frame with an intensity that seemed capable of rending apart the thin little chest. Pina was concerned about her condition and complained to Fronti that she could become very ill indeed if medical attention was not soon forthcoming.

Fronti ridiculed her request for professional attention. "You are being naive. Whoever heard of people like us calling in doctors to attend to their guests? You really are too silly for words, mees. What we *will* do is to get some medicines from the little grocery store in the village. Then the girl can take those and hope for the best. It was my intention to move from here in the morning. However, my plans are fairly flexible and a delay of one day will make but little difference to the general scheme of things. But as we have really been too long in this cave, for it is known to very many people from the past, then whatever her condition we will move the day after tomorrow. Giorgio shall go to the village tomorrow as early as possible and shall buy a bottle of linctus. Then you may play at being a nurse. But as for calling in a doctor - don't make me laugh!" He turned on his heel and stalked out of the cave.

Stella lay before the fire, wrapped in the filthy piece of blanket that Giorgio had tossed to her when they first arrived in the cave. How long ago was that? Pina had no way of telling how time had passed. They might have been prisoners ten days, maybe even longer. It seemed like a lifetime since Fronti had met them at La Poltrona. Their general filthiness did not, could not, aid Stella's recovery. The main trouble was the damp chill of the cave. Never could the fire, no matter how well and often it was refuelled, warm the place to a bearable temperature. They roasted in front as they froze behind. It was small wonder that Stella had succumbed to this infection with its accompanying hacking cough. Pina put up a prayer to Sant'Antonio that the trouble would not worsen and turn into pneumonia.

The child stirred restlessly and whimpered every time she moved. "I'm so terribly sore. Every time I cough, it hurts here." She indicated the lower part of her chest towards the back. Pina warmed her hand at the fire and slipped it gently under the girl's dress to massage the part. The ribs stood out like laths from the poorly-

214

fleshed frame.

Giorgio, displayed much concern about Stella's condition. "When I was a boy, my Mama used to rub me with goose fat," he told Pina. "Pity we don't have any of that up here! You could try rabbit fat; it would be better than nothing. I'll see if I can get down to the shops today if Fronti will let me go. There's still time before the shops shut."

"What time is it, then?" asked Pina.

"What! Don't you know how the time goes? It's just about noon."

"How could we know about time? Here in the cave we can't tell night from day! Even if we were wearing watches, we could not read them."

"That's true. I never thought of things like that!"

As he appeared to be in a communicative mood, Pina asked, "How long have we been prisoners?"

"Let me see. Today is Thursday - no, it isn't, it's Friday. You came up on Saturday evening, so you see it's not all that long - a mere six days. There was that young German mees who was held in Sardinia for nearly a year. It takes time to get ransoms and things organised, you know, but I would think you ought not to be our guests for more than another month or two. Fronti is a very good business man, and he wants to get this all over and paid up as soon as possible."

Pina's heart sank as she heard this estimate. She was quite sure that Stella could not endure such a long captivity in these spartan conditions. She continued with her massaging of the child's chest, feeling that though it might be ineffective, it showed that someone cared for her.

Fronti returned to the cave. "I've made a signal to our friends below. You'd better get down there right away. Tell them we cannot move for another forty eight hours because of this brat's trouble, but then, no matter what her state of health, we shall move to the hut. They can start getting fuel and food there as soon as they like. And while you're down there, get something for the kid's cough - goose fat, linctus, anything that they stock in the alimentari. Don't give any secrets away; just use that minuscule atom of grey matter the good God handed you when you were born. I'd go myself if that damn track wasn't so difficult for my old legs. You can get down and back again before I can reach the end of the path." As Giorgio began to prepare himself in a leisurely manner, Fronti snarled, "And HURRY!!" The younger man ran out of the cave - he had a wholesome respect for his leader.

"Make up the fire!" he commanded Pina as he sat on some fir branches opposite Stella. As Pina rose to obey, he added, "And for God's sake stop that coughing. You'd drive a man mad! Cough, cough, cough, all day and all night! He subsided into near silence as Pina threw an armful of fuel on the fire, grumbling to himself about children who kept their elders and betters awake all night. He held out his hands to the blaze as the wood flared up. "It's enough to freeze a man to death out there," he told Pina. "All the same, I think I prefer it there. At least I don't have to listen to her hacking away like that. Shut UP!" he yelled at Stella, who cringed, holding her hand before her mouth in a vain effort to muffle the coughing fit that was assailing her.

Angelo came into the area lighted by the blaze. He gave Pina a leer and a ponderous wink. She shuddered. She hoped that Fronti's control over the man was strong enough to keep him in check. "Dio, it's cold out there!"

Fronti stared up at him. "Don't I know it! Haven't I been out there half the night, protecting these innocents from ravening beasts like bears and rats and people who would try to take them away from us by force. STOP COUGHING!!" he screamed at Stella. "What are you doing in here? You're supposed to be on guard."

"There's a party of walkers coming along from the west. What do I do?"

"You walk along to meet them. You tell them that there's been a frana - a landslide - further to the east. You are one of the working party trying to restore the path. You turn the walkers back and get them to use the upper path, and you go with them to ensure that that is just what they do. You will be very polite, but very firm, and extremely concerned for their welfare. But whatever happens, they are not to be allowed to get near the entrance to this happy home."

Angelo went out, repeating to himself the instructions he had received. Fronti, his eyes gleaming redly, said, "I rather feared that we might have some walkers coming this way. If too many come - and they may, because this is the weekend, after all - if too many appear, I say, then we shall move this night, no matter how bad that brat is. Get as much rest as you can. When we move, our departure will be hurried. There is far to go and you will have to walk every centimetre of it. At least you will not have a lot of luggage to pack and carry!" He grinned sardonically at his little joke.

After a while, Angelo returned. "I turned them off - they went like lambs. I told them just what you said. Only trouble is, they may look over the edge and then they'll see it was all a pack of lies! They said if they met any other walkers they would tell them about the frana. It's getting a bit late in the season; maybe we shan't have any more walkers."

"Let's hope so," grunted Fronti. "Get back to your post, and if any more interlopers come by, pitch them the same yarn. Just make certain that you stop any strangers in good time, before they reach the adit." He resumed his contemplation of the fire as Angelo went out again. Fronti only broke his train of thought to hurl a curse from time to time at Stella, when she was quite incapable of stopping her attack of coughing. Pina continued massaging Stella's chest. It seemed to afford her a little relief. Time dragged by on leaden wings.

It was perhaps four o'clock when Giorgio returned with some linctus for Stella. Pina seized on the bottle and quickly made up a dose with warm water from the billycan. After she had taken the dose, the child seemed to cough a little less. There must have been some kind of opiate in the mixture, because soon she slept. Fronti sat before the fire, absorbed in his thoughts. The fire crackled. There was peace in the cave.

TWENTY SEVEN

On Saturday morning, just before nine o'clock, Annibale roused Sandro and they, together with the rest of the party, gathered in the office once more. Annibale inspected his army. One ageing politician, who though he had been a member of the partisans, had never heard a shot fired in anger; one majordomo, brave enough, it was true, but more likely to be a liability than an asset, by reason of age and generally poor physical condition; one policeman of some sort or other, value completely unknown; one ancient cavalryman, with a game leg, but who would die to save his master's child; and one vainglorious boy, never tried in any sort of critical situation, but on whom, nevertheless, the greater part of any physical activity must depend. It was a pitiably weak force with which to assault a stronghold which, as he knew from the days of yesteryear, was to all intents and purposes impregnable. He could only hope that his planning, with the blessing of Providence, would bring about a good result.

As they tore at the bread rolls and drank the coffee that Elsa had provided, Annibale said, "There is no necessity to waste time on further talk. Each one of us knows what is to be done, and how to do it. Just check watches once more. It is precisely a quarter past nine." Every man inspected his watch, Sandro doing so with ostentatious pride. Annibale continued, "All agreed? Right. Sandro, you get away now on your moped. Let me stress once again that you are not to give yourself away as you take post. Remember that the signal which will indicate that action is to start will be a shot from my gun - fortunately it has a very distinctive bark, which most of us know, having heard it when I have been shooting in the grounds. Any further questions?" The last question was directed at Sandro.

Not even he had anything to ask, so Annibale despatched him immediately, and very soon the howl of his moped reached the ears of the little party in the office. All were silent, each occupied with his own thoughts. Carlo was glad that at last there was to be some action - action which would be sharp and summary. Don Stefano was trying to recall what little he knew of the cave, from reports he had received from the brave men who had held it long ago - how it had a cold damp atmosphere that seemed to tear at a man's vitals. He prayed that Stella had not been too badly affected by the conditions up there. Annibale was tingling with excitement at the prospect of the coming battle. Like an old war-horse neighing at the sound of the trumpet, he thrilled at the chance of once more smelling the acrid smoke of gunpowder used in earnest. Passi was resigned to whatever might happen. He was fatalistic about the whole affair, as he had been about most of the happenings during his life. When the moment of truth arrived, he knew that he would perform his duty with the same cold efficiency that he displayed when he was working on the estate accounts. He hoped sincerely that none of the party, most of all himself, would be hurt. However, if it was ordained that someone would be wounded, he hoped that any suffering would be borne with a decent fortitude.

Breakfast completed, Annibale ushered the little party out to the waiting cars. With the Rolls leading, driven by Don Stefano with Passi seated beside him, the tiny convoy moved off. Traffic was light and they made good time to Teramo, where they took the road to Montorio. Midway between that town and the Ponte Rio Arno, the cars drew into a layby and the quartet gathered in the Rolls for a final consultation.

"Here we part company," said Don Stefano. "I wish you good fortune in your endeavours. If we fail, which Heaven forfend, let us at least fail like men, and die in our failure! But let us not talk of such an ending to this sorry tale. I fear that if we are unsuccessful, our loved ones will receive short shrift from these banditti." They all got out of the car, and Don Stefano took each man's hand and shook it warmly. "When we emerge from this victorious, as I hope and pray we will, I shall give you all proper thanks. But let me say here and now that I am truly grateful to you for your sympathy and loyalty in this dreadful time of worry and anxiety. Now, Luigi, let you and me press forward. We shall all meet again in victory, I am certain!" Tears hung on his eyelashes as he entered the car and took the wheel. Carlo found that he, too, was choking back a tear. In normal circumstances he would have considered Don Stefano's emotion to be mere histrionics, but this time things were different - he himself was involved personally and emotionally!

The Rolls glided away. The big Fiat stood in the sunlight, the bodywork still gleaming from the attentions of Sandro's wash leather. A small creaking came from its internals as the engine cooled after the drive. All around them the high hills stood guard. Their summits glowed in the bright morning light. High on the tops of the two Corni, snow gleamed and winked. The north facing slopes were already beginning to show blue shadows as the sun crept round, and the deep green of the pines assumed a more sombre hue as the light fled from them. Far below their parking place, a stream laughed and gurgled noisily as it rushed over the small cataracts that lay across its path. Some sort of bird hung on lazy wings in the bright autumn sky, wheeling and rising and falling without a motion of its extended pinions. Annibale rolled himself a cigarette. With evident pleasure he inhaled deeply and expelled the smoke from his nostrils. Seated on the low stone wall that guarded traffic from the sheer drop to the stream below, he was the picture of a happy and contented man. He looked like any normal tourist, interested only in the scenery around him, and the pleasant savour of his cigarette smoke mingled with the air that at this season was starting to hold a certain crispness.

He and Carlo did not speak. All there was to say had been said earlier. They simply had to while away the time until the hour arrived for them to move into their place and explode into violent action. Annibale rolled another cigarette and smoked it leisurely. At last he threw away the sodden stub, and said, "Time to move." They took their seats in the car and Carlo drove the Fiat up the steep winding hill to Prati di Tivo, by-passing Pietracamela. Carlo looked along the white road where he had sustained his head wound. With careful fingers he touched the place where a scab was already beginning to form on the wound. Annibale saw the motion and laughed, "I thought of it, too!" They arrived at the broad carpark of the Prati. The chairs of the seggiovia were moving in their stately silent dance up and down the side of the mountain, the grey-green grass below them forming their dance floor. Glancing round the carpark, Carlo noted that the only other vehicle parked there was Sandro's moped.

Parking as close to the lower station as possible, with Annibale at his heels, Carlo made his way to the ticket office. The old woman was eager to talk, but Carlo dismissed her inconsequential chatter as politely as he could. When a chair arrived, he slipped into it without effort, but Annibale was not so adept, and had to let a chair pass before he too, was safely installed and ascending into the clear mountain air. Looking back from two seats above the old man, Carlo could see him fumbling with the safety bar as at the same time he tried to hold his shotgun securely across his lap.

Above them the mountain stood bleak and stark in the sunshine which glanced off the small patches of snow that remained from the last winter. Carlo hoped that he would be able to pinpoint the precise location of the cave, but could distinguish nothing that remotely resembled a cavern or the entrance to one. Annibale had said that the spot was well concealed, and evidently he had spoken no less than the truth. He could appreciate the military thinking that had gone into making this the place to lie hidden from opposing forces. No one could possibly imagine that up there, just below the snowline, there lay hidden such a refuge. Carlo hoped that Pina and Stella were not feeling the cold too much, but consoled himself with the thought that even if the cold did bite, as it most assuredly did in this exposed chair, in a very few hours from now, the prisoners would be safe in the warm comfort of Tre Boschi.

On arrival at the upper station, Carlo leapt nimbly from his chair, disdaining the proffered assistance of the attendant. Annibale alighted less gracefully; he stumbled and his gun fell between his legs, threatening to trip him. The attendant, accustomed to such awkwardness, hastened to help the old man, and Carlo also rushed to his aid. Between them they extricated Annibale from imminent decapitation from the following chair as it swung towards him. The attendant smiled, and said, "The signore is plainly no skier! What do you hunt today?"

"Rats, mostly," growled Annibale, before Carlo could answer for him. The man raised a questioning eyebrow, but gained no further enlightenment from the passengers. He stood and watched them as they left the station through the wicket gate and up the stairs that led to the shrine of the Black Madonnina. Annibale paused to read the inscription on the plinth of the statue which stood above them smiling benignly into space. "Do you know the story, signore?" he asked.

"It is dedicated to a skier who fell to his death from the mountain. I can read, you know!"

"That's only for tourists! I meant, do you know the true story?"

"If it's not too long in the telling, I'll hear it. We have a few minutes in hand."

"It's short enough. Many years ago, some shepherds were up here with their flocks. They found the statue right here, laying on the ground. It seemed all wrong to them that such a beautiful work should be abandoned like that, so they lifted it and began to carry it down the hill with the idea of mounting it in the church at Pietracamela. But the further they got it down the slope, the heavier it became. They dropped it on the path and went for reinforcements to help to tote it. They returned with some helpers, among the parish priest, but again, the lower down the slope they carried it, the weightier it grew until they barely lift it from the ground. The priest suggested that they return it to where it was found, and to their amazement, the higher it was carried up the slope, the lighter it grew until it was the same weight as it had been when first they found it. So the priest said that it was clear that the statue did not wish to leave the spot where they had first discovered it. He and the shepherds eventually built this shrine and dedicated it to all men who love mountains. The inscription on the plinth came many years later. I am not a religious man, but perhaps we might as well take out insurance by putting up a prayer to the Madonnina before we move on to the work which awaits us!"

With bowed heads, they stood for the space of time in which a man might count up to thirty, and then clambered over the handrail and took the path which Sandro had used the previous night. On each side of the ridge was a vertiginous drop. Far below, Carlo could see the roofs of the hotels at Prati di Tivo. To his left, even further down, lay the view afforded by the Gran' Sasso and the Campo Imperatore. They were too far away for him to distinguish details, but here and there he could see some small moving white dust clouds raised by a vehicle moving along a narrow unsurfaced road, Annibale, leading on without a glance to left or right, stopped at a path which forked to their left. "This is where Sandro should have gone. Now we must be silent. Along this path to the right lies the cave. We cannot go far along the track without coming into view of anyone who may be on guard."

They moved along the lower path. Now the great shoulder of the Corno blocked the view to the left, rising thirty metres or so at their elbows. The track diminished to a perilous narrow ledge, barely a metre wide. The view to the right was tremendous. Far, far below the smoke of a hidden fire curled lazily upward in the still air. Trees marched up the slope until not even the hardiest of them could gain foothold or sustenance from the meagre soil and the scree took over completely. Then even the scree had to concede victory to the smooth glacis, too steep and too exposed for even the bravest of herbage to survive. Even a fly, thought Carlo, would have trouble in finding foothold there. He would not like to miss his footing on this path. To do so would mean a drop of at least one hundred metres bouncing from sharp rocks to scree back to rocks again until one ended up as a mangled and broken body among the trees. He shuddered at the conception of such a death.

Annibale had ceased to move forward. Carlo came close up behind him. The old man said, "In just a few metres, there is a buttress and there the path bends. If we go round that buttress, we shall be in full view from the cave. We are in good time. In ten minutes, I shall give the signal!" They moved on towards the buttress and stopped just before it, resting their backs against the towering cliff. The silence was almost palpable. There was very little wind. There seemed to be no living person within thousands of kilometres - they might as well be on a desert island, thought Carlo. His heart was filled with pity and rage - pity for the captives and rage against the kidnappers who had brought them to this desolate place.

Annibale broke his shotgun and slipped a cartridge into the breech. He lifted the weapon to his shoulder and discharged the shot into the air. Echoes rang out all around, reverberating from the blank wall of the mountainside. He reloaded and stepped out of his cover, gun held at his hip. Giorgio was on guard. He shouted, and waved Annibale away. When he took no notice, he threw a rock at him. Annibale ducked and the rock hit Carlo in the chest before falling over the precipice. Annibale took a quick potshot at Giorgio, who ducked into the adit out of danger. Annibale reloaded.

Carlo was coughing from the effect of the blow in the chest that the rock had given him. When Annibale questioned him, he replied that it was nothing but a slight attack which would quickly pass. When at last his coughing subsided, he crept beneath Annibale's arm and looked along the ledge, his handgun held ready before him. Seeing nothing, he crept forward another metre or so. There was a sharp crack and a bullet hit the rockface above his head, to whine away into the distance. "So," thought Carlo, "One of the bandits is armed, and he's not a bad shot either!" The pistol might be only a small bore weapon, but in the right hands, it could do a lot of damage.

He retired swiftly to the safety of the buttress to consider the next move. The fleeting glimpse that he had been able to take along the path had revealed no sign of the presence of Don Stefano and Passi, and of course it was impossible to see if Sandro had gained his position. Annibale moved nearer to him. "Well, they know that we're here and since they threw lead at you and a rock at me, there must be something that they want to hide. Now what?" Without waiting for an answer, he moved round the buttress into an exposed position. "Come out with your hands up!" he shouted. "We will not shoot if you do not! Do you hear me?" His challenge was greeted with contemptuous silence.

Along the path came the dull report of a heavy pistol - Carlo was sure that it was Don Stefano's old army .45 which emitted a sound completely unlike that of the little pistol - a Beretta, he thought that might be. There came a crack from the pistol as though to give support to his opinion. A shout reached his ears, "Come out and see what we have here!"

They moved out from behind the abutment, and stood on the short straight path that ran before the cave. At the further end of the straight, Don Stefano stood, and behind him, Passi. The heavy .45 pistol hung from the senator's right hand. Between the two pairs of rescuers and in front of the cave, Fronti stood. He was holding Stella before him as a shield. In his hand was a small pistol. Close to him, one on each side, stood two men, each holding a rock ready to throw.

"One step further, Capriotti, and your brat will get it! And you two behind me, the same applies! Tell me if they move, Angelo!"

One of the men replied, "I'm watching them, Fronti!" He spoke loudly so that everyone could hear him.

Don Stefano cried, "Don't shoot my daughter, Fronti! Don't shoot her!"

"Make no stupid move, Capriotti, and she will be safe. Listen. I am going to pass the girl to Angelo here. Then I am coming along the path to talk to you. Try any tricks, and my chap will sling the brat over the edge! He won't hesitate!" Ostentatiously he passed Stella to Angelo, who grasped her tightly. Stella then saw her father for the first time, and emitted a piteously cry. "Papa!" Then the rough hand of Angelo was clamped over her mouth to stifle any further utterance.

Under the watchful eyes of Angelo and Giorgio, Fronti, gun in hand, made his way along the path to where Don Stefano stood. "Well, Capriotti, we seem to have reached stalemate. You cannot move without imperilling your daughter and I cannot go either way

without running into one wing or another of your army. But I hold
the whip hand; I have the trump card! One of your people makes a
false move and both the women die! So this is my suggestion. You
order your men to withdraw to the shrine for three hours. I will take
your kid and the mees to another hiding place. When the three hours
have passed, you may seek me out if you care to try. All the time that
you act wisely, I will guarantee the safety of your brat. The only way
you can anger me is to attack me. My men don't mind dying - they
would prefer that to a long spell in gaol. But if you play me false
over this truce I offer, the women go over the edge, I swear it!"

"You blackguard, Fronti! May you rot in hell!"

"Words, Capriotti, words! They mean nothing to me. Be
sensible. Withdraw to the shrine and give me the three hours I
demand. Break that truce, and the women die! Don't think, I beg
you, that I do not mean what I say. I am in deadly earnest. And once
I have gained the place of safety that I seek, we will restart dealing
and haggling, though I hate the process."

"Let me consult my friends there behind you."

"No. Only you can make the decision. Your friends must abide
by whatever that decision might be." He looked keenly into the
senator's face. "I give you two minutes to make up your mind. If
you would rather not accept my generous offer, then over the edge go
the women and we men can have a battle all to ourselves!" He turned
his back on the senator and began to walk back towards the cave.
"Call out what you have decided, in two minutes, remember!"

Don Stefano bit his lip. He could think of no action open to him,
other than acceptance of Fronti's 'offer'. It seemed inevitable that he
must do as he was ordered by the bandit. Perhaps when they were all
gathered at the shrine together, di Felippo or Annibale could come up
with some other scheme, but for his part, his brain seemed numb.

Passi moved forward, slipping by his master. He called, "We
accept your offer."

Fronti turned. "Very well. I will allow you to pass before the
cave to join your friends. I can be magnanimous in victory!"

The three bandits, with Angelo still holding Stella, went into the
adit. Don Stefano and Passi moved along the path to join Carlo and
Annibale. They had just passed the mouth of the adit when Fronti
came out and called to them. Once again, he was holding Stella.
"Look," he cried. "You see that she is safe and has been well-

treated."

Stella gave a little cry at seeing her father so near. She wriggled in Fronti's grasp. On that narrow path, there was danger in such movement, and involuntarily he loosened his grip slightly. Stella fell to the ground as he sought balance and she scrabbled away from her captor by about a metre. She was progressing painfully along the rough track when Sandro decided to take a hand in matters.

He raised himself to his full height on the lip of the cliff. Memories of yet another film flooded into his mind. "Geronimo!" he screamed at the top of his voice. Fronti, startled by the shout, ceased his attempts to regain his hold on Stella, he looked up. Raising his pistol, he took careful aim and shot at the precise moment that Sandro launched himself into space. The shot hit the boy in the solar plexus.

He was dead as he hit Fronti full in the chest with his two feet. There was a strangled scream of terror from the cattle dealer turned bandit. He sought to recover his balance, teetering back and forth on the extreme edge of the track. Then a final crescendo scream of panic escaped his throat and he followed Sandro a hundred metres to the scree below, provoking a miniature avalanche as the pair of bodies rolled onward until they were brought to a halt by the first of the trees.

Annibale ran like a mountain goat along the track, leaping over the prostrate form of Stella. He was closely followed by Carlo, and the pair brushed by Don Stefano and Passi, fortunately without precipitating anyone else into the abyss. As Don Stefano picked up his daughter to hold her tightly, covering her face with kisses, Angelo and Giorgio emerged from the adit. Annibale brought up his gun. Angelo stared at the fate that could not be avoided. Shot in the stomach, he dropped like a stone. Giorgio stood in the adit, holding up his hands as Annibale reloaded. His face was grey with terror; his whole body shaking; he was weeping copiously. "Shall I spare the gaolers trouble and shoot him, too?" asked Annibale.

"No. He will give no trouble." Carlo brushed past the two men and entered the cave. His eyes took time to accustom themselves to the gloom. Then he saw, crouching on the further stile of the fire, the sobbing form of Pina. He bounded over the fire and lifted her into the comforting strength of his embrace. She was shaking violently as she dropped her head on his chest.

"There now," he whispered. "It's all over, sweetheart! You're free and thank God, unhurt. There, there. Please don't cry." She clung desperately to him repeating his name over and over as he sought to comfort her.

Annibale entered the cave. "Well, it hasn't changed at all! Same old smoky fire, same old water running down the walls. Thank God Sandro found you, mees. This is no place for a stay of any length, and particularly a stay by gentle young ladies!"

Gradually, Pina recovered from her shaking. Womanlike, she ran her fingers through her matted hair and smoothed down her tattered dress. "I must look a real sight," she murmured, tremulously. "We didn't have much opportunity to keep ourselves clean and we didn't expect visitors this afternoon!" She gave a little smile that set Carlo's heart beating wildly. "Dio!" he thought. "This woman of mine has courage!"

Annibale grinned. "We'd better get back to Tre Boschi as soon as possible, mees. It will soon be dark out there, and the track is dangerous enough even in daylight!"

Carlo agreed. "That's true. The path is bad enough in daylight. I wonder how you managed to get up here at all! Can you walk, dearest?"

"With you near me, I can do anything! Anything in the world!" She took his hand and they emerged into the fading light of day.

After the long spell of darkness in the cave, the little light that remained outside tore with fierce intensity at her eyes. She was unable to detect the love and pride in Carlo's eyes as he looked hungrily down at her, all filthy as she was. She was able, though, to see that Stella was locked in Don Stefano's arms while Passi, standing nearby, wiped tears from his unsentimental eyes. She saw, too, Giorgio, ignored by those who had captured him, but making no move at all to escape.

Annibale prodded him none too gently with the muzzle of his shotgun. "Please be kind to him," pleaded Pina. "He was good to Stella and me, as far as he was permitted to be kind."

"He is a rat, mees, and rats should be killed on sight, as were the other two. It is a pity that he did not put up resistance, as they did, and so die with them!"

"You mean that Fronti and Angelo are dead?" she breathed.

"Darling, Fronti fell over the cliff, and the other rascal managed to get himself shot!" She burst into tears at hearing this. Carlo wondered if he would ever be able to understand why. If she could weep over those two, who must have treated her roughly, what would happen when she learned about Sandro, who had given his life for her and for Stella? He decided that he would keep this news from both of the girls until much later. They had both endured about as much as they were able, so far today.

Slowly the little party made their way along the track towards the seggiovia station. Annibale led, followed by Don Stefano, carrying Stella. They were followed in turn by Passi, who cast continual untrusting looks at Giorgio who was immediately behind him. Pina followed Giorgio, while Carlo brought up the rear. From time to time, Pina was glad of his helping hand over the worst and most dangerous parts of the trek along to the station.

Every member of the party, for his or her own personal reasons, heaved a sigh of relief when at long last the narrow track expanded into the wider path that ran over the crest, and they were finished with the slow and painful progress that was forced upon them by their fear of high and perilous places. At the shrine, Stella would have her father turn off the path to allow her to offer thanks to the Madonnina for their wonderful delivery, and Pina, standing beside her in front of the black statue with the kindly but weather-beaten face, sent up an additional prayer of thanksgiving to Sant'Antonio as well as to the Madonnina.

At the station, the attendant gazed in astonishment at the raggled appearance of the women of the party when they trooped into his café for a warming drink. Their talk was hushed. Each one carried evidence of the strain so recently undergone. Then, when they had drank and were warmer, Don Stefano, at his most senatorial, commanded the attendant to stop the machinery and allow everyone to mount the chairs in comfort without haste. Annibale, trusting to no one, seated himself beside Giorgio and all the way down kept his gun pushed hard into his prisoner's ribcage. Don Stefano and Stella shared a seat, naturally, as did Pina and Carlo. Only Passi travelled in solitary splendour, his nostrils flaring from time to time as the flimsy perch swayed over the ground far below them.

The party were honoured by the woman at the lower station stopping the chairs to allow them all to alight; she had been warned by her colleague that these people were no ordinary party, and it might be politic to see that they were well served. Leaving the station, Don

Stefano used the telephone at the taxi rank to call a cab to convey him and Stella to Tre Boschi. Carlo persuaded Pina to make a third member of that party, as they would be travelling directly to the house. He, with Annibale and a somewhat dispirited Giorgio, would go in the Fiat to the barracks, where Giorgio would find lodging for a few months until his trial was arranged. Other matters had to be arranged. A search party would have to go out to recover the bodies of Fronti and Sandro, and another party would have to get up to the cave to bring down what was left of Angelo, who had hurriedly been dragged into the cave by Passi. The bears in the Gran' Sasso are hungry beasts and it would be unwise to leave corpses out in the open a moment longer than was needful. And finally a guard would have to be mounted over the Rolls at Prato Selva until someone could be sent to collect it.

After some argument, Passi agreed to travel with his master and the two ex-captives in the taxi. He seated himself in a front seat beside the driver and the little party set off on the trip to Tre Boschi. As the taxi wafted its way down the hill, Don Stefano tapped his majordomo on the shoulder. "I should like to know on what authority you told Fronti that I had accepted his terms for a three hour truce."

Passi allowed a fleeting smile to crease his usually immobile features. "Signore, you are a gentleman, and a gentleman's word is his bond, as Fronti well knew. Had *you* said that the terms were accepted, we should have had to abide by them. I... I am no gentleman. The thought struck me that if some way presented itself whereby the terms might be broken, then I, being no gentleman, would lose nothing, whereas, in a similar situation, you, senator, would have lost your honour!"

TWENTY EIGHT

Il Capitano Leonardo Bianchi, Commandante of the Carabinieri at Fortalezza, sat in his green leather swivelling chair, with his heels resting on the desk before him, and admired the immaculate jackboots that adorned his well-turned legs. He drew deeply on a cigarette, and each time he spoke, a thin spurt of smoke came from his lips. He had an audience of only two people, but he was playing to the gallery, so to speak, with all the élan that a dashing officer of an elite corps should display. Carlo and Pina, on the opposite side of the desk, were not unduly impressed.

"I think," said the Capo "that we have tied up and tidied up that little abduction very successfully. We have had to put Giorgio under a little... er... pressure, shall we say, but he doesn't seem to know a lot about what was going on. He is not exactly gifted with great brain power. All he knows is that when the affair was successfully completed, he was going to receive a reasonable amount of ready cash. One or two things emerged during our... er... conversations, and led us to other members of the gang - the smaller fry, one might say."

"Fronti was, of course, the brains, the master mind. As a cattle dealer, he travelled not only all over Italy, but also to other countries and he had many foreign contacts. It is obvious to me that it was he who dreamed up the idea of copying the abductions committed by the Brigate Rosse - the Red Brigades. Signor di Felippo has told me, signorina, of your adventures during your journey to our country, and for all of those you can thank Fronti. Sadly for his plans, he had not made allowances for our friend here, who so gallantly came to your rescue."

"Giorgio and Angelo were but tools. Had we not scotched their plans, both men would have become, by local standards, rich men; that is, of course, contingent upon Fronti keeping his promises to them. Of the even smaller fry, we managed to pick up the men who collected the ransom money from the culvert. Here I would take issue with you, Signor di Felippo, but no matter now - however, you should have kept me informed. But that is all in the past. Even so, I should like to know your reasons for being so secretive."

"To tell you the truth, Capo, I had, and in fact, I still have, more than a suspicion that someone in your command is untrustworthy. I'll say more of that later. To return to the ransom money, did you recover any of it?"

"Following your example, I intend to return to that later! But I will say that the men who picked up the case and the money, and also provided people to run errands for the band, all lived in Pietracamela. They also were responsible for providing food supplies. They would carry rations part way up the mountain and deposit them where one of the men from the cave could pick them up. By means of a rough signalling system, they could keep Fronti informed of all that they were doing. This system was a sort of wartime relic, of course. The disadvantage of their supply system was that in a small place like Pietracamela, they could not buy in quantity without tongues wagging. That, signorina, if you are interested, was the reason for such frequent trips down the mountain being made by Angelo and Giorgio."

"Now, about the money. Would you believe that we found it intact, still in the case, under a bed in the cottage of one of the rascals! Seems incredible, doesn't it? A fortune, hardly concealed at all, in a small cottage in a mountain village! But that was the kind of people we were dealing with - the rankest amateurs! It's a great pity that we did not get Fronti alive. When my men got to him he had been pretty well smashed up by his fall, and then the wildlife had had a go at him. Sandro was close by him, and he, too, was in a bit of a mess. As for Angelo, we found him in the cave, just where you had left him.

"Fronti's ideas were too grandiose for his capacity to follow them through. He needed a much larger body of helpers, for one thing, but that would have meant smaller shares for every member of the band. His detail planning was poor, too."

Carlo interjected, "You are wrong, capo! Fronti was not the brains of the affair at all. He was just the greedy tool of more ambitious people!"

The Capo's look showed his surprise. "What?"

"Well, I cannot really put it succinctly. I hope that this long rigmarole will not be too boring. But this is my side of the story. I was sent to dig out a few facts about some rather massive drug smuggling. Not the more common marijuana, but some really high quality heroin. We knew the stuff came from Albania, and we had a shrewd idea that it was entering our country by one of the east coast ports. But we didn't know where the gang on this side of the Adriatic was based. Albania is chronically short of hard currency, and they used our friends to distribute the drug all over Europe - it didn't stop here in Italy. Our friends were only middlemen, mere carriers. That was where Fronti proved so useful. As a cattle dealer, he could carry large sums of cash without arousing suspicion; everyone knew him as a much-travelled dealer in prime cattle.

"My masters thought the drugs might be entering Italy through one of the great ports like Pescara or Ancona. They really clamped down on those places, and went as far north as Venice and south to Brindisi. But always we drew blank. Then someone up there," he nodded in the direction of Rome, "had a rush of brains to the head and thought we ought to look at smaller ports. Fishing ports were really ideal, because the fleet put out every night and came back every morning to unload their catches. What was to stop them meeting some equally innocuous Albanian fishermen in mid-ocean, making a swift transhipment, and each returning to his home port? Customs men rarely search fishing vessels for contraband, as you may know, Capo. So they, my masters, shoved a man in at San Benedetto to look at all the ports northwards, while I got posted to Giulianova and my parish ran south to Pescara.

"I spent a lot of time - and government money - in the fishermens' bars and I listened more than I spoke. I bought people a drink here, and a drink there, and in due course, I was led to Fronti. But to me, it was pretty plain that while he was fairly high-ranking as far as the smuggling went, he was definitely not the Great White Chief!

"I would say here and now that the abduction of Stella Capriotti and my fiancée was intended to allow the gang to cease their trade of smuggling drugs - they sensed that we were getting too close to them. They needed sufficient money to let them all retire. They felt, too, that as middlemen, they were taking all the risks and not getting a fair return for their efforts. Those above them in the pecking order were getting all the cream while they were running all the risks. All the time they were satisfied with such pickings as they were getting and were obeying orders, it would have been hard to track them down; they were safe, although I modestly say I was making some slow progress. The kidnapping of Stella Capriotti was an attempt to make a huge haul. It was also a tremendous error of judgement on their part.

"Fronti was not, as you so wisely remark, Capo, equipped

232

mentally or materially to run a successful abduction. Neither were those who guided him. They were too susceptible to the lurid publicity given to the public about the Brigate Rosse. The Press is never able to, nor is permitted to tell the whole story, and the plans of our friends were built on false foundations. When Sandro boasted that Don Stefano was hiring a bodyguard for his daughter, they decided that it could be worth their while to snatch the child, or so I believe. There may have been other motives, of course, with which I am not acquainted.

"Unfortunately they chose the wrong victim. They did not thoroughly assess what the market would stand, and so they demanded far too much ransom money. This was a basic error which professional kidnappers would not have made. No doubt Sandro was much to blame, but then again, his bragging and boasting were notorious all over the Abruzzo, and Fronti and his bosses should have been very well aware of his faults."

The Capo listened intently, completely absorbed in Carlo's recital. "And who, may I ask, were these bosses? I notice that you have at all times referred to them in the plural. I do assure you that I had no idea of such goings-on in my area of command! If your masters in Roma did not play their cards so close to their chests, we people in the lower echelons would be able, perhaps, to take the necessary action. I can say with some honesty that on the whole I run a fairly tightly controlled operation here in Fortalezza!"

"You could not know, Capo! Maybe your chaps might have been able to dig out a little more than they did - maybe, even, they did in fact find out such things. But if they did, then the information did not reach you, and in a moment or two I shall explain how that came about. I think I can explain why much information was not allowed to reach your ears. I admit that I have been lucky in my investigations. Certainly I had my suspicions early on. There were always niggling little thoughts at the back of my mind. I thought perhaps I was being stupid and that my ideas were without foundation. But a chance remark by one of my suspects supported my suspicions. The comment was that one day, very soon, they were going to receive a pile of cash that would enable them to realise an ambition that they had long cherished. I called up my masters, and they did a little investigation for me. Capo, did you know that Fronti was the illegitimate son of Maria, Sandro's aunt, the paralysed one? And that with Mina, the one who translates for her, those two are responsible for two-thirds of the villainy that goes on in your district?"

The Capo's incredulous smile broadened.

"Oh, I assure you that it's true, all right! I visited them in their little shop, my two pretty suspects. I helped Mina to roll up some material - the trade term is bolts of cloth - and in each bolt there is a cardboard tube, larger or smaller according to the size of the bolt.

In a number of the bolts I handled, there was a package forced tightly into the tube halfway down. Now, heroin has a very distinctive odour, and a single sniff was enough to teach me a lot! I don't think a visit to the shop would pay you now, though. I expect the dear girls have taken fright, and every single tube you inspected would be clean as a whistle! But an occasional visit by one of your chaps might help to keep the girls on the strait and narrow!"

"You cannot be serious, di Felippo!"

"Oh, but I am! However, neither you nor I will ever be able to pin anything on the old dears now that Fronti has gone, and with him the greater and most important part of their organisation. You would find that he will be made to appear responsible for any and every thing! They had hoped to groom Sandro for stardom, but his wagging tongue made them alter their minds about that idea. As things were, Fronti was just the man for them - ambitious, avaricious, and although not too well endowed with grey matter, always obedient.

"Now to explain to you why I have been unable to tell you as much as you would have liked to know and I would have liked to tell. At the same time, you will find the reason why information from your men was not getting through that door. Look well at your staff. If, among them. you find a distant relative of those two old women in Bellante, you need look no further. Or maybe you might find someone who owes the old women money. Whoever he is, that person kept the women informed of your every move, and would not have failed to tell them instantly had we given you any information about our reactions to the demands of the kidnappers. Or about our plans to attack the cave. The hostages would have been whipped away to another hiding place, and we should have been returned to square one. No, believe me, it was not you that I distrusted. But I am sure that a person in your office, one with a post of some authority, has been passing information to the gang as soon as it reached his ears, and that person is capable of withholding information

234

from you. The trouble is that when you find your man, you won't be able to pin a thing on him! He will be far too clever to allow that to happen. I would recommend a swift transfer out of harm's way. You may even have to promote him to get him moved. Who said that crime doesn't pay?"

The Capo drew a deep breath. "I'll kill him!"

"You won't, Capo, and if you think for a moment, you'll know that you won't because you can do nothing. There's nothing concrete to work on; just my suspicions, and if you boil things down, they're not worth a lot. Your only solution is a transfer. You couldn't even have him discharged without good sound incontrovertible reasons!"

The Capo's face was scarlet with suppressed anger. To cover his confusion, he turned to Pina. "And how do you feel now, signorina, after your ordeal?"

She gave him a flashing smile that restored his equilibrium a trifle. "Oh, I am almost completely recovered now, thank you, Capo. It was a most unpleasant experience while it lasted, but it's all behind us now. Stella is recovering nicely from her chest infection now that she is receiving proper attention. Of course, the prospect of being a bridesmaid is helping her no end on her road to complete recovery."

"A bridesmaid, signorina? Who is getting married, then? I did not know that the senator had any close relations!"

It was Pina's turn to blush bright red. She took Carlo's hand in her own and pressed it. "This is my prisoner, capo!"

"Well, I'll be... Congratulations to you both!"

Carlo grinned. "It's a fair cop," he said in English. Then in Italian he added, "I told you that someone was suppressing information, Capo!"

The Capo pressed the bell on his desk, and rose to his feet. His brigadier came into the office. "Get my car out, brigadier. I want two men to go with me." The man acknowledged the order and left the office.

The Capo went on, "Can you spare the time to accompany me to Bellante? I would like you to be present when I talk to the old ladies."

Carlo nodded. "Pina, dear, can you take the car back to Tre Boschi? And will you permit me to go with the Capo?"

"So long as the Capo promises to return you to me as soon as possible, I agree! I will spare you for a short while. I must learn to be a good wife to a policeman!"

The Capo's teeth gleamed white below his moustache. He smiled his thanks to Pina. To Carlo he said, "I see already that you are going to be very much under petticoat government." His smile took the edge off the remark.

TWENTY NINE

It was the hour of siesta. In more go-head towns and cities, siesta did not happen so late in the year - siesta was only for the hot months. But here in Bellante, all doors were shut tight and bolted while the inhabitants took their rest for an hour or two, shedding for a brief time the need to scratch a living somehow. Let those who dwelt in the great conurbations dispense with siesta if they so wished - during the cooler months, that is. The Bellantesi, by long established custom asserted their inalienable right to a rest in the afternoon, and would not forgo that right even if it snowed, which sometimes it had been known to do.

In the sisters' shop, all was quiet. In the morning, during a slack period, Maria had washed some of her underclothes and now those garments, mostly constructed of man-made fibre, were spread on the rack above the cooker, so that they could dry out more speedily than if put outdoors in the tiny courtyard where the sun rarely penetrated. Now Mina, half asleep, was reclining in her armchair, while Maria, safe from the prying eyes of customers, sat on one of the hard kitchen chairs at the table. She had chosen that particular chair because the very hardness of the seat came as a welcome relief from the soft clinging upholstery of her usual chair, in which she played so well the role of an invalid. Her fingers drummed ceaselessly in a devil's tattoo on the scrubbed table top. Her face wore a worried preoccupied look. Below her chin the massive pendant dewlap shook from time to time as she wagged her head, trying to dispel the black thoughts that insisted on invading her mind. Intuition told her that something, somewhere, was radically wrong, yet she was unable to put a name to the cause of her feelings.

Mina stirred, then rose. She stifled a yawn with her fat little hand. "Coffee?"

Maria continued her drumming, not even stopping to nod. Mina lighted the largest gas burner. It flared yellow. "We need a new cylinder," she said. "This one is almost empty. I will go to the smith in half an hour or so and ask him to bring us one." Again Maria nodded. Mina doubted if she had heard what was said. The coffee pot was charged with water and freshly ground coffee. Mina put the machine on the burner and, as was her custom, turned up the gas so that the flames rose high all round the pot. She then crossed the kitchen and rummaged in the high cupboard over the sideboard, seeking cups and saucers, sugar bowl and all the paraphernalia that was needed for the coffee drinking ceremony.

A cry from Maria made her turn round. One of the articles of clothing above the cooker had ignited and was sending up a thin black smoke signal. Mina moved as quickly as she could round the table, with the intention of seizing the garment and throwing it into the sink, where it could safely burn out. Maria moved round the table with the same errand in view. Both were moving with all the speed they could muster when they collided. Both lost balance. Mina fell first, and Maria landed on top of her. As she fell, Maria caught her head on a corner of the cooker. Blood was running from her head, and she lost consciousness. Her weight on top of Mina caused her to lose the power to get from under her sister, and prevented her from breathing properly. A scrap of the burning material fell on the top of the cooker, flared up and set fire to another garment on the rack. Smoke grew denser as more items of clothing ignited. A piece of blackened gauze material floated lazily upward in the heat given off by the cooker. It hit the ceiling, bounced back, and still smouldering, fell on to Mina's chair.

The plastic upholstery quickly caught fire, glowing redly, to reveal the foam padding that gave the chair its luxurious softness. Now this also began to smoulder, adding its quota to the fumes which were rapidly filling the kitchen. The espresso machine hissed and bubbled on the cooker, but Mina, pinned under the dead weight of Maria, was incapable of lifting herself to turn off the gas tap. She thought a rib had been broken when Maria had fallen so heavily on her. The painful struggle to relieve herself of Maria's weight was tiring her. The ever increasing black fumes were making her cough, she was coughing, she was cou... Each cough racked her body and made her ribs hurt more.

Her chair did not burst into flames. The flame retardant padding of the seat and squab merely smouldered sullenly. With each extra square centimetre of padding that smouldered, more suffocating smoke was added to that already filling the kitchen from floor to ceiling. The deadly fumes thickened. Soon Mina ceased to cough so painfully. She lay inert under her sister, unconscious and only faintly breathing.

The black smoke filtered into the shop, filling it as well as the kitchen. From the gaps between door and frame, little trails of smoke puffed out into the street. An early riser from siesta who was passing along the street raised the cry of "Fire!" Windows were hastily thrown open, doors swung to allow people to enter the narrow street. At the entrance to the sisters' shop a solemn conference was soon taking place as men tried to decide what to do for the best. Some were trying to peer through the little window, but the fumes were too thick by far to allow them to see anything. A man ran into the church and began to ring the bell to raise the alarm throughout the whole town.

Three men of the town's fire brigade arrived. They were all volunteers under the command of the grocer. One of the men attacked the shop door with his axe while the commander organised the neighbours into a bucket chain. Under the blows of the axe, the shop door soon collapsed and the axeman ran inside the shop, to retire very quickly, choking and spluttering. The grocer tied a wetted handkerchief round his nose and mouth and entered the shop, but he too was beaten back before he could reach the kitchen. Some person had telephoned for an ambulance and with siren blaring, the vehicle had reached the top of the street. There it had to stay; it was much too wide to attempt to get near the scene of the fire. The first aid men dashed down the slope with a stretcher, but were prevented by the fumes from entering the shop. The neighbours had seen that there was small sense in carrying water to a fire that they could not reach, and now stood discussing the tragedy in the only way people *can* talk of such matters - at the tops of their voices. Into this babble and generally ineffective activity, Carlo and the Capo arrived with the two carabinieri.

A rapped command from the Capo sent one of the policemen scuttling back to their car. He returned very quickly, bearing gas masks. Both the carabinieri donned a mask apiece, and disappeared into the shop. They reappeared bearing the unconscious form of Mina. Gently they laid her body on the pavement and the first aid men leapt upon her and began to give her mouth to mouth resuscitation. The carabinieri re-entered the shop and presently emerged with the body of Maria, who was promptly given the same treatment as her sister was receiving.

In obedience to another command from the Capo, the gas-masked carabinieri moved into the shop bearing buckets of water. The bucket chain quickly declared a moratorium on further speculation and returned to the task, less interesting but more useful, of delivering water to the policemen. The smouldering fire was at last doused. The kitchen window was opened, and the evening breeze which had already begun to waft down the street, began to clear house and shop of all fumes, although the after effects of them were bitter on the palate for a long time after they had dispersed. By this time, it was full dark. The Capo stood down his sweating men from their task. A friendly neighbour produced a bottle and two tumblers for their heroes, and the Capo affected not to notice that his men were drinking while on duty as he and Carlo entered the shop.

They went directly to the kitchen. The cylinder had long run out of gas, but Carlo turned off the tap and disconnected the pipe. It was a simple task to build up a picture of how the tragedy had started, for charred remnants of clothing still lay on the cooker rack, and Mina's blackened and distorted chair stood in its customary position, the upholstery now non-existent. There was little the two men could do. They observed the preparations that Mina had made for coffee, looked round to be certain that there was no danger of the fire flaring up again, and went into the shop.

Carlo lifted down a bolt of cloth. He pointed it towards a street lamp and said, "Now you may see what I have been talking about! The centre of this tube is blocked. Remove the blockage, and you will find the parcel of heroin there to be of the highest quality you've ever seen!"

The Capo looked down the tube. He called to one of his men and sent him to the car with instructions to use the radio link to call up three more men and a police van. "I'm going to have every scrap of this material moved to the barracks for thorough investigation," he told Carlo. "I shall put a guard on the place until morning, and then we shall sift through everything. And when we have the evidence we require, - and I think that we have that already, thanks to you - I'm going to ensure that those two old women are put away for the rest of their natural lives! They're going to regret that they ever got mixed up in this racket, I promise you!" He paused for a moment. "But what about you? Basically, this is your case."

"I would have passed it to you in due course. I am not expected to make arrests and the like, as you know. I shall be called upon to give evidence anonymously when the case comes up for trial. But you may have the kudos. Yours, all yours!"

They stepped up into the street. The ambulance men were carrying a stretcher up the slope to the ambulance. The body on the stretcher was covered and the face hidden by a white cloth draped over it. Carlo raised a questioning eyebrow. One of the men shook his head. "Not a hope, signore. In truth, they were both dead before we tried to bring them round, but we had to make the attempt. It was useless, and we knew it right from the start." He turned away. He seemed to be exhausted by his efforts. It is always sad when a patient is lost, even two old ones such as Maria and Mina, and the man seemed to be near to tears. Slowly the men went up the slope with their burden.

Carlo said, "Well, it's your baby now, Capo. As far as your parish is concerned, the drug smuggling is at an end. But do not doubt that it will break out again somewhere else. Our friends don't give up too easily when vast amounts of cash are involved. As for me, I am certain that there, on one of those stretchers, goes the brains of the kidnap as well as the most important middleman, or middlewoman, rather, of the drug trade around here. I don't know which of the pair was the actual leader, although I suspect Mina - the other one seemed to be too decrepit to engage in any serious planning beyond that of her next meal. But I'm ready to bet that she was involved to a certain extent. It's a great pity that they will never talk to us now - we would have learned a lot, I know."

The two men walked up the hill to their car, pushing through the now crowded street. Many ghoulish sightseers had gathered, although there was nothing to see. The guard at the shop was being kept busy as he tried to push back those who wanted to get right into the scene of the late action. Winter was approaching; there was a bite in the air now. Carlo did not mind that - he could foresee no coldness in his future!